COPYRIGHT © 2022 DONALD HOUSER

ISBN: 978-1-7339175-6-8 (Donald Houser)

CLIMATE TRAVELS

TIME TRAVELS TO

SAVE THE PLANET

DONALD HOUSER

The distinction between the past, present, and future is only a stubbornly persistent illusion.

Imagination is more important than knowledge. Knowledge is limited. Imagination encircles the world.

Albert Einstein

ACKNOWLEDGEMENTS

Any resemblances to real people or places in this book are purely coincidental. This novel is entirely a work of fiction.

I want to thank my editors John Voorhees and Marianna Versteeg for all their help.

1- JUNE 6, 2045

Arthur stopped his run as soon as the temperature became unbearable. He was drenched in sweat as he walked the remaining distance to his apartment. The sun had been up less than two hours, but the temperature was already near 100° F. There were only a few clouds in the sky. If only it would rain soon. More clouds would be welcome and would help the heat. At least the smoke had cleared somewhat from the latest wildfire. He took a quick shower, grabbed his laptop and papers, inserting them into his back pack, and left for his laboratory at the University of California at Berkeley. When he reached the campus, he was sweating again. It seemed that summers were endless sweats and smoky skies nowadays.

As he climbed the steps of the Physics Building, he stopped and looked out at the scurrying students in their shorts and tee shirts. They too were sweating with the heat. There had been some progress in his life of 28 years in reducing carbon emissions in the US and Europe, though not nearly enough. Much of the other historical big carbon burners had not made the same progress. There were still coal burning power plants in much of the world. The global mean temperature had already exceeded 2.0° C above the baseline temperature in 1950 and the temperature at the poles was nearly 6° C above. The tropics were almost unlivable and climate refugees were clamoring to get into Europe, North America, Russia, China, Australia, Argentina, Chile and South Africa.

He stepped into the air conditioned building and immediately felt the relief of the cooler temperature. The energy needs for air conditioning around the world had skyrocketed. He descended the stairs to his basement laboratory where his work in particle physics and energy sometimes felt like a useless pursuit. He should have become a climate scientist and helped to stop the runaway warming that was threatening life on earth. His current pursuit to build an Einstein-Rosen Bridge, commonly known as a wormhole, theoretically required tremendous amounts of energy— more energy than was physically possible at present. Sometimes the futility of his research seemed absurd. Travel though time had been a dream of his since he was a little boy. Einstein had been his hero much to the amusement and delight of his family.

Outside the door to his laboratory, he placed his eye close to the optical scanner. In his peripheral vision, he saw the lanky woman hurrying past and watched her retreat as the door clicked open. Her shapely image in her baby blue, tank top and navy shorts as she scurried away remained in his mind. He tried to recall the brief glimpse of her striking face. He didn't think he had seen her before, but something seemed familiar about her. Maybe he had seen her before. But where? What was she doing in the basement of the Physics Building? He had an urge to run after her, but what would he say to her if he did catch up to her. 'Hey, what were you doing in the Physics Building basement' sounded accusatory.

Against his better judgement, he pushed the door closed, then ran down the hall and up the stairs. As soon as reached the outside, he looked both directions before he spied her walking quickly down the sidewalk her smooth leg muscles stretching and contracting beneath her shorts. He hesitated a few seconds, wondering if pursuing her was crazy. Nevertheless, he sprinted after her.

When he was nearly abreast, he slowed to a walk matching her pace and casually said, "Hello, how's it going?" How lame could he be? Was that the best he could come up with? She was probably thinking he was some kind of dork or pervert.

She stopped abruptly and with a furrowed brow stared at him. "Do I know you?" Her beauty was intimidating up close— prominent checks flushed by the heat, a long smooth nose, and sumptuous beckoning lips in their rose colored lipstick. Her expression changed to one of surprise, her pale gray eyes cutting him to the core, her face framed by her jet black hair. Her surprised expression suddenly erupted into a smile. "It's Professor Brown isn't it? I took your introduction to quantum mechanics course. You're the youngest full professor at the University."

He was thrown by her recognition and couldn't seem to find the words to respond to her comment. He smiled back, bathed in sweat, feeling discombobulated by her intense gaze. Finally after what seemed like long seconds, he was able to respond to her questioning countenance. "Yes, that's correct. When you walked past me in the basement, I thought I knew you from somewhere, but now realize I've never met you. So sorry I accosted you like this."

"Don't be sorry. It's an easy mistake to make." She held out her hand. "I'm Rose Manning. I'm working on my doctorate in climate science." She blushed slightly and looked down at her sandals. "I was just going to breakfast. I came in early to do some work on my thesis. If you're not busy, would you fancy joining me?"

"Oh, I don't want to intrude."

"Don't be silly. Have you already had breakfast?"

"No, I don't usually eat breakfast."

"Whenever you eat your first meal of the day no matter what time it is, it is breakfast." She smiled, her perfectly formed teeth shining bright in the sunlight and laughed. "You can at least have a tea or coffee and keep me company." She grabbed his arm. "Come on let's get out of this heat."

2- JUNE 6, 2045

"I'm so glad you agreed to accompany me here for a chat," Rose said while focusing on his handsome face. He looked very casual in his green short sleeved shirt and black jeans for a full professor. The coffee shop just off campus was busy, but they were able to find a table in the back after placing their orders at the counter and filling their cups with coffee. "I must confess I've been walking through the Physics Building for a few weeks." She took a hurried drink of coffee. "It is a short cut of sorts, and it's nice to get the brief cooling from the heat." She had almost thought of telling him she had hoped on her excursions that she would run into him, but was too embarrassed to confess.

"Yes a pleasant but brief cooling in this heat is always welcome." Arthur watched her face as she blushed and looked away briefly.

What the heck, maybe being honest was what was called for if she wanted this meeting to lead to something more than a coffee. "I must admit that my travels through the Physics building was also in hope of meeting you."

"Why would you want to meet me?"

His surprised expression gave her a chuckle. "People say you're a genius... another Einstein."

"Who says?" He grinned awkwardly. "That's absurd. Einstein definitely was an amazing genius. Me, I'm just a mediocre scientist working on my research, which is progressing nowhere, and teaching a few classes to maintain my professorship."

"I enjoyed your class on Introduction to Quantum Mechanics. I found it fascinating." The photograph of him in the physics building did not do justice to his handsome face. No wonder when he accosted her, it took her some time to recognize him.

"Quantum mechanics is a long way from climate science."

"I like all kinds of science and love learning new things." She watched his spreading smile. His amazing greenish tinted, hazel eyes behind his glasses seemed to sparkle when he spoke. She had audited his class but had sat in the back, a good distance away in the large auditorium. The front row was full of young women, who were obviously taken by the young handsome professor, but they were a minority. Most of the class were men. His class was one of the most sought after classes in physics. He made a complex subject quite interesting, speaking with enthusiasm and a sprinkling of humor. She remembered his joke about the Schrodinger's cat being quite a phenomenal cat being both alive and dead at the same time.

"I'm glad to hear it. Where would science be if people were not interested in learning new things? What is your doctorate thesis on?"

"Permafrost thawing and the future contributions to global warming."

"What would you say the prognosis of this thawing will be?"

"Nothing good. The tremendous amounts of carbon and methane locked in the permafrost will only provide further warming."

"Yes, I read as much. Too bad we hadn't started earlier on our quest to reduce carbon pollution. It seems our new President is sincere on doing all she can to reduce greenhouse gas emissions. She was able to get Congress to pass an overdue increase on the carbon tax. Her support for a carbon reduction incentive payment is a welcome stand. She has personally travelled to China and India to try to get them more on board in reducing fossil fuel use. I believe she is sincere about making progress in reducing climate warming and seems to be a go getter."

"You're quite well informed on climate news. I wish more of the populace and especially scientists had your interest."

"Climate warming is the most important issue confronting humans and all the other life forms. Sometimes I wish I had pursued climate science rather than physics."

"Isn't your research about energy? That's very important for the future of the planet and climate. Our energy needs are driving climate change."

"In a manner of speaking, yes, you are correct. My specialty is trying to produce a working prototype of an Einstein-Rosen Bridge, which could be a futile pursuit since to maintain such a structure would require a tremendous amount of energy. Sometimes I think I'm wasting my time."

"Well, probably all scientific pursuit can seem difficult for the time period involved. Unfortunately, the first climate scientists were very ineffective on getting people and governments to recognize the importance of decreasing carbon dioxide and other pollution."

"Very true. Big Oil knew back in the 1970s that fossil fuel burning was harmfully heating the planet, but were very effective in sowing doubt." He looked around the small café. "I've heard this cafe was a popular spot, but have never been. It's very pleasant sitting here with you, but I have a class in a about an hour, so I should be leaving." He watched her face without speaking as if he was working out an internal puzzle.

What was causing him to hesitate, she wondered. She enjoyed his company and felt relaxed talking to him. She was disappointed that he had to leave. Oh well, she had met him and wouldn't need to go out of her way to walk through the Physics Building anymore. She was foolish to think he would be as interested in her as she had been about him.

The scuttlebutt around campus was that he was unattached. He had dated an attractive history graduate student for some time, but they had recently stopped seeing each other. When she learned of the break up, she had begun cutting through the Physics Building in hope of meeting him. She didn't know why she wanted to meet him. All her fellow female graduate student friends thought he was a dreamboat, but the rumor was that he was uninterested in women because he was so caught up in his research. One of the reasons his girlfriend had broken off dating him.

Rose wondered why she had been so determined to meet him. Maybe it was the challenge he presented— a handsome man uninterested in women— or maybe it was his reputation as a budding genius. Well, she had managed to meet him and had gotten him to accompany her to breakfast— a triumph of sorts. She would be the envy of her fellow students. Would that be the end of it? She studied him as he fidgeted in his seat in obvious consternation, wondering what was causing his discomfort.

Suddenly, he leaned forward. "Would you be interested in having dinner together sometime?" he asked, fidgeting with his hands. "I've enjoyed talking to you, and I am interested in hearing more about your thesis."

She sat erect in surprise. "Oh... ah... yes, I would love to have dinner with you." She smiled widely, feeling more successful then she had imagined possible. She was truly excited— something she hadn't felt since her breakup with William— and was looking forward getting to know this man better. William had been too full of himself and his proclivity for denigrating climate science had eventually been too much to accept.

"How about Friday evening?"

"Umm." She squished her lips together and looked up at the ceiling. She didn't want to appear too anxious and easy. "Yes, that would be good." She fished in her purse and withdrew a small notebook. She wrote out her address and phone number. "What time were you thinking?"

"Do you like to eat early or late?"

"I like to eat later when it's not so hot, and I like eating outside. The air-conditioning in many restaurants is like a deep freeze. What do you fancy?"

"My sentiment also. How about I call for you around 7:30. I'll make arrangements for an 8:00 reservation. Do you have you any preferences on restaurants?"

"No, you pick, but they have to have a number of vegan options. I've been a vegan most of my life. Surprise me." Was she being too demanding? Probably not. Most people concerned with climate warming were not big meat eaters. The land use required to grow crops for animal feed had been devastating to the planet. Factory animal farming was waning, and the last deadly avian flu pandemic seven years after the terrible SARS2 coronavirus had opened the eyes of many to the dangers of the meat and poultry factory production. Not to mention the cruelty involved.

"Excellent, I'm mostly vegan myself. Until Friday then." He rose and bowed. He stood motionless for a time. She would have loved to know what he was thinking. "Goodbye," he finally said and strode away.

3- JUNE 9, 2045

"This is pleasant. I've not been here before," Rose announced. "Excellent choice. This courtyard is beautiful. Lovely landscaping."

They were sitting at a table on the open air patio close to the thick bushes of purple fuchsia and pink bougainvillea. The half-moon, surrounded by a halo, was prominent in the slightly smoky sky, and the temperature was comfortably in the mid-eighties.

"I'm glad you like it," Arthur replied. "It is considered quite the up and coming restaurant."

"What do you fancy getting? There's lots of vegan choices."

"I was leaning toward the assorted mushroom and rice stuffed tomato and pepper. What are you thinking?"

"I'm going to get the vegetable curry. Of course I'll want to sample yours as well." She smiled and fixed her gray eyes on him.

Her gaze felt like a *Star Trek* tractor beam lifting him from his seat. He focused on her elegant hands to break the spell of those gray eyes with their subtle bluish tint. "Of course we have to sample each other's dishes."

She was beautiful in her yellow-flowered sundress with its spaghetti straps. She had a compact bosom and her small Adam's apple accentuated her long neck. He was so glad he had found the courage to ask her to dinner. He wondered how old she was. He guessed she was about his same age. He had completed undergraduate at 18 and his doctorate in Physics at 22. He was made a full professor at 25. He suspected she was probably around twenty-six or so. She looked younger with her smooth complexion and lanky body. Why had she been determined to meet him? He had heard his students calling him the young genius. Was this what caused her to seek him out? Was he like some exotic animal to her?

"You seem quite contemplative," Rose said. "A penny for your thoughts."

"Oh... I was just thinking of all the sumptuous dishes I would like to try here." He was actually thinking how alluring Rose was and wondered if she would like him enough to continue seeing him. Her close presence made him swoon. He was getting way ahead of himself. He thought about her expressions— 'a penny for your thoughts' and 'what do you fancy'. "I've noticed you have used a number of expressions from England. Have you spent time in England?"

"Yes, I did a semester during undergraduate there. I almost went to Cambridge for my post graduate. It's such a lovely University, but I thought the faculty here at Berkeley was more advanced in climate science, and I've always liked the bay area of northern California."

"Cambridge... yes that's such a quaint and interesting city. I did a summer seminar there a few years ago. I was reluctant to leave. Although I must admit I never got used to the frequent rains.”

“Yes exactly, although they are waning with the decrease of the North Atlantic Drift. Without the rain the island wouldn’t be so green. The changing weather caused by the weakening of the Drift will be detrimental to all of Northern Europe. England is quite a contrast to the US West. Here we would love having half of England’s rain. Especially with the increasing drought.”

“I’ve read how global warming is affecting the ocean currents in the Atlantic. The effects of the warming and acidification of the oceans are so detrimental. Coral has become nearly extinct. The polar caps are melting at an alarming rate, undermined by the warming water underneath and the less reflective melting surface.”

“Yes indeed. It’s so sad about the coral. I remember my Dad, who was an avid recreational diver for years, complaining about what ocean warming was doing to the coral formations around the world. Coral is such a beautiful and productive organism. It’s terrible that coral has all but disappeared. The Australian Great Barrier Reef is 80 percent dead.” She picked up the wine menu. “Are you interested in any wine or beer?”

“Sure, I could go for a glass of wine. I’m not much of a drinker, but yeah.”

"The bottles are quite expensive. I'm up for just a glass of white wine." She handed the menu toward him.

As he reached out for menu, he looked up into her eyes. Suddenly he was lost in her eyes and held the menu as if frozen before gaining his momentum and opening the menu. "I think I'll have a glass of the Pinot Grigio. What would you like?"

"I'll have the same." She looked toward the waiter, who saw her glance and moved to their table.

"We'd both like a glass of the Coppola Pinot Grigio," Arthur said. "I'll have a mixed salad to start and the mushroom stuffed tomato and pepper for my entrée." He handed his menu and the wine menu to the waiter, who turned to Rose with a big smile.

Rose smiled back. "I'll have a pear salad to start and the vegetable curry."

Arthur waited for the waiter to accept her menu and leave. He felt a semblance of pride being with Rose, especially after observing how the waiter was enthralled by her beauty. He felt so lucky that he had met her. "So tell me about the thawing of the permafrost."

"Well it has already begun. Today the release of carbon dioxide from permafrost thawing is estimated at contributing the equivalent of 6 gigatons of CO_2 a year and an unknown quantity of methane. We are at 70 gigatons of equivalent CO_2 now and 450 ppm of carbon in the atmosphere. Further permafrost thawing will be catastrophic. The amount of hydrates of methane in the Arctic Ocean shelf is unknown. There is significant bubbling visible already. Methane as you probably know is a more potent greenhouse gas, 84 times that of CO2 for 20 years and 28 times over a hundred years because it dissipates over time while CO2 takes more than a hundred thousand years to dissipate."

"Wow that is kind of frightening."

"It is, but as you say the US has been making better progress on reducing emissions since the influenza outbreak in 2027. The horrible President Trump was a disaster for the climate. He increased fossil fuel use and destroyed environmental regulations. I remember my Dad railing against Trump when I was a kid. The US was slow to begin reduction in fossil fuel use compared to Europe. Biden tried to reduce fossil fuel use and promote clean energy, but the Republicans and the oil and gas industry and their backers stopped him from making much progress."

She paused and studied him a moment, then took a drink of wine. "President Harris actually began the first reduction in fossil fuel use with the first national carbon tax after the Republicans lost big in 2024. Mayberry was good in 2032 in increasing the tax to an amount that significantly affected the petroleum and natural gas industries. President Baker has done a great job in promoting clean energy. Most of the transportation sector is now electric. The goop hydrogen fuel cells for large transport and trains has further reduced greenhouse gas emissions. We still have too many natural gas electric generating stations. If we could get China, India, and the rest of the countries to increase their carbon taxes and do more to transition to clean energy, we could hopefully avoid the dreaded 3° C warming."

"I like your positivity." He paused to focus on her smile. "I feel better about climate change talking to you. Sometimes the news is so disturbing. After Trump supporters tried to rig state elections in favor of the Republicans, the country could have veered toward fascism and runaway climate catastrophes. I think the US squeaked by. If Congress hadn't passed the voting rights act, who knows what would have happened." He shook his head.

"Yes, the US definitely squeaked by. The fossil fuel industries and their backers were doing an excellent job of creating misinformation. If the Republicans had been successful, we would have been doomed. On the other end of the spectrum though, the doomsday cult about global warming is counterproductive also. We need to provide accurate assessments of climate change, highlight the successes we have had, and what can be done in the future to improve the situation. Overly pessimistic projections are not helpful. The situation is dire, but not hopeless. There is so much we can still do. The technology exists to totally eliminate CO_2 from entering the atmosphere. Dickerson being elected in 2040 was a setback. Thankfully he was a one term Republican President. His failure to get congress to decrease the carbon tax was fortunate. The increased use of clean hydrogen in the manufacture of concrete, steel, and aluminum has helped in decreasing the US carbon footprint along with carbon capture. Hopefully India, China, and the developing world will make more use of the hydrogen technology and carbon capture."

He was utterly impressed by Rose's oration. She was so smart and so convincing, not to mention unbelievably enticing. "You would be an excellent spokesperson for getting people interested in totally eliminating fossil fuels. You need a public forum to get the word out."

"I'm not very good at public speaking." She took a drink of wine to hide her embarrassment. "This wine's good." She shifted in her seat. "I think you are quite a good public speaker. As I said, your class on quantum mechanics was so interesting. However, I never was able to get my head around the many worlds theory for the collapse of the entangled wave function into particles even for remote viewers once the initial observation is made." His concentrated stare caused her to take a quick breath. "Where are these other parallel worlds?" She leaned back with a semblance of a smirk to await his reply.

He suddenly realized as she leaned back that he was staring at her too much, but found it hard to stop. "Yes, I'm not a big proponent of the many worlds theory. I think the collapse of the wave function after observation at present is unexplainable. The world of particle physics is different than the macro world. I don't know if there will ever be an acceptable theory for the wave collapse upon observation. This bothered Einstein as well."

"Oh, well, I'm glad I'm in good company then."

"Where do you parents live?" Arthur asked.

"They live in Palo Alto. My Mom was a professor of chemistry at Stanford where I went to undergraduate and graduate school before transferring here. My Dad is a biographer and quite successful. One of his most famous biographies was of Einstein."

"Wow, your Dad is John Manning. I read his biography of Einstein when I was a kid. The biography had an immense impact on me. I adored Einstein and all his amazing theories and discoveries." He paused and smiled as he remember how enthralled he was reading her Dad's biography of Einstein.

"What about your parents, where are they?"

"They live here in Berkeley," he said. "They're retired high school teachers. My Mom taught science, and my Dad taught history. They had me late. My sister is ten years older than me."

"What does she do?"

"She's a math teacher at a Sacramento High School."

"Quite an academic family you have."

"Your family is academic as well. Do you have any brothers or sisters?"

Rose looked down and took a shuttering breath before looking up to answer. "My younger sister was killed in an auto accident."

"I'm sorry to hear that."

"Yes, it was devastating. I was in graduate school when it happened. I dropped out for a semester before transferring here. My Mom and Dad never got over it. My Dad never wrote another book and my Mom retired soon after the death. I tried to comfort them, but I was just as devastated, and of little help to them. We all loved her so much. She was such a delightful sister. I miss her terribly. I transferred here in part to get away from my parents, I'm sorry to admit." Her eyes dripped tears as she dabbed her face with her napkin. "It was so hard to be around them with their terrible grief and my own debilitating grief."

"I can sympathize with your need to get away. The death of a child or sibling is the most difficult death to deal with, I'm sure." He looked away at the approaching waiter carrying their dishes, glad to change the subject. "Ah here's our dinner." He held up his glass. "Here's to health, happiness, and a better world."

She opened her sad eyes wider as she clinked her glass with his. "Health, happiness, and a better world."

He felt for her, wanting to kiss and caress her to dispel her sadness. "This smells great." He cut into the pepper and stuffed a fork full in to his mouth. "Hmm, this is delicious."

She scooped up a fork full of her curry and rice. "Yes, this is lovely too. Want a bite?"

"Of course." She scooted her plate toward him, and he took a bite. "Nice, quite piquant. Here, try the stuffed pepper." He cut a bite for her and shoved his plate toward her.

She scooped up the fork full. "Yum, that is good. I love mushrooms."

After they finished their meal, Arthur asked, "Would you like to go for a drink and hear some music. I have a friend, who is playing folk guitar at a bar near here." He didn't want to leave her. He felt an exhilarating energy being with her. She had captured his heart so quickly. He was amazed. He had never felt like this before.

She smiled and stared at him for a minute before answering. "Yes, that would be nice. What kind of music does he play?"

He felt a tremendous relief that she would accompany him, and he would get to know her even better. "All kinds— Dylan, James Taylor, old blues, modern songs... he can play anything. He's really good."

"Sounds exciting."

4- DECEMBER 10, 2046

Arthur was infatuated with Rose from the start, and after over a year of dating, he decided that he wanted her to be in his life always. Since she had completed her doctorate and had secured an assistant professor position at the University Climate Science Department, she would be present in Berkeley for a good while. They got along well, went out often, and even were compatible in difficult situations. Their vacation together to Hawaii had been sublime with never a cross word.

When Arthur met Rose's parents, John and Mary, he talked both of their ears off about Einstein, possibly going overboard on how much he had enjoyed John's biography of Einstein. He professed that John's book had spurred him to pursue physics. He talked about his work on trying to prove the existence of the Einstein-Rosen Bridge, which both John and Mary were very interested in. Mary was a delight and could hold her own on Physics and Einstein. He could see where Rose had inherited her beauty and intellect. Mary was an intelligent, stunning beauty in her own right.

When he and Rose went to dinner at his parents, Frank and Olivia, his parents fell in love with Rose. They were older than Rose's parents and were sometimes a little absent minded. Arthur was glad they lived in Berkeley, and he could offer assistance when needed. Often when he was alone with his parents, they would ask when he was going to marry the wonderful Rose and give them some grandkids.

He didn't know if he wanted children given the future that the continued warming climate would portend. There was slow continued progress in eliminating fossil fuels in the US, but much more was needed. Many of the other countries outside Europe were not making the same progress. The fact that he often worked late in his laboratory, he thought might be an impediment to marriage and certainly wouldn't be ideal for fatherhood.

His Project was finally looking like he might ultimately prove the existence of an Einstein-Rosen Bridge. He had persuaded the Energy Department to fund the construction of a triple-wall, stainless steel enclosure, which could be cooled by liquid helium, and several immense electromagnetic controllers, which surrounded the structure and would be used to produce the vortex and control the swirling ionized atmosphere. A banked, computer network was also included for programing and controlling the electrical energy and the vortex of a future Bridge.

He believed from his calculations that to produce an Einstein-Rosen Bridge inside the structure he would need a tremendous amount of electrical power. The electrical power he could obtain from the University grid did not seem to be of sufficient strength. He built a bank of capacitors that could ramp up the power for short bursts, hoping that this burst of energy from the capacitors might be enough to begin the formation of the Bridge.

He had assembled a good and loyal team. His chief computer specialist, Violet, was a vivacious, beautiful, delightful, young woman whose computer skills were amazing. She had a master's degree, and was somewhat of a workaholic. His chief mechanical and electrical engineer was an older pleasant man, Billy, who had amazed Arthur from the start. It seemed Billy could build anything that Arthur envisioned. His other engineer, a younger man, Harold, was very astute also. All, except possibly Jason, the other computer specialist, seemed to be thoroughly committed to the Project.

Arthur and Violet had formed an uncanny partnership over the year working together. Her ability to write code for what he envisioned was as if she could read his thoughts. He fell in love with her. Not a sexual love, but a love of intellectual comradeship. He enjoyed her company and would have done anything for her.

Their work to set up the equipment had gone well. Everyone pitched in and they all seemed to get along. Violet was a lively participant, who would often get everyone laughing. He was very happy with the progress they were making. When he noticed the discord developing between Violet and Jason, he was concerned. He had sensed soon after hiring Violet that her sexual preference was for women even though she hid her orientation well.

Jason's teasing of Violet, trying to get her to go out with him, was making Violet angry. Jason had a high opinion of himself and thought he was the superior computer programmer when in fact Violet could run rings around him. Arthur didn't feel it was his place to inform Jason about Violet's sexual preference, but he didn't want Jason's pursuit to cause Violet to leave.

Arthur decided he needed to speak to Jason and asked him to come into his office. After Jason took his seat, Arthur began, "Jason, I've noticed that you've been teasing and pursuing Violet. It is making her angry, and I would like you to stop. She is very important to the Project. I don't want your antics to drive her to quit."

"Hey, my personal life is my own business. Who I want to go out with is none of your concern."

"I agree, but what happens at work on my Project," he said with increased vehemence, "is my business." He focused intently on Jason. "You need to maintain a professional relationship with Violet here at work. What you do when not at work is entirely your own business. Have I made myself clear?"

"Jesus, I was just having a little fun. This is not the military."

"No it isn't, but make no mistake I am in charge."

"Okay, okay. Can I go?"

"Yes, sure, go back to work. The last computer sequence you wrote doesn't look right. I believe it needs more detailed steps and safety protocols." Arthur stood.

Jason rose slowly from his seat with a frown. "All right, I'll see what I can do to improve it."

"Thanks for your understanding, Jason. Talk to you later."

Arthur watched Jason leave his office. He suspected Jason wouldn't stay with the Project much longer. He thought Jason's presence was a distraction for the team. He wouldn't fire him, but would be glad when he left.

After his talk with Jason, Jason stopped teasing Violet, which made the work much more enjoyable for all. Jason continued working on the Project, but his work was often a little shoddy. Arthur had had no other qualified initial applicants for the computer specialist position, and he knew no one who could take Jason's place. He didn't want to saddle Violet with all the computer work, so he kept Jason on while putting feelers out for a replacement.

When he told Rose about the situation with Violet and Jason, Rose said if she was Arthur she'd have no qualms about firing Jason. She thought he sounded like a jerk. She thought Violet would welcome Jason's removal. Instead of firing Jason, Arthur became more critical of Jason's computer work, hoping Jason would get fed up and leave of his own accord. Firing someone at the University required endless paperwork and hearings. Arthur was so intent on his calculations for the Einstein-Rosen Bridge power requirements and structure inputs, he felt he had little time to go through a firing process. He could tell that any criticism greatly angered Jason. He also knew from phone calls asking about Jason that Jason was looking for another job. He thought Jason wouldn't be around very long.

He was surprised that Jason stayed on for nearly six months, but, when Jason resigned to take a job at Tesla, he was delighted. He disliked Jason somewhat, but wished him well at Tesla, and had given him a good recommendation. The day after Jason left, Violet was visibly ecstatic, positively beaming, joking with Billy and Harold and whizzing around the laboratory. She started working more hours, coming in early and staying as long as Arthur.

When Arthur asked her why she was working so much, she replied, "I need to correct a lot of the programming Jason worked on. You should have fired the idiot a long time ago."

Arthur suddenly realized he had caused Violet more work by keeping Jason on. He had been wrong to think he was helping Violet by not forcing all the computer work on her. His tolerance of Jason had done the opposite from what he intended. He had been so caught up in his calculations for the energy input and the sequencing that he had not reviewed Jason's work as he should have. "I'm sorry Violet. I knew he was not nearly as good a programmer as you, but I'm afraid I did not check his work as I should have."

"Not to worry, Boss. I'll straighten his work out. You've got other fish to fry if we're going to get the correct energy inputs necessary to form an Einstein-Rosen Bridge in the structure. I have every faith in you. What we have accomplished so far is utterly amazing. I'm with you, Boss, all the way." She got up from her computer terminal. "I'm not the only one who's glad Jason is gone. Billy and Harold thought he was a dunce also. The team is rock solid now and ready and willing. When do you think we can ramp the structure up and see what she's capable of?"

"Soon... I think I've figured out how best to connect the electrical inputs if my calculations are correct. I'll get Billy to reconfigure the input electrical cables and we'll fire her up next week if you'll have the computer code ready to go by then?"

"You bet, Boss. I've already corrected most of Jason's work, and I'll definitely have the computer program ready for your review later this week. I'll be ready. You can take that to the bank."

"Okay, Violet, sounds great. Thank you for all your hard work."

Violet stepped up to Arthur and gave him a hug. "Oh, Boss, I love working for you. You're the best."

Surprised, Arthur shook his head and quickly stepped back. "Thank you, Violet."

When Arthur told Rose about Violet hugging him and his embarrassment, Rose laughed. "Do I need to be jealous?"

"No, of course not. I'm totally yours, which brings me to what I've been intending to do for a while." He got down on one knee and removed a box from his trousers, which he opened with a big smile. "Rose, I love you more than words can say. Will you marry me?"

Rose tackled Arthur, and she rolled with him on the floor. "Arthur, I would love to marry you." She took the ring from the box and held it out for Arthur, who slipped it on her finger. "How does it look?"

"Like it belongs on your beautiful hand."

She grabbed him tightly, rolling and laughing. She stopped the rolling and stood up, extending her hand. "Come on, this requires a thorough vetting of my spouse to be. I need to put you through your paces to make sure you have the stamina to be my husband."

"Oh I've got the stamina and then some." He jumped up, took her hand, and led her to his bedroom.

Violet had been totally thankful and excited when Arthur offered her a position on his Project. When she came for the interview after she saw the job posting at the University, she didn't know what to expect, but the posting sounded interesting. At the interview where she learned of Arthur's work to prove the existence of an Einstein-Rosen Bridge and his hope to actually produce an Einstein-Rosen Bridge, she had nodded and played along as if she knew what he was talking about, but in fact had no clue. Immediately after the interview, she had gone to the library and read everything she could find on the Einstein-Rosen Bridge. Her research had enlivened her wish to be hired. She had been working for a bank maintaining their computer network and solving computer problems as they came up. The work was easy for her, and she wanted something more challenging.

Arthur's Project sounded like just the type of work she was looking for— something that would stretch her abilities. She had always liked reading science fiction, and the job was actually a science fiction pursuit— proving the existence of a wormhole and trying to produce an actual wormhole. She was totally psyched about the job. She soon fell in love with Arthur— a brotherly love. He was such a calm mild-mannered man and not at all supercilious even though it was obvious to her that he was a genius.

Although she deeply loved Arthur, her sexual preference was for women, something as a young girl she initially fought, but as she grew older eventually embraced. She had tried to be heterosexual in high school, but it left her unsatisfied and rather sad. She kept her sexual orientation secret from her parents. They would never have understood. She had trouble understanding it herself. She tried to be bisexual in college, but that didn't work either. She had to face it she was a born lesbian. When she went home for her second summer break from college, she came out to her parents. They were appalled and asked her to leave. She never saw her parents again. She immersed herself in the lesbian scene in college and had occasional flings while she worked at the bank, but many of her liaisons were superficial, and she grew weary of new encounters.

After going to work for Arthur, she had become something of a sexual recluse. Occasionally she would try a lesbian encounter, but most left her feeling unsatisfied intellectually. She wished often that she would find a woman that stimulated her as much as Arthur and that would be someone she could form a lasting relationship with, but realized the probability of finding such a mate was small.

5- JULY 6, 2047

Rose was deep in thought as she sat at her desk, looking out the window of her office, listening to the lone song bird nearby as she watched the students parade by in the blistering sun. The bird population along with the insects they fed on had been decimated by climate warming. The US government had not done nearly enough to stop the burning of fossil fuels. Nevertheless, she was happy about her personal life. The handsome genius and she had been married for almost a month. Their civil ceremony had been a small affair with their parents, siblings, and friends, since neither being particularly religious had wanted to involve a church. Ever since the ceremony, she felt sublime, immersed in a soothing bliss and feeling of fulfillment. To top it off, she had been offered a full professorship at Berkeley.

She had been worried that she would be passed over and remain an assistant professor. To become a full professor, she had thought that she might have to move to another University. Something she would have only contemplated if it was within commuting distance to Berkeley. Arthur would not have moved. He was thoroughly committed to his Project, a Project she had only a vague idea of how far he had progressed toward his goal of proving the existence of an Einstein-Rosen Bridge. She secretly thought he would never be able to produce the Einstein-Rosen Bridge even for a fleeting moment. It just sounded too much like science fiction to her.

It was amazing the amount of funding Arthur had been able to secure from the Department of Energy. He had spent millions building his laboratory with its large structure to contain the Einstein-Rosen Bridge and the computer networks to formulate and maintain such a Bridge. She knew he could be very convincing with his enthusiastic, mild-mannered speech. He had convinced her she should marry him when marriage was the last thing from her mind. It seemed he had a presence that made him stand out without really trying very hard. She was thoroughly mesmerized by Arthur and wholly appreciative of their life together. She really didn't mind that he spent many hours at his laboratory because when he was home, it was as if his world revolved around her. She could feel his love for her deep in her bones, which tantalized her and comforted her in a way that made her quake with joy.

After their marriage, she had enjoyed moving into Arthur's two bedroom apartment that was within walking distance to the campus. His apartment was bright and cozy, much nicer than her former dingy apartment. Although his apartment was quite adequate for the two of them, it would be cramped if they were ever going to have children. Something she and Arthur had discussed, and both truly wanted even though the world was still warming drastically from the continued use of fossil fuels, and the future was looking chaotic.

She had been working hard trying to convince other countries to follow the US's lead in reducing the use of fossil fuels through her articles and international travel as a participant in the Intergovernmental Panel on Climate Change. Most of Europe, except for some of the eastern countries, were quite a bit ahead of the US in eliminating fossil fuels, but in the rest of the world, progress was far behind. Her recent trip to India to meet with climate scientists there had been disappointing. She was still hopeful however that her continued activism would help the people of the world to come to their senses and force governments to make the necessary changes to avoid a climate apocalypse.

Several months after they were married, she began to look for a suitable house they could buy. She was in no hurry. She wasn't ready to have children, but she knew finding a suitable house that they could afford in Berkeley would be difficult and would probably take time. Arthur was pleased that she was looking for a house, but he had a few adamant requirements that made her search even more difficult. He wanted a house that was within walking distance to his Physics Building Laboratory and had a pleasant backyard. She spent months casually looking when she had free time for the perfect house. She found many that she would love, but most were too far from campus or too expensive. She agreed with Arthur's two requirements, but wondered if she would ever find a suitable house. Her increased trips to Europe, South America, Africa, and Asia for her research and outreach kept her busy and left little time for house hunting.

When at a retirement party for the Director of the Environmental Science Research Department, she met an English Professor, Michael Adams, who was going to retire in a few months. Professor Adams's wife had died, and he was planning to move closer to his daughter in Seattle after he retired. He had a house near the campus that needed many repairs, and he professed that he wasn't looking forward to getting it ready to put on the market. She asked him if she could look at the house since she was in the market for such a house. Professor Adams was agreeable to her visit, and they set a date.

In November, Arthur and Rose moved into the house that they had purchased from Professor Adams. Arthur was so happy that Rose had found the perfect house. The detached, white clapboard, two story, three bedroom house was less than an hour walk to his laboratory and had a lovely landscaped backyard. There were many repairs needed. The shingle roof had to be replaced, the bathrooms needed updating, and everything outside and inside needed repainting, but on the whole the house was a real find. They hired workmen to make the repairs and updating, and had them remodel the kitchen, opening it up and installing larger windows.

Things were also going well at Arthur's Project. The Oakland Fusion Electric Generating station had begun operation after years of delay. The Department of Energy had agreed to the installation of cables to his Project. He hoped with the increase in electrical energy the Fusion Station could supply that he could make more progress on the forming an Einstein–Rosen Bridge.

When Arthur invited Violet to dinner after they had renovated their house, he was apprehensive that Rose would not like Violet. Her enthusiasm was sometimes a little over the top, and her directness could turn people off. He liked Violet immensely and hoped Rose would feel the same.

Arthur rushed to the door when he heard the sound of the doorbell. As he opened the door, he was surprised to see Violet in an alluring red print dress with white flowers and a plunging neckline. At work, she was always in jeans and baggy shirts. "Violet, your look great. Come on in."

"Hey up, Boss, here's some Champs," Violet said and immediately hugged Arthur, causing him to blush, before swishing past him to admire the house. The living room held two navy blue cloth sofas with an oak coffee table and a large Persian carpet with a medallion center of white, red, and green surrounded by a deep blue field that matched the sofas and a border of the same colors as the medallion. Still life and landscape water color paintings, made by Rose and her mother, decorated the walls. "Boss, you and Rose have really made the house beautiful. I love the watercolor paintings." She continued into the dining room with its older looking oak table and chairs and breezed into the kitchen.

When Rose, dressed in a purple dress and wearing a multicolored apron, turned around from the stove, Violet erupted in laughter. "Rose, you look just like I imagined— except you are far more beautiful. How did a beanpole like Arthur snag such a beauty?" She slipped up close to Rose and held out her arms. "Can I give you a hug?"

"Certainly, Violet. It is such a pleasure to finally meet you."

Violet wrapped Rose in her arms, staring at her face momentarily before kissing her cheeks in the French manner. "Hmmm, you smell fantastic." She stepped back. "Gardenia and rose essence is it?"

"I'm not sure, but now that you mention it, yes. Arthur bought it for me."

"It suits you to a tee." She stepped around Rose and studied the cook top. "What have we got cooking?"

"Spaghetti marinara sauce with shitake mushrooms."

"Smells wonderful." She pivoted and walked back into the dining room. "Arthur, don't just stand there. Open the Cham, and let's have a toast."

Arthur popped the Champaign that Rose had brought and poured three glasses. Rose had followed Violet into the dining room.

When all three had their glass of Champaign, Violet raised her glass. "Here's to two amazing and wonderful people and to their lovely house. Good health and happiness."

"Good health and happiness," Rose repeated.

"This house has good vibes. I can feel that you two are going to be so happy here."

"Thank you, Violet. Yes, I believe we will."

That evening after their dinner as he and Rose were getting ready for bed, Arthur asked, "So what do you think of Violet?"

"She's a funny and delightful young woman. She's totally in love with you."

"Rose, she's more likely to be in love with you."

"Oh, I know she's a lesbian, but she's infatuated with you intellectually. If she was hetero or bisexual, I'd be very worried about the long hours you work together. If I was so inclined, I'd fall in love with her myself. She's one of a kind person. You are lucky to have her."

"Don't I know it." He laughed. "It's almost if when I talk to her about a concept I think we need to incorporate in the Project, she has already read my mind and has visualized a way to integrate it into the computer software."

"You think you'll ever form an Einstein-Rosen Bridge?"

"I certainly hope so. I'd hate for all the time and money we've devoted to the Project to have been a waste. Sometimes I feel guilty in spending so much government money. Money that would probably have been better spent trying to mitigate climate change and stopping the use of fossil fuel."

"Gargantuan amounts of money for climate change would be available if the US would cut back more on its absurd spending on military equipment. It's a stupid waste of money. What you spend on your Project is a drop in the bucket compared to the wasted money spent making weapons to destroy countries and people. There has been some progress in reducing the so called defense spending, but still the amount is way too much. They should call it offense spending. The American people have been duped with the nationalism and hype on display to convince them of the need for the bloated defense budget." She frowned as she slapped her pillow. "Upgrading nuclear weapons that can never be used if life on this planet is to continue at a cost of billions is the dumbest thing I could imagine."

"I totally agree. Maybe someday we can get countries to destroy all nuclear weapons."

"Don't hold your breath."

"Come here you vixen. I'm in bad need of a kiss and a hug from my beautiful and astute wife."

Rose's frown turned into a big smile as she slinked to Arthur, allowing him to encapsulate her in his arms. "Oh Arthur, what would I do without you?"

"Don't you ever try to find out."

6-   SEPTEMBER 14, 2049

Rose welcomed the addition of Diane Johnson to the Climate Science faculty. She had been on the panel interviewing Diane and had fought hard to get the panel to offer Diane the position. She was so happy to have a climate scientist of African American descent to help with her teaching and her research. She felt the faculty was way too Anglo Saxon. Diane and she had gotten along well right from the beginning. Diane was as passionate about mitigating climate warming as Rose and was a jolly addition to the staff. She often had Rose in stitches with laughter. She was a head shorter than Rose's more than six feet and quite seductively curved. Her short curly hair framed a beautiful chestnut face that more often than not was locked in a smile or bursting with laughter.

Diane for her part seemed happy to call Rose her friend. She was often at Rose's and Arthur's house for dinner and loved playing backgammon with Arthur, her raucous laughter filling the house. Since their new home was within walking distance of the campus, Diane would often park her car near Rose's house, and they would walk to campus together. They worked together on climate projections and papers on their research findings about what continued fossil fuel use would do to the climate. They came to be inseparable friends.

Rose was often trying to fix Diane up with men she and Arthur knew, but none of the men proved to be a good match for Diane. She was a strong independent, outspoken woman, who wouldn't suffer fools for long.

Rose observed that Diane seemed to get along better with the white men she dated than the black men. She had been raised by her Jamaican mother. Her white father had died from cancer five years after Diane was born. Rose thought maybe she was seeking a type of connection to her father with her proclivity for white men.

Rose and Arthur both thought Diane was a beautiful fun loving woman. Arthur however thought Rose should stop trying to fix Diane up. He sensed that since Diane never had a dad growing up that she might be leery of and at the same time fascinated by men. He thought it would be better to let Diane pick out her own male friends without Rose's help. Rose took Arthur's suggestion with a grain of salt.

When Rose was having trouble with her climate simulation program, she went to the computer science department for some advice. As soon as she met Simon, a handsome black computer scientist, who was very friendly and offered to look at her program, she immediately thought of Diane. Simon accompanied Rose back to the Climate Science building and made some changes to the code of her climate simulation software that improved the speed of calculation. When she introduced Simon to Diane, she believed there was a spark of concentrated interest from both parties, so she quickly made an excuse about something she needed to do and left the two alone.

When she returned to the office after a walk and a coffee, she strode into Diane's office and sat down. "Well, Diane, how did it go?"

"How did what go?" Diane replied.

"You know... with Simon."

"He said he had made some minor adjustments to the calculation code and the simulation should compute much faster now. I ran the last simulation we did again with the changes Simon made, and it certainly was faster and seemed more accurate. He's good."

"I don't mean about the software. I mean you and him. Did he ask for your telephone number?"

"No."

"He didn't? I'm sure he was quite taken with you. How long did he stay?"

"He was here about 20 minutes."

"What did you talk about?"

"Easy, Rose, with the third degree and trying to fix me up. I thought Arthur told you to cool it."

"Hey, I'm concerned about you. I want you be as happy as I am with my wonderful husband."

"There aren't many handsome budding geniuses about like Arthur."

Rose laughed. "I doubt you're looking for a budding genius. Simon seemed quite intelligent. He recognized the problem in the software and corrected it in no time."

"How do you know I'm not looking for a budding genius?"

"All right, I'll leave it be. Still... you do think Simon's handsome?"

"Yes, Rose, he was a handsome man."

"I bet he calls you or comes to see you."

"Okay, I'll put five dollars that says he won't."

"Okay then." Rose held out her hand. "Five bucks says he will." They shook hands.

Rose breezed into work on Friday glad it was the end of the week. When she started up her computer, looking at the profuse emails she needed to review, she balked at the number, decided to take a break, and went to Diane's office.

As soon as she entered Diane's office, Diane slapped a five dollar bill on her desk. "You won."

"He called?" Rose replied, smiling with raised eyebrows.

"Yeah, we're going out to dinner tonight."

Rose scooped up the five dollar bill and laughed. "I knew it. I told you."

"All right... all right, don't rub it in."

"You're happy about this, aren't you?"

"Yes, I am."

"I have a good feeling about this."

"Good."

"Where you going for dinner?"

"I was going to let Simon choose."

"Why not go to the Garden Sanctuary. That's where Arthur and I had our first date. It has great vegan options and a beautiful courtyard. Very romantic."

"Maybe you should go in my place, Rose, since you want to plan the date."

"Hey, I'm just trying to be a good friend."

Diane rose, laughing, and gave Rose a hug. "I'm just kidding. Thanks for the suggestion. I'll suggest the restaurant to Simon."

Simon couldn't believe his luck in meeting Diane. Something about her immediately seared his heart. She was such a friendly, smart woman— a scientist at that. He was excited about taking her out to dinner. He had dated many beautiful black women, but most didn't have the aura that Diane exuded. She was a joy to talk to and had him laughing easily. Her colleague, Rose, was a beautiful woman also, who could have easily been a model with her lanky sensuous form. He felt Diane was as beautiful as Rose, but in a different way with her compact, buxom body and face that entranced him so much that the surroundings seemed to disappear. Her full lips were like a siren's call.

He had been an all-star running back in college at UCLA. His 6 foot 5 inch, muscular frame sometimes intimidated women. Not so with Diane. He thought Diane was someone he could respect and have fun with. With those thoughts swimming around in his mind, he rang the doorbell of Diane's apartment.

"Hello Simon, come on in," Diane said. She was wearing an African print dress, the tans, browns, and black earth colors complementing the beautiful chestnut color of her skin. He was wearing an African print yellow shirt and blue trousers. "I like your shirt. Seems we had similar thoughts about our dress."

"Yeah, you look fantastic. That is a beautiful dress." He followed her inside the small apartment. African carvings were displayed on the top of the bookcase. Photographs of another older woman were above on the cream colored wall. He stopped to peruse the photographs. Diane came up next to him.

"That's my mom. Isn't she beautiful?"

"Yes she is," Simon answered. "Where does she live?"

"In Columbia, Missouri where I grew up. She's the cleaning supervisor at the University of Missouri, but will be retiring soon. She grew up in Jamaica where she met my father, who was there on vacation. He was the Director of Maintenance for the University." She thrust her arm toward another photograph. "That's me as a kid with my Mom and Dad."

Simon moved to get a better look at the photograph. "You look happy."

"I was. Little did I know there that my world would soon fall apart." She paused and took a deep breath, blinking to stifle her tears. "My Dad died soon after this photo from pancreatic cancer."

"I'm sorry to hear that. It must have been difficult."

"It was. My Mom worked so hard to provide for us and made sure I got a good education. She insisted I go to graduate school. I wanted to get a job to help out, but she wouldn't hear of it."

"He pointed at another picture. "Is this when you graduated from graduate school?"

"Yes."

"Great picture of you and your mom."

"Thanks. Well, shall we be off?"

"Sure let's go."

After a pleasant meal at the Garden Sanctuary restaurant, Simon asked, "You up for desert?"

"I'm full to the brim," Diane said. "But I do love deserts. Maybe we can share one."

"Of course. What were you thinking about?"

"The vegan carrot cake sounds enticing."

"I'll go for that." Simon signaled the waiter and placed the order. "So how do you like your job?"

"I love it. Working with Rose is a delight. She is so kind and wise. She and I have a great time together.

Her husband, Arthur Brown, is a professor in the Physics department. Everyone calls him the young genius. I'm over at their house regularly. Arthur and I are backgammon fanatics."

"I'd a thought a genius would be a chess player."

"Do you play chess?"

"Yes indeed. Do you play?"

"I can play, but I'm very poor at it."

"We should play. After dinner, would you like to come back to my apartment and have a quick game?"

"Yeah, that sounds enjoyable as long as you don't make fun of my poor chess skills."

"Wouldn't think of it."

"Where are your parents?"

"They're deceased. I grew up in Detroit. Not a great place to live although I was able to excel there. Mostly because of my football prowess. It got me a full scholarship to UCLA. My parents were so proud. My Dad wanted me to enter the NFL draft, but I didn't want to be butted about anymore and end up with repeated concussions. College football is hard physically, but nothing like the pros. I was more interested in intellectual pursuits. My father worked at a glass factory owned by the Chinese. He had worked for GM before they closed most of their plants in Detroit. My mom didn't work until the plant closed, then she established a day care center in our home. I was the oldest of the children. My two sisters married good men and still live in Detroit. My brother is in

Texas. I don't how he stands it there. It'd be way too hot for me. The heat even here in the summer is hard for me to tolerate. Year round heat in Texas would be hard for me to take, not to mention the racist idiots there. The Democrats finally won the majority there, but the right wing Republicans still have a lot of power."

"Yeah, I know exactly what you mean. I had plenty of run-ins with racist idiots in Missouri. The Republicans are still trying to divide the country with their overt racism. Luckily it hasn't worked for them so well nationally, but it's still rampant in Missouri and the rest of the South."

"No shit. Excuse my language. The more things change the more they stay the same. I'm so glad that people like you and Rose are trying their best to get the world to come to their senses and totally eliminate fossil fuels. What would you say the prognosis is?"

"It's not good. We are headed for 3°C global mean temperature increase. It doesn't look like— unless things radically change— that there's any way to stop it, and 3° will lead to 4° and higher. I wish I could be more optimistic."

"Damn, I don't like the sound of that."

Diane enjoyed her date with Simon immensely. His size was daunting, but he seemed to be a gentle soul. She wondered how he had felt about her. He was very attentive throughout the night. He had been kind when he quickly defeated her twice at chess back at his apartment and complimented her chess play. He had not tried any intimate moves on her back at his place. He was quite a gentleman. After he drove her back to her apartment, he kissed her gently when he said good night. She felt a throb with the kiss and thought he was someone she would like to get to know better. He was the first black man she had dated in Berkeley, who stirred her emotions.

When he called the next day to invite her to dinner at his place on Wednesday, she was greatly pleased and hoped the dinner together would lead to additional dates and greater intimacy.

Sunday, Rose invited Diane to dinner. She was dying to find out how the date with Simon had gone. Diane waltzed into their house wearing a pink dress that emphasized her sensuous curves with a big grin and a bottle of wine as Rose opened the door.

"Thanks for inviting me. All these sumptuous dinners are creating havoc with my figure."

"You couldn't tell that by me. You look great."

"You look beautiful yourself. I like your black dress. Wish I had legs like yours to show off."

Arthur came up to give Diane a hug. "Glad you could come, Diane." He glanced at Rose. "Be forewarned, Rose is going to interrogate you about your date. "

"Oh, I figured as much. Nice Hawaiian shirt. Very festive."

"Well, how did it go?" Rose asked.

"Easy, Rose, let's sit down and have a drink first," Arthur said.

"Okay." Rose grabbed Diane's hand and dragged her into the dining room.

Arthur opened the wine and poured each a glass. "Here's to health, happiness, and clean energy."

"Exactly, health, happiness and clean energy," Diane responded and took a drink of her wine. "This wine is pretty good. What do you think?

"It's superb," Arthur said. "It has great body and is very smooth. Thanks for bringing it. Pinot Noir is one of my favorites. I'll just go get our dinner." He brought in a dish of brown rice and a pot of curried vegetables."

"Yum, curry. I was hoping you were making your signature vegetable curry, Arthur. Smells delicious."

"Okay, Diane, stop stalling," Rose said. "How'd it go with, Simon?"

"It was fun. We had a good time."

"What happened after the dinner?"

"He invited me back to his apartment for a game of chess."

"Oh, I see. He's a chess player."

"Yes, and a good one. He made short work of me."

"And...."

"He's got a nice two bedroom apartment near campus. Very spacious and nicely decorated."

"And...."

"And none of your business."

"Has he asked to see you again?"

"Rose, stop with the third degree," Arthur said.

"It's okay Arthur. She can't help herself." Diane laughed. "Yes, we arranged to meet again. He's making me dinner this Wednesday."

"So he can cook. All right, sounding good."

7- JUNE 20, 2050

Arthur awoke with the hum of the air conditioning cycling on and rolled up to watch his beautiful wife as she slept, her dark hair draped across her cheek.

Rose rolled toward him as if she sensed Arthur's gaze. She smiled at him as she opened her sleepy eyes. "It's my handsome husband." She scooted toward him and gave him a quick kiss before throwing off the sheet and starting to rise.

He thrust out his arm to restrain her "Hey, where do you think you're going? It's still early. You've got plenty of time to get to work."

She shrugged off his hand. "Don't worry, Big Boy. I'm going for a pee. I'll be back." She laughed as she hurried to the bathroom and sat in full view on the toilet.

He watched her with anticipation. How had he managed to impress such a smart, beautiful, fun loving woman to marry him? It was too good to be true.

Rose was enjoying her full professorship at Berkeley. Her research on permafrost had been recognized globally, and she was often asked to speak around the world on climate change solutions. He was so proud of her. Her assistant professor, Diane, was a wonderful help to her and a good friend, whose company he enjoyed immensely.

His own situation was looking up. He had made progress on the Einstein-Rosen Bridge Project now that energy was available from the Fusion Oakland Power Plan. The Fusion Plant was an amazing technological achievement at an astronomical cost. It was a wonder that it ever got built. The gargantuan amount of electrical energy that the Plant could produce, and the additional electric supply lines installed to the University finally could provide the extreme energy requirements in theory that the Einstein–Rosen Bridge needed.

"Hey, you voyeur, do you get a kick out of watching women pee?" Rose shouted with feigned anger.

"You bet. It's a turn on."

She finished with a smirk and ran laughing back into the bedroom, diving onto the bed. "I've got your turn on, Mister."

"That you certainly do," he responded and grasped her in his arms, kissing his way down to the dark triangle, tonguing her to climax, before entering her for a luxurious slow coupling, leading to a strong embrace, their faces relaxed in rapture.

After several minutes, Rose slipped from the bed and went into the bathroom to shower. "Don't forget that Diane is coming for dinner tonight with her new boyfriend."

"Who's cooking?"

"Ha, ha, you know full well the answer to that."

Diane swept into the foyer in her tight fitting midnight blue sleek dress, pulling her muscular boyfriend in with her, as Rose opened the front door, wearing a green full skirt dress with short sleeves and a scoop neckline. "Hi, Rose. You look incredible. Isn't she so beautiful?" She pulled her boyfriend closer. "Let me introduce you again to Simon."

Rose gave Simon, wearing blue slacks and a light blue shirt, a kiss on the cheek. "Welcome, Simon, to our home." She turned to Diane. "You're most welcome too, Diane."

"I should hope so," Diane responded.

Arthur stepped forward in his Hawaiian red print shirt and jeans. He grabbed Simon's hand and gave it a strong shake. "Come on in and have a seat in the dining room. I've nearly got dinner ready."

The couple followed Rose and Arthur into the dining room, which was separated from the kitchen by a green granite topped, oak island. Rose poured each a glass of Pinot Noir while Arthur continued into the open kitchen, stepping around the island.

"Diane, you were still working when I left," Rose said after taking a drink of wine. "How did the computer simulations work out?"

Diane studied Rose with her dark eyes and frowned. "I am not happy with the projections. We still are emitting too much carbon. We've got to completely phase out the remaining natural gas generating stations. The projected elimination of the remaining coal fired plants in India helped the simulations immensely, but I'm still projecting we will surpass 3° C even with the dissolution of the Indian coal plants if that ever comes about." There were beads of moisture near Diane's hairline, shining on her chestnut full forehead.

"We suspected that would be the case. We need to send the simulations to the IPCC. The US and most of Europe have phased out a good deal of the gas generation. We've made meaningful progress, but we need so much more. Of course if we'd have started sooner, we'd be better along." She stopped and watched Diane. "You're sweating. Hasn't it cooled down outside much? What's the temperature outside now?"

"It's still in the mid-90s. Not too bad... considering what it was when the sun was still up. I worked up a sweat from the car to your house. We parked down the block. You know me, I can start sweating at the drop of a hat. Just think of the immigrants baking on the southern border, hoping to get into the country. I heard on the radio on the way over that there has been more killings on the border and deaths from heat stroke. The climate refugees in Mexico are getting restless. We need to allow more in to the country. We are largely responsible for their plight."

"Yes, the climate refugees are burgeoning, and, as you say, we should be honor bound to help." She took a drink of wine and turned toward Simon. "Simon, I was so thankful when you fixed our climate simulation software. You're a computer whiz."

Simon smirked. "I can hold my own, I suppose. I wouldn't characterize myself as a whiz." He laughed, then smiled broadly lighting up his ebony face. His hair was cut short and his face was strikingly handsome. "I feel I'm stagnating in the computer science department. I've got the mainframe churning along well. I'd say the University's computing power is one of the best if not the best in the country. I could go for a new challenge."

Arthur came around the island carrying a tray of dishes and set the rice and two Thai style curries on the table. He set the tray on the oak sideboard and took his seat. "Don't be bashful. Grab a dish and help yourself."

"This smells wonderful," Diane announced and selected the rice, piling a mound on her plate and passing it to Simon. "This looks too delicious. I'll have to restrain myself." Her laugh shook her full figure, her ample breasts bouncing, her black bushy hair framing her smiling face. "I'm tryin' to lose my excess pounds."

"What excess pounds?" Simon replied. "You're fabulous just as you are."

Diane's smile could not have gotten any bigger as she caressed Simon's muscular arm.

"Simon, I heard you comment about wanting a new challenge," Arthur said. "I'm looking for a computer expert to help with my Project." Arthur leaned back and studied Simon. The guy must be an athlete Arthur thought. He puts my skinny body to shame. "When you have some free time, I could show you the Project. You'll have to sign a secrecy agreement before you can visit. You think you might be interested?"

"What kind of Project is it?" Simon asked, leaning forward slightly. "It's not for the defense industry is it. I'm a dyed in the wool pacifist."

"No... no. It's an energy project of sorts. My other former computer specialist left more than a year ago. He was offered a lot more money by Tesla than I could possibly match." He wasn't going to tell Simon that Jason had been a jerk, and he was glad he was gone, but felt bad for all the additional work Violet was doing. He had been looking for a suitable replacement to no avail. Experienced computer scientists were in much demand, and the University pay scale made offering a competitive salary difficult. "He helped my main computer specialist get me on the right path, so you wouldn't be starting from scratch. My main computer scientist, Violet, is very astute and totally amazing at writing code. I've never encountered anyone like her. I'm lucky to have her."

"From what you've told me, I'd like to have a look see. You reputation precedes you. You're highly regarded around campus. I'd at least like to see what you're working on. I think you and I could get along well."

"Great, I'll work on setting it up and give you a call." He looked around the room with a smile. "Well let's dig in. I slaved over a hot stove to produce these dishes." He laughed. "I sure hope you like them. Actually we have an induction cook top so I'm exaggerating about the heat."

"Your house is pleasantly cool, but not cold," Diane said. "I don't like cold air conditioning. Many of the restaurants around town are way too cold. It's a waste of energy and not healthy."

"I agree," Rose added. "The University's policy of maintaining 75°F in the buildings should be adopted nationwide."

"Well, we keep the mainframe and storage at 55°— heat is detrimental to computers," Simon said, before turning to Diane. "So you think we're headed to break the 3°C over the 1950 baseline. That's terrible. Won't that make growing cereals in the US nearly impossible?"

"Some of the new wheat and rice strains show promise," Rose said. "Canada, Russia, Mongolia, Argentina, Chile, and South Africa are going to become the bread baskets of the world, but the land available for growing is diminished by the areas with permafrost. Photosynthesis works best between 50° and 68° F. It totally ceases at 104° F and is very poor below 50° F. Greenhouses that are temperature controlled can work it hotter and colder situations, but they require energy. Sometimes I get so distressed about the historical lack of progress on greenhouse gas emissions. I wished I had been born in the past when I could have helped make real progress in reducing greenhouse gases. Just think of all the gigatons of CO2 the world has spewed since 1950 that is wreaking havoc now and will continue creating chaos."

"Aren't they scaling up carbon air extraction plants around the world?" Simon said.

"Oh yes, but we couldn't build enough extraction plants to make a significant difference," Rose replied. "The plants have to be sited in suitable locations where they can discharge the CO2 underground into volcanic rock where it is converted to limestone. Plus it takes a lot of energy to power the extraction fans and pumps, so you need access to clean power as well. We've lost most of the Amazon rainforest that was a huge carbon sink. Efforts in organic farming and forest building are helping somewhat in sequestering carbon as well as increased hemp farms."

"There's a clamoring amongst some scientist to start spraying sulfur dioxide or pulverized limestone into upper atmosphere to block sunlight," Diane said. "I'm not ready for white skies. Whatever they spray has to eventually come down, consequently they have to continue to do it periodically. The US is still burning way too much fossil fuels. Our government needs to be more proactive. We need a much stronger carbon tax and increased incentives to sequester carbon. We could be much better on promoting plant based diets and organic no till farming. The United Nations needs to be more aggressive on getting the other countries still burning significant fossil fuels to transition to clean energy."

"Not to put a damper on you climate activists, but have you read any good books or seen some good movies, Simon," Arthur asked. He didn't want the difficulties of climate warming to dominate the conversation.

"What was that detective series we saw on PBS, Diane?" Simon asked. "It was really engaging. I thoroughly enjoyed it."

"The Seattle Murders."

"Sounds macabre," Rose said. "I could go for a good comedy."

"Speaking of macabre, I've got a killer vegan cake from the Sunshine Bakery for dessert," Arthur announced.

"Bring it on," Diane said. "You know I've got an absurd sweet tooth." Her laugh was infectious and they all joined in.

Diane was surprised that Simon would want to change jobs. He was the lead manager of the computer mainframe and was well respected. She suspected that the mysteriousness of Arthur's Project was what enticed Simon. She knew that Arthur was working on a monumental physics project that many of the faculty wondered about. Rose had said that he was trying to produce something that had been predicted by

Einstein but had never been found to exist, but, when questioned further, had demurred stating it was all top secret, and even she didn't understand what was going on.

Diane and Simon became enamored of each other, and they went out often. She had fallen in love with the man, who made her feel wrapped in a warm glow of enchantment. She so enjoyed their nights together, often spending the night at Simon's apartment. He was a gentle tantalizing lover. She had never felt such profound love. Rose often teased her about how glowing she often looked after a night at Simon's.

Arthur waited in the lobby of the Physics building, watching for Simon's approach. He was nervous about showing Simon his Project. He hoped he could showcase the Project well, and Simon would be interested in joining the team.

When Simon wearing a light-blue, short-sleeve shirt and khaki shorts came up the steps, Arthur stepped outside in the hot sun to greet him. "Glad you could come," Arthur said as they shook hands. He led him into the building and steered him to the administrative office. He showed Simon the secrecy form, which Simon carefully read.

Simon looked at the secretary behind the counter, then focused on Arthur. "What are you working on? This secrecy agreement sounds draconian."

Arthur smiled and tilted his head from side to side. "Let's just say it is cutting edge. Many countries would like to learn about our progress. A lot of my funding comes from the Department of Energy. They are a worrisome sort." He laughed. "If you feel you don't want to be involved in such secrecy, we can end it here."

"No, now, I'm really intrigued." He signed the form.

Arthur handed the form to the secretary, who issued a visitor badge for Simon. He clipped the badge to his shirt and followed Arthur to the basement. Once inside the laboratory, Simon stood in amazement. "What is that immense stainless-steel tube?"

"It's the enclosure for what I hope will be an Einstein-Rosen Bridge."

"A wormhole? They don't exist. No one has ever found one in the universe."

"No, they haven't. We've found an amazing number of black holes though. The theory that Einstein-Rosen Bridges are possible I believe to be very sound. If there have been Einstein-Rosen Bridges in the past, they would have collapsed quite easily. That's what the enclosure is for to maintain the structure if we can ever produce the Bridge."

"It's cold in here"

"Yes we maintain the temperature at 55° F. Once we ramp up the energy, this place gets very warm. Well actually I should say hot even though the enclosure hollow walls have circulating liquid helium."

"What are those immense structures around the tube?"

"Electromagnetic devices."

"You've taken the entire basement of this building, and it has been excavated down several stories. The cost of the Project must be astronomical."

"It's an expensive endeavor. Let's walk down to the floor." They were standing on a cat walk that encircled the large room.

Simon followed Arthur down the stairs and to a bank of computer terminals. "Have a seat." Arthur said, indicating the chair in front of one of the terminals. "Are you interested in learning more, or have you seen enough to know you're not interested. I know it looks overwhelming."

"Oh, I'm interested all right," Simon said as he sat down.

"Great." Arthur stepped away a few feet. "Hey, Billy and Harold, come out wherever you are and meet Simon," he yelled.

A slim, older, gray haired man came around the stainless steel enclosure followed by a younger, blond man, both wearing white coats. Arthur went to the wall and took down two white coats. He slipped one on and gave the other to Simon. "You'll be more comfortable wearing this."

Billy and Harold, this is Simon from the Computer Science Department. He's come to see if he might be interested in joining us."

Simon stood and shook hands with the two men.

"Hey what about me," a young woman with short red hair with a blond streak and a long stride, wearing black jeans, a red tee shirt and white lab coat, said as she came from a nearby room.

"I didn't think you'd be in today?" Arthur said before turning to Simon. "And this is Violet, our lead computer scientist."

Violet shook hands with Simon. "Glad you came to have a look at us. These men have been trying to work me to death since Jason left."

"Jason was our other computer specialist, who left quite a while ago, and, yes, we've relied on Violet immensely since he left." Arthur gave Violet a quick smile.

"Relied immensely... nicely put, Chief," Violet said sarcastically and gave Arthur a dig in the side with her elbow. "Go ahead and sit back down," Violet said to Simon as she took a seat at another adjacent computer terminal. She typed rapidly on the keyboard, and a cutaway schematic of the enclosure came up of the large screen. "Isn't she a beauty? Bet you've never seen anything like it." She looked over at Simon and laughed before tuning to Arthur. "Okay, Boss, give him the spiel." She swirled back to look at Simon. "He's quite engrossing if you give him a chance."

"Violet, is the lively one among us," Billy said. "She keeps us entertained."

"Easy there, Billy. I'm not here for your entertainment."

"Of course not, Violet. You are essential to the Project and an amazing computer programmer. We are lucky to have you."

"Thanks, Billy."

"You are, though, very entertaining."

"You Devil," Violet said, rising as if to go after Billy, but instead sitting back down and laughing.

"To produce the Bridge," Arthur began in a loud voice in hopes of producing a serious mood, "we have to introduce a huge amount of energy on the inside of the enclosure walls and maintain that energy at levels never before seen. The electromagnetic devices keep the enclosure from bursting, pull the energy away from the walls, and hopefully concentrate and revolve the energy enough to spin the atmosphere inside the enclosure in such a manner to form the Bridge. If we are ever successful at maintaining and controlling the energy, we may be successful in producing an Einstein-Rosen Bridge, which if we program correctly, would theoretically allow travel in time."

"Well said, Wunderkind," Violet announced. "Pretty amazing isn't it, Simon?"

"I'm speechless. You actually think you can a make a wormhole or whatever you want to call it that would allow time travel?"

"I'm reservedly hopeful, yes."

"Wow, this is unbelievable. What would I be doing?"

"You and Violet have to come up with the software to control the energy and electromagnetics within narrowly defined parameters and establish the control basis of travel in the past. Violet and Jason have begun writing the software, but we're still working on the parameters."

Violet leaned back. "What he means is he's working on the parameters. We've got to figure out how to keep the parameters steady and not blow up the campus."

"Violet is exaggerating. There's little possibility of an explosion, but a meltdown could destroy the enclosure and the laboratory. The electrical energy we will be using is gigantic and will have to be closely monitored and controlled. We have a direct feed from the Oakland Fusion Generating Station and a bank of capacitors that can increase the electric flow quickly when needed."

"So, Simon, do you want to join our team?" Violet asked.

"Violet, let the man think about it. He has a lot to consider. That's all I can tell you today, Simon." He placed a hand on Simon's shoulder. "I'll walk you back out. You don't have to say anything now. Leave the coat on the chair and let's go."

Simon did as instructed and followed Arthur up the stairs.

"Glad to meet you, Simon," Billy called. "I hope you decide to join us."

When they were in the hall, Arthur stopped. "Violet, is very enthusiastic and sometimes a little over the top, but she is a superb computer programmer. Between her and Jason she was the most innovative. I'm thankful she has stayed with us. Jason was good, but I suspected he wouldn't stay for the entire Project. He didn't really believe we would ever be successful."

"Man, I'm in a daze. I almost feel like I stepped into another world. Does Rose know what you're working on?"

"Somewhat, but not completely. It's top secret. You can't even hint what we're working on to anyone else. I know this is sudden, but I didn't know how else to explain to you what you'd be working on. I trust you Simon." He had formed a good opinion of Simon when he first met him. Arthur placed a lot of stock in his intuition.

8- JULY 18, 2050

Simon entered the basement early in the morning. Violet was the only team member already there. "Hey, Violet, how's it going?"

"I'm glad you're here. This algorithm I came up with doesn't seem to be working properly. I've made some error, but I can't figure out where I went wrong. Come have a look."

Simon descended the stairs quickly, grabbed a lab coat and sat next to Violet. "What time did you come in?"

"About four. I ran over from my apartment and took a shower here. I can't run once the sun is up. I can't take the heat. I like a morning run to get the blood circulating." She shifted her shoulders as she was running. "Here take a look." She punched the keys energetically on the keyboard and a series of equations came up on the screen.

"Gosh, I don't see anything right away. I remember Arthur was talking about the electromagnetic field being wobbly on the simulation. Is that what you mean?"

"Yeah, it fails to control the field under simulation."

"Umm, maybe we need to change the current in smaller increments to stabilize it. Maybe the algorithm needs a qualifier."

"Jesus, why didn't I think of that?" She punched Simon on the arm. "I'm sure glad you came aboard. You've been here less than two weeks and you have helped immensely."

"Hey, I'm still shooting in the dark."

"We all are except for Wunderkind himself. Just imagine if we get this thing to work."

"Yeah, it would be the biggest scientific breakthrough since the glass sodium battery."

"That was an amazing scientific discovery. Now we don't have to tear up the world for lithium or worry about batteries catching fire. But establishing an Einstein-Rosen Bridge would be the most significant scientific breakthrough since Einstein's theory of general relativity." Violet began frantically typing code. "I think this new equation will do the trick for the algorithm. We'll show Arthur when he gets here and maybe he'll agree to another simulation."

"Great. How long before we actually initiate a real test run?"

"That's up to Arthur. I can't wait. It's going to be so cool."

Simon had been leery of Violet when he first started, but her vibrant personality quickly grew on him. She was an amazing code writer, seemed to have a photographic memory, and was fun to be around. He speculated on how old she was. She looked to be in her early 20s, but he suspected she was older than she looked. He wondered why she seemed to work long hours. He would have thought someone as attractive as her with her red hair, blue eyes, high cheek bones, and slim but enticing frame would be going out often. Arthur emphasized to everyone on the team that they needed to have fun and a life outside the lab. Violet didn't pay much attention to his admonishments about working so much, and, aside from the admonishments, Arthur didn't berate her. Arthur and Violet had a very close bond. It seemed to Simon that they often knew what the other was thinking. Violet's adoration of Arthur was quite apparent.

The lab door buzzed open, and Arthur strolled in. He smiled down on Violet and Simon. "Good morning. You guys are here early." He walked down the stairs, put on his lab coat, and walked over to the two. "Did you guys beat the heat? It's already nearly a 100° out."

"It was pretty hot when I came," Simon said. "I didn't pay attention to the temperature. Knowing it just makes me hotter."

"Hey, boss, I think I've corrected the algorithm that wasn't keeping the electromagnetism steady as it ramped up."

"That's great."

"Can we run another computer simulation to check it out?"

"Definitely. We'll run it as soon as Billy and Harold come in and get the enclosure cooling going. After the computer simulation if it shows promise maybe we will ramp up power on the enclosure and see how the cooling goes. No electromagnetics though. I had a thought on how we can increase the field. Billy and Harold will have to do some mechanical adjustments and we'll need to run new power cables from the capacitor bank to the electromagnets." Arthur walked away whistling. "I'm making tea. Anyone want a cup?"

"Oh yes," Simon and Violet answered simultaneously.

After lunch the team assembled in the conference room, which served as the break room as well, at Arthur's request. "The computer simulation this morning was excellent. Thanks Violet and Simon, you've done a great job. Billy and Harold, thanks for running the new cables and adding the bypass to the liquid helium. I think we're ready to bring up power on the enclosure and see how she fares."

The team was silent.

"Do any of you have any reservations?" Arthur asked.

"How hot are we going to allow the enclosure to get?" Billy asked looking worried.

"I don't know. What would you suggest we allow today?"

"I wouldn't want to go over 800 ° C."

"Well, I wasn't thinking anything close to that. Let's see if we can keep it under 500° on the outside and no more than 70° C on the inside."

"Yeah, that sounds good," Billy replied

"Okay, stations everyone. You all have your beepers. If anything at all seems out of line, beep repeatedly, and we'll shut it down nice and slow. Any questions?"

"I have one," Violet said. "Where will you be?"

"I'll be standing behind you and Simon." He stood up. "Any others?" He looked from each team member to the other. "Okay, let's do it."

Violet went out to her terminal and pulled up the startup sequence on the big screen. On the other screen, Simon pulled up the measuring indices. Violet swiveled around and looked at Arthur.

"Okay begin initiation," Arthur said.

Violet hit enter, and the hum of the electricity heating the enclosure began along with the sound of the liquid helium pumps.

Simon announced after half an hour, "The enclosure has reached 100° and is holding 20° inside."

"Second stage initiate," Arthur called.

Twenty minutes later. "200°," Simon announced, "and 25°C inside.

"Keep it steady," Arthur said.

"300° and 30° inside."

"Third stage initiate."

Thirty minutes later. "400° and holding and 50° inside," Simon said.

An hour later Arthur held up his hand. "Looks fantastic. Power her down."

"How's it looking, boss," Violet asked.

"Better than I expected. The cooling is working wonderfully. I was surprised that the inside temperature remained so cool. Of course the electromagnetics when employed should affect the inside temperature dramatically." He clapped his hands. "Did you hear that Billy," he shouted. "Great design change you came up with the bigger pumps and additional lines. For the amount of electrical current and power we fed her, she remained remarkably cool." He wiped his forehead with his handkerchief. "The room got hot, but not unduly. Great job everybody. Violet and Simon, good catch on the algorithm. Once we've got everything shut off and locked down, I'm buying at Jim's pub. You're all coming, no excuses. You hear that Violet."

"Yes sir, Captain. Make mine a double scotch." She laughed raucously.

After several rounds of drinks at the pub, Arthur walked to his house, feeling very satisfied. He was reasonably sure they could keep the enclosure from overheating when they went to full power and engaged the electromagnets. The big question was: would the electromagnets be able to form the Bridge and keep it from collapsing. Another thought that was niggling him was, if they produced a stable Einstein–

Rosen Bridge, could they program it to a specific time and could anything transverse inside the Bridge without being destroyed by the forces within. Well, he was getting ahead of himself. Time would tell.

When he arrived at his home, Rose's bicycle was locked in its rack. In the morning, he had left before Rose. She had said she'd be working late. Could something be wrong? He hurried into the house. There sat Rose on the living room couch reading the newspaper. He felt a surge of relief. "You're home early. I thought you had a 5 o'clock class and had other work to finish."

"Diane is taking the class for me. I thought I'd surprise you. Why are you late?"

"We ran a heat simulation today that went better than I expected. So I took the team to the pub to celebrate."

Rose opened her arms. "Come here, Big Boy, and give me a hug and snuggle, you handsome devil."

"Well, all right. I like the invitation." He sat down on the couch and pulled her to him, kissing her passionately. "I hope I'm not too late for whatever you had in mind."

"No, not too late. Shall we retire to the bedroom and work up and appetite for some curry from India Palace?"

"By all means." He rose, pulled her up, and led her up the stairs to the bedroom. As soon as they were inside, she began disrobing and dived onto the bed.

Once he was naked, he hurried to the bed his arousal already apparent.

Simon walked to his apartment, feeling excited about their simulation, ignoring the late afternoon heat and sweat that had soaked his shirt. He was so glad he had taken the job with Arthur. He wondered if they would ever be successful with the Wormhole. The cooling success of the Wormhole tube was heartening. Violet seemed to put a lot of faith in Arthur. He had to admit what Arthur had built was amazing. How Arthur had got the funding for the Project was a mystery. Simon had on several occasions subtly questioned Arthur about the funding. Arthur had replied that he had good friends in the Energy Department, and the University was very supportive as well. Violet didn't know anything about the funding either. It didn't matter really. He put it down to Arthur being a curious sort. If funding was pulled and the Project shut down, he'd be okay. He could always go back to work for the Computer Science Department. He hoped the Project would continue. He would be, if they were successful, part of one of the most important scientific breakthroughs in history.

When he saw Diane's car on the street, he quickened his pace, ignoring the heat. It had to be over a hundred. Once inside the apartment he was disappointed that Diane was not present. She must have driven to his place and walked to campus. She'd be along when she finished at the University.

He went to the refrigerator and grabbed a cold beer. He sat down on the sofa and held the bottle to his sweating forehead before he took a big swig. He thought about watching the news on TV, but decided he didn't want to spoil his mood, so he turned on the stereo and switched on his MP3 player. As BB King sang out 'Ain't nobody home', he stretched out and savored the beer.

He must have dozed off when he heard the click of the front door. Diane rushed in. "Oh, it's hotter than hell still. Please, get me a beer. I'm dyin', Honey."

"Will do, Babe, but first I need a kiss."

"I'm dripping and probably smell horrible."

"I don't care about getting wet, and you never smell horrible." He wrapped her ample frame into his arms and kissed those deep-red, full lips. "That's nice." He released her and sauntered to the kitchen, coming back with two beers.

Diane grabbed the beer and took a long drink. "Phew, that tastes so good. I'm burning up. I gotta take a cold shower. Do you mind?"

"Not at all." He gazed at her sideways with a wry smile. "Is it all right if I join you?"

"Excellent idea, My Love. Let's get down and dirty."

"You mean down and clean."

9- NOVEMBER 12, 2050

Rose finished her lecture and stood talking to some of the students before heading to her office. She sat down at her desk and pulled up the article she was working on about the increase in methane discharge from the Artic shelf. Her last trip to Russia had been frightening. The amount of methane being released would increase the warming immensely. There didn't seem to be any way of preventing the 3° C increase in global mean temperature. She slammed her fist down on the desk. To hell with the article. She needed cheering up. She texted Arthur that she was heading home, and she would really like for him to join her.

She unplugged her laptop and left her office. She retrieved her bicycle and leisurely road home. Her shirt was nearly soaked when she arrived. The temperature was in the high 80s. She went inside, but Arthur was not home as she had hoped. She went into the bedroom and took a quick shower. When finished, she felt a little better. She poured herself a glass of chilled white wine and settled on the sofa to await Arthur.

After several hours as she sat wondering what was keeping Arthur, she became agitated. Arthur usually responded to her texts asking him to come home. Something must be happening at the Project. She told herself to relax. He would be along soon. When she heard the front door, she stood and hurried toward the door.

"Hey honey, sorry I couldn't come sooner," Arthur said as soon as he saw Rose approaching. "What's up? Has something happened?"

"I started to write my article for *Climate News* about the methane emissions from the Artic shelf and felt so despondent, knowing that there's no way to stop us from exceeding 3° C." She squished her face together and exhaled forcefully. "I couldn't continue."

He folded her into his arms. "My Sweet Love, I'm sorry. Your work is so important. I know it can be depressing."

"It's already still in the 80s in November. It's crazy."

"December should be better."

"We're going to have an ice free Arctic Ocean probably through the winter this year. When I was in Russia, I met idiots in the government that were excited about an ice free Artic Ocean. They thought global warming was an economic boon for their country."

"Come on, let's have some wine, and I'll tell you a secret."

"What secret?"

"In good time." He escorted her into the kitchen and poured himself and her a glass of white wine. "Sit down. I must ask you to keep secret what I'm about to tell you."

She studied him closely before sitting on the stool in front of the kitchen island. "Okay I promise I'll keep your secret."

"We initiated an Einstein-Rosen Bridge and stabilized it enough that we were able to send a probe back in time and retrieve the probe after several hours."

"What!" She watched Arthur's smiling face. He was pulling her leg to cheer her up. Sending a probe back in time... that was crazy. She had always thought his top secret Project was purely theoretical. "I know you're trying to cheer me up. Thanks." She took a long drink of wine. "You are such a wonderful husband. Wouldn't it be great to go back in time and get the world to begin reducing carbon fuels when it would have been easy so we wouldn't be facing the catastrophe that's coming?"

"I was thinking the same thing. It might be possible. I thought for sure the probe would be destroyed because of the forces necessary to maintain the Bridge. I never thought in my wildest dreams that we could retrieve the probe."

The wine glass slipped from her hand and crashed to the floor breaking into small fragments. "You're not kidding?" Her face was stretched as she shook her head. "You really sent something back in time and retrieved it?"

"Yes it's true. It's really true."

"Was Simon there?"

"Yes, the whole team. Everyone is ecstatic and in a daze. We did it."

"How far back in time?'

"Two years."

"How do you know it was actually back two years? Could it have been an illusion?"

"I don't think so."

"Think? You don't know for sure?"

"I'm sure," he pronounced quickly, tipping his head to the side. "Hey, I want you to come to our next Bridge production and see for yourself."

"Bridge Production? Sounds like you're making a movie. I thought you had to keep your Project completely secret. What if your sponsors found out you let other people see what you've done?"

"I'm not going to tell them."

"Do your sponsors know you actually produced a 'whatever' Bridge and sent something back in time?"

"No."

"What happens when they find out?"

"They can't find out."

"What do you mean?"

"My Project in the wrong hands could be used for terrible things. I never thought I could make an actual working Einstein-Rosen Bridge. I was working toward a fleeting Bridge— not one that would remain stable... let alone allow time travel."

"So what happens next?" She still couldn't believe what he was telling her. It was too much like a science fiction movie.

"I want to send an animal inside a probe back and retrieve it next week."

"Why?"

"To see if it will survive."

"You mean it could die? That's cruel."

"I know, but the sensors in the probe maintained suitable temperature and pressure. I think if we provide the cat with oxygen, it will survive. I know of no other way to test the viability of life in time travel."

"What are you saying? Life viability in time travel? I can't grasp what you're telling me. Are you thinking that humans could travel back in time? That can't be… it can't be possible."

"Perhaps not. Don't you think we should try?"

"To what end?"

"As you said to get the governments to do more about reducing greenhouse gas emissions earlier in the past."

"You're dreaming. It's a great dream, I'll grant you, but it's crazy. I don't believe it's possible."

"We'll see."

Simon left the lab in a daze. He couldn't believe what they had just done. An object had traveled back in time. Was it an illusion? Maybe they had sent the probe somewhere nearby where it disappeared, and then they retrieved it. Maybe it was like some kind of magic trick.

Simon so much wanted to tell Diane about it and get her take on it, but he couldn't. He was sworn to secrecy. He understood why secrecy was absolutely necessary. If the military got hold of the Bridge, Jesus …. If they altered things in the past how would that affect the present? Could alternations in the past lead to the destruction of the present? He wanted to talk about what they did more with Arthur, but Arthur said he had to go home. Something had happened to Rose.

When he reached his apartment, he hoped Diane would be there just to reassure him that life was unaltered by what they had done. He opened the front door, and Diane came to greet him.

She kissed him, then held him at arm's length. "What's happened? You look like you've seen a ghost."

"It was a grueling day at the Project. When we finished, Arthur left hurriedly saying there was something up with Rose. Do you know anything?"

"Well, she's been bummed out ever since her trip to Russia about the methane bubbling on the Artic shelf and what that means for warming. I left before her. She was going to work on her article about the methane for *Climate News*. Other than that. I don't know anything."

"Maybe that was it."

"So what happened at the Project?"

"Oh, nothing. Just one of our simulations was difficult to execute and took longer than we had estimated. No big thing. I could sure use a cold beer."

"You stay right there," she said patting his sweat soaked chest. "I'll get us both one."

Simon accepted the cold beer and took a big swallow. "Thanks. This sure hits the spot. It's still almost like summer out. This methane bubbling sounds ominous."

"Oh it is. It's going to insure we exceed 3° C. We may be headed for geoengineering spraying in the stratosphere."

"Is that safe?"

"Rose and I don't think so. We're running out of options though."

Simon took another large swallow. "Yes, the world leaders haven't done what they should have... what was necessary." He pulled Diane to him.

Diane looked up at him, grinning mischievously. "Let's forget about that." She snuggled against him. "What else are you needing?"

"I'm glad you asked," he replied, smiling widely, "but first let's go out and eat."

"You don't want to work up an appetite first?"

"Let's save that for the rest of the night, Sweets." He kissed her and squeezed her full body tighter to him. "You know keeping two places is crazy. Why don't you give up your apartment and move in here."

"You want us to live together. You know I'm an old fashion woman."

"I know." Simon got down on his knee and removed the ring from his pocket he had been carrying for over a week. He took a deep breath. "Diane, My Love, will you marry me." The time travel had affected so much he felt he couldn't wait any longer to propose.

Diane brought her hands to her face and let out a soft scream. "Oh, Simon, of course I'll marry you." She pulled him up and held his hand with the ring. "It's beautiful. I'm so happy."

He placed the ring on her finger and kissed her, feeling the delicious embrace of her soft body.

Arthur had Rose come to the Laboratory to witness his experiment sending the cat back in time and hopefully retrieving it. He had Billy design a special graphene probe capsule with recording sensors that would hold a cat with an oxygen mask.

Rose watched Violet and Simon bring the enclosure up to temperature. See couldn't believe what she was seeing— a massive structure that seemed to vibrate as the hum of the electromagnets filled the room and the heat from the structure caused her to start sweating. She wondered what the temperature must be inside the probe as the heat intensified, and she worried that they were killing the cat.

The hum of the electrical current and the electromagnets grew to an almost deafening intensity. She found it amazing that the enclosure outside temperature was so much higher than the inside temperature as the sweat slid down her forehead and cheeks. She lifted the hair from her neck to cool herself off. When the outside enclosure temperature reached 500° but the inside was only 55°, she was amazed. How had Arthur been able to make such an amazing machine?

Simon shouted, "Phase four holding. Bridge formation beginning. Bridge stable. The cat is away to 1980."

Rose couldn't believe her ears. How could it be possible that the cat was gone? She had trouble accepting the cat had left and wondered how they could tell that the cat was away to 1980. There were no cameras inside of the structure. Without being able to see the inside of the structure there was no visible proof. Were they fooling themselves?

Arthur had Simon reduce the power, and Simon announced the Bridge had collapsed. They kept the power and cooling on. The temperature in the room dropped slightly as Simon announced they were maintaining structure temperature at 300°.

After an hour and a half, Arthur had them bring the power back up to maximum and program the return of the cat. When Simon announced the Bridge had reformed, Arthur, shouted, "Bring her back."

Violet started typing furiously.

Simon after a few minutes declared, "She's back."

"Shut the enclosure down slowly," Arthur said, excitedly

After about 20 minutes, Simon shouted "Internal temperature at 45°C."

Arthur and Billy both wearing furnace gloves went to the enclosure hatch and opened it up. Billy announced, "Probe has returned."

Arthur broke in a large grin and laughingly said, "We did it. Hallelujah."

Billy climbed inside and brought out the probe. He set it down and opened the probe up. He pulled out the unconscious cat. "She has a faint heart beat," Billy said.

Arthur knelt and stuck a hypodermic needle into the cat. "A little adrenalin to get her heart beating stronger," he announced.

Rose watched the proceeding dumfounded. Arthur removed the oxygen mask from the cat and carried it into the breakroom and placed it in a soft cat bed. "Her heart beat is improving." He looked at Rose. "We did it. The forces inside the Bridge can possibly sustain life. We won't be sure of that though until the cat recovers."

"How do you know the cat actually went to 1980? Where did she go in 1980?"

"The software confirmed she went to 1980," Arthur said. "She would have ended up where the enclosure sits now but in 1980. In 1980 this wing of the Physics Building wasn't built. She would have been in an open field inside the probe for the two hours."

"Where's the proof the cat went to 1980?" Rose said.

"The software is accurate," Violet said with vocal enthusiasm.

"How do you know?" Rose asked. "The cat could have remained inside the enclosure. You don't have cameras to prove the probe actually left."

"There are no cameras that could withstand the forces inside the enclosure," Arthur said. "Besides the swirling ionized gases of the Bridge would be opaque."

"I'm not convinced," Rose said, shaking her head. "I don't believe it's possible."

"Well, I assure that the cat went to 1980, and we were able to bring it back," Arthur said as he approached Rose and put his arm around her. "The big question is will the cat recover. She seems to be in a coma. She's probably dehydrated as well." He turned to Simon and placed a hand on his shoulder. "Can you set up a drip of saline solution for the cat? We'll need to takes turns caring for the cat until she recovers. I'll take her home first and bring her back in the morning. I hope she recovers. Perhaps the forces inside were too much for her. She's alive, but may never regain consciousness."

"I still have a hard time believing this cat went back in time to 1980," Rose stubbornly said.

"Yes, My Love. It is hard to believe. I and my team believe that the cat went to 1980 and returned." He rubbed Rose's back. "Perhaps when we send me back to 1990 and bring me back, you'll believe."

"There's no way I'm allowing you to get in that machine and travel back in time. What you are saying is completely crazy."

Violet strolled out of the Physics building in an exhilarating daze. They had made history. Time travel was possible. It was hard to believe that they had actually been successful. She thought back about Rose's reaction that it was not real. She understood why Rose couldn't believe the cat traveled back and forth in time. There was no real evidence of what had happened other than the software completion.

The years she had worked on the software programming and the amazing insight that Arthur had provided turned out to be so worth it. She had had her doubts along the way, but strongly believed in Arthur, who she adored beyond reason. If she would have been heterosexual, she would have loved to have a partner like Arthur. Her work on the Project alongside the genius of Arthur she found so rewarding. She would remember this day, November 19, 2050, as a high point in her young life. They had accomplished the almost impossible feat of sending a living being back in time and retrieving it.

When Simon came on board, she slowly developed a deep friendship and bond with him. Maybe it was the discrimination that Simon had experienced being black somehow fit with the discrimination she experienced over her sexual orientation. Simon was a good computer programmer, and they fed off each other. She doubted that she would have been so successful with the software for time travel if Simon had not joined the team. Jason had been a relatively good programmer, but often sloppy about his work. She never got along with him. He was a misogynist, stuck-up egoist, who had asked her out repeatedly. He was so interested in himself he never cottoned onto the fact that she was a lesbian. She had developed a mask about her sexual orientation that most people couldn't penetrate. Arthur had figured it out, she knew, soon after working together.

She hoped to hell that the cat recovered. If it didn't, the possibility of human travel in time seemed out of reach unless there were ways of lessoning the forces inside the Bridge. Time would tell.

10- NOVEMBER 24, 2050

Rose hurried to the door when she heard the doorbell, opening it wide as Simon and Diane waltzed in. "The happy couple. Welcome. You two have been so secretive. When Diane told me about the marriage proposal, I was so happy for you both. Have you set the date?"

"December 3rd," Diane said, "and you are going to be my bridesmaid. No hemming and hawing."

"Oh, how wonderful. I accept graciously. Thanks for including me."

Arthur came and greeted the couple. "I'm so happy for you two love birds. It's going to be a great day. Come on in to the dining room. Rose has been cooking most of the day."

"What's on the menu?" Diane asked.

"You'll have to wait and see."

They walked to the dining room, and Rose asked them to be seated. Arthur opened the beers and passed them around. Rose went to the kitchen and returned with a red and orange casserole, a dish of refried beans, a small dish of vegan sour cream, and a mixed green salad. She set out the dishes and sat down. "Pass me your plates and I'll serve you."

"Red enchiladas," Diane exclaimed. "One of my favorites. Oh boy, my mouth is already watering."

Once everyone was served, Rose said, "Bon appétit."

"This is delicious and nice and hot," Simon said. "I adore hot chile. What else is in here?"

"Swiss chard, onions, two kinds of vegan cheese and plenty of red chile sauce. If it's too hot, the sour cream will cool it down."

"Woo, it is hot," Diane said. "Pass me the sour cream."

Rose was happy everyone was enjoying the meal. "So Diane, what will be your wedding color scheme? Are there going to be other bridesmaids?"

"I thought purple would go well. My friend, Sandra from college is coming to be the other bridesmaid. You'll like her. She's even taller than you. I will look stunted next to you two and Simon."

"I can't wait to meet her."

"Speaking of the wedding, Arthur, I would like to ask you be my best man?" Simon said.

"I'd be honored, Simon." Arthur thought Simon would have chosen another friend as his best man. He hadn't known him that long, and he didn't think many men would want their boss as their best man, but he would be happy to oblige.

"No tuxedos. I thought simple, dark blue suits would be nice. I want a relaxed ceremony nothing extravagant."

"I like your idea," Arthur said. "Our wedding was a small affair, and I enjoyed it immensely. Although, I was quite nervous."

"You never told me you were nervous," Rose said.

"Who wouldn't be nervous wedding the most beautiful and accomplished woman they ever encountered."

"Nicely put," Rose said, laughing. "Flattery will work wonders with me."

"Who would have thought?" Arthur rose with a smirk. "Who needs another beer?" Everyone assented. Arthur went to the refrigerator.

Rose watched Diane surreptitiously as she drank her beer. She felt apprehensive about how Diane would react to what Arthur wanted Diane to help with. He had convinced Simon of the idea, but Simon didn't feel he could ask Diane. He had insisted that Arthur had to ask Diane. Arthur was the expert, and his gentle manner was very persuasive.

When Arthur had explained to Rose what he wanted to do, she had thought the idea was completely insane. Even after she had witnessed the traverse with the cat, she couldn't believe it was true. She thought it was just an illusion. It took Arthur a few days to convince her that the cat had actually traveled back and forth in time. When he suggested sending a human back in time, she had adamantly argued against it. Arthur would not drop the idea. Eventually, his continued arguments of why his idea was important and nominally safe, finally won her over.

After they had finished their meal and were sipping their coffee, Arthur scooted his chair back. "There's something I want to ask you, Diane. Please don't feel obligated, but we would really like your help." He took a sip of beer to wet his mouth and inhaled deeply. "I know that Simon has been keeping what we are doing at work on my Project secret. I'm sure you're very curious, and I imagine Simon has been acting strange lately."

"Yeah, he has," Diane said, glancing at Simon before returning her gaze to Arthur.

"What I'm going to tell you will come as a shock and will seem unbelievable. The reason I'm going to reveal what we have been doing is because I think you'll want to be involved. First though, I'll need you to promise to keep what I tell you and what you will further learn absolutely secret."

Diane looked to Simon, who nodded, then to Arthur. "Okay, I can keep a secret."

"Great. My Project has been more successful then I or anyone ever imagined. We have built an Einstein-Rosen Bridge, a Wormhole, which will allow travel back in time." He waited while Diane's face dropped.

Diane looked around the room at everyone and began to laugh. "You almost had me. Nice try. Did you and Simon cook this up? Wouldn't that be something if it were true? Yeah, travel back in time and get people to do something about climate change long ago." She laughed again. "What a concept."

"I'm actually serious, Diane."

"He's telling the truth," Simon added.

"I know it sounds unbelievable," Rose said. "I was there when they sent the cat back to 1980 for two hours and brought her back alive."

"Wait a minute. How gullible do you think I am?"

"Darling, it is not some trick," Simon said. "We really did send a cat back to 1980 for two hours and brought it back. Cross my heart."

Diane opened her mouth, her eyes wide, and shook her head. "Truly."

"Yes, truly."

"So why are you telling me this?"

"We want your help," Arthur said. "After your wedding, I'm proposing that I be sent back in time with information that will be helpful to climate scientists so that they can use the information to try to get our government to actually start reducing carbon emissions."

"You can't do that in two hours," Diane said.

"No, of course not," Arthur replied. "We all will need to decide: who I should talk too and what I should say to help the chosen advocate in his or her endeavor to convince the US Government to take serious actions to reduce fossil fuel use and transition the economy to clean energy. I will need to spend probably at least a week, maybe more."

"Is this time travel safe?"

"Not really," Rose added. "He's been at me for weeks trying to convince me he should do this." She shook her head. "I'm still not convinced. I thought if anyone should go back, it should be me. I'm the expert, but yesterday we learned that I'm pregnant. He is afraid the strain of time travel would be too much for the baby. The cat that came back was in a coma for several days after its return, disoriented for over a week, and didn't really recover completely for many weeks."

"Congratulations," Diane exclaimed. "How wonderful that you're going to be mother. That's so great." She smiled briefly before adopting a stern expression. "If the cat came back in a coma, wouldn't that happen to Arthur?"

"Probably," Arthur said.

"Where would you go?" Diane asked. "How does this work?"

"I would end up in the same place as I began, the basement of the lab in a past time. There was a lab in the same spot in 1990, the year I propose to go back to. I would want to go at night so I could hopefully recover after I materialized and make my escape with the capsule enclosure before anyone came to the lab and discovered me. I would set up an automatic infusion of adrenalin upon my materialization to help spike me from the coma. Since the cat traversed both ways, the effect of the transverse was double what I would experience on the single passage."

"This... this is too crazy," Diane said. "I think it sounds too risky. Not something a father to be should be doing."

"I know, Diane. It is no doubt very risky. I don't want my child to grow up in a world with runaway climate degradation. I'm willing to risk my life for my child."

"Rose, are you going to let him risk his life like this?"

"Believe it or not, I am. What's happening to the climate is putting enumerable lives at risk. People are already dying in the thousands from extreme hot spells, and sea level rise is displacing enumerable groups of people. The last heat wave in India was a terrible devastation. Water scarcity, terrible storms, climate refugees…." Rose exhaled strongly and paused briefly. "Arthur thinks he can change what is happening by getting people in the past more interested in transitioning from fossil fuels. He believes that by changing the past he will change the present. I'm not sure I totally agree, but he has convinced me it's worth a try."

"I'm not asking for your answer tonight, Diane, and I'm sorry to spring this on you before your wedding, but I'm afraid that the secret of the Einstein-Rosen Bridge could get out." Arthur extended his hand across the table and grasped Diane's hand. "I believe if my sponsors discover what I have achieved, the Project will either be taken away from me or shut down. There's no way they would let me do what I'm proposing."

"You don't trust your team?"

"I trust my team explicitly, but the sponsors may find the false reports I've been sending them not as productive as they would like for the immense sums the Project is costing. Time is of the essence, I believe. I want to travel on December 6th or there about."

Arthur paused and took a long drink of beer. "Thanks for believing me, Diane, and thanks for coming to dinner. I look forward to your wedding. Go home and think about what we have discussed. Talk it over with Simon. Give us your answer in a few days if possible."

Rose got up and came around the table to help Diane up. "Think about it. If you're leery of being involved, we will understand. I've already started working on the materials he'll need to take with him, and I sure could use your help." She hugged Diane, then escorted Simon and her to the door.

"See you soon," Rose said as she ushered them outside.

"Enjoy the rest of your evening," Arthur added. "See you tomorrow, Simon."

"Goodnight," Simon called as he escorted a speechless Diane to her car in the moonlight

As Rose was lying in bed in Arthur's arms, she asked, "Do you think Diane will want to help?"

"I don't know. Of course she was shocked by what we told her. If she's reluctant, I'm confident you can provide me with the information that I will need to present."

"The science of climate warming was already known to climate scientist in 1990," Rose said. "Fred Hinson spoke to Congress about global warming and the need to reduce carbon emissions in 1988. I don't know what additional information we can provide that will help convince the powers that be to begin reducing the use of carbon fuel. The oil and gas industries, banks, and other moneyed interest won't want to change. In 1990 they did everything in their power to stop any meaningful action on global warming. Look at the history. I don't know how you can get them to change."

"It's not I who will get them to change. It will be Doctor Hinson and his colleagues, who will hopefully get the powers to be to change. I assume you have settled on Hinson as the person I should talk to and provide the information and technology."

"Yes I believe so. But I... I know I tentatively agreed to your travel, but I'm having serious reservations." She pulled away and rose up on her elbow. "What would I do if you never came back or died upon your return? You had the cat stay only two hours in 1980. The wing on the Physics Building had not been built then. The cat was out on the grass for two hours. You'll end up in the Physics building basement. What if someone sees you?" The more she thought about Arthur time traveling back, the more she didn't like it.

"There shouldn't be anyone in the Physics Building Laboratory at midnight."

"Shouldn't be? There's no guarantee. What if you're apprehended and charged with breaking-in the laboratory?"

"I'm fairly sure this is unlikely. If so, I believe I would be able to talk my way out of trouble. If I am detained, it wouldn't be for long. That's why we'll set additional specific times and dates for me to rendezvous in the lab basement in case there are unforeseen circumstances. Violet and Simon will have to power down the Bridge after I'm sent and repower it ready for the set date and time. If I don't appear, they'll do the same for the alternate dates."

"What if you're delayed for some reason and don't make any of the rendezvous, or they can't reconstitute the Bridge?"

"That won't happen." He pulled her to him. "I'll make one of the dates, I promise. Violet and Simon will be able to reconstitute the Bridge. Have no fear. I don't want to miss the birth of my child."

She punched him on the chest. "Your damn right you better not miss the birth of your child. You have to come back. If you don't, I might be tempted to be sent back to join you."

"No way is that going to happen."

11- DECEMBER 9, 2050

Everyone on the team as well as Rose and Diane were present. They had chosen Friday night as the best time for Arthur's travel to 1990 so that he would arrive on a Sunday. The excitement and apprehension of the group were apparent. Arthur had converted a large sum of money to gold that he could exchange for the funds he would need for expenses to travel and meet with Fred Hinson, who worked at the NASA Goddard Institute For Space Studies in New York City and to set up a bank account for Doctor Hinson to aid his work to publicize the importance of reducing greenhouse emissions. He had printed a fake 1990 Driver's License for his identification needs and a Swedish passport.

He also was taking a laptop and a portable hard disk that would work with a 1990 computer. They had debated about him taking a laptop. The technology was so advanced compared to portable computers in 1990 that it was important that no one see it. He would have to be careful about keeping it secure. If necessary, he could use the laptop to download the information to another hard disk or print out the information in case the hard drive he took with him didn't work.

They had chosen December 16th, another Sunday, at 12:00 PM as the retrieval rendezvous, giving him one week to travel from Berkeley to New York meet with Fred Hinson and return. Seemed simple enough as long as he wasn't detained with illness or something else. The alternate rendezvous would be December 23rd or December 30th, if he didn't materialize on the 16th.

"Everything seems to be in order. We should begin." Arthur hugged Rose. "See you in a week, My Love."

Rose looked like she would faint. "You come back to me, you hear. No ifs ands or buts."

"I'll be back. Don't worry."

"Hah, don't worry," Rose blurted out angrily. "Oh, he's just going for a little excursion 60 years in the past. Nothing to it."

"I know... I know. Okay, Simon and Violet, are you ready? Billy and Harold take your positions."

Diane took Rose's hand.

Arthur hoisted the graphene capsule that Billy had manufactured, donned his helmet, connected the oxygen pack on his back, and waved before entering the enclosure and securing the door. He placed the capsule in the center of the enclosure, opened the capsule hatch, and climbed inside. "I'm all set," Arthur said into his microphone. "Capsule secured. Automatic adrenalin in place. Begin initiation of the Bridge."

Violet looked back at Rose and gave a thumbs up. She turned to Simon. "Here we go. Stage 1 power initiating, liquid helium circulating, and temperature rising."

"Stage 1 looking good. All parameters within range," Simon said after twenty minutes.

"Stage 2 initiating," Violet announced. "Temperature rising, electromagnets ramping up, initiating revolving current." She took off her lab coat as the room temperature started to feel hot.

"Stage 2 parameters within range," Simon said after ten minutes.

Rose squeezed Diane's hand as she grit her teeth, ignoring the sweat beading on her face.

"Stage 3 initiating, circulating current reaching maximum, enclosure temperature holding at 500°, inside temperature at 50°."

The temperature in the room was very hot. Rose wiped her crimson face with her handkerchief, her knees bending as she started to swoon. Diane let go of Rose's hand and hugged Rose to her.

"Stage 3 parameters have stabilized," Simon said. "You still conscious Arthur?"

"Just barely. I can feel the pressure building. I love you all. See you in a week."

"Initiating stage 4, temperatures holding, current at maximum. Bridge formation beginning." Simon looked back at Diane and Rose before turning to Violet and nodding. "All parameters good. Bridge complete. Arthur is away to year 1990."

Violet jumped up. "Give 'em hell, Arthur."

Rose burst out crying and fell to her knees. "You come back to me, Arthur, you hear."

"Wow, we did it," Violet said smiling at everyone in turn. "Okay, beginning the powering down."

"Parameters good, temperature is decreasing, everything still looks good," Simon said. "God speed Arthur." He leaned forward and placed his head on the console desk, the sweat beads running down his neck

Diane helped Rose up. Once Rose recovered her equilibrium, she walked up to Violet. "How do we know if he made it?"

"We don't for sure," Violet answered as she looked up at Rose's troubled face. "The software indicated he was sent to 1990, but there's no way to actually verify that."

"Are we sure he left?"

"We'll have to wait for the enclosure temperature to cool some more, then we can open the enclosure to verify he's gone. But all indications of the program are he's now in 1990."

Arthur felt a tremendous pressure on his body before he blacked out. When he started to regain consciousness, he raised his arms and moved his legs. He had a splitting headache, but his body seemed responsive. He opened the capsule. He was in a dark room. He slowly pushed himself from the capsule and rolled onto the floor. He switched off the oxygen and removed his helmet. Hearing no movement, he removed his transit suit, placed the oxygen pack that still had plenty of oxygen, the helmet, and the suit in the capsule. He donned his back pack and walked to the door of the laboratory. He stuck his head out. Nobody seemed to be around. He looked at his watch— 11:40 PM. He had been unconscious around 30 minutes. The lab door had a keyed lock. It would be easy to break back in. He went back, hoisted the graphene capsule, and went out into the hall. He walked down the hall and stopped in front of a bulletin board displaying a flyer for a concert the night of December 15, 1990. He had made it. Now the difficult work would begin. He hoped he would be able to complete the mission and return for the rendezvous. He could do it. Nothing would stop him. He had to get back, or all would be in vain.

He walked up the stairs slowly. He was somewhat disoriented and dizzy, but feeling quite good considering. He headed out from the building and went to a wooded area of the campus. He sat down on a bench to await the coming day when he could change some of the gold for money and acquire a hotel room for two weeks where he could leave the capsule to await his return to the room hopefully in a week to prepare for the trip back. He stashed the capsule in front of him so that he could keep an eye on it. The capsule had been made by Billy to look like a large bass fiddle instrument case and hopefully wouldn't garner undue interest. He thought he might catch a nap, but he was way too excited. He had succeeded in his boyhood fantasy of time travel. Who would have ever thought?

Several hours after the sun was up, students and faculty started to appear. The students looked very much like the students in 2050. Amazing how little dress had changed in 60 years. He was glad he had a warm insulated jacket. He guessed temperature was in the high 30s or low 40s. When it was 9:00 AM, he went in search of a coin merchant. He found one in town and exchanged a number of gold coins for cash, then went to the Graduate Hotel and paid for a room for two weeks. He received no questions about the capsule at the hotel other than the desk clerk asking if he was here for a concert.

In the room, he settled down on the bed. It was quite comfortable. He wanted so much to lie down, but pushed the thought out of his mind. Ignoring his fatigue, he called the airline and reserved a flight to New York for 6:00 PM. He then set the alarm for 1:00 PM and crawled to the center of the bed and laid back, exhaling a long breath and closing his eyes.

When the alarm began to beep, he rolled over, and stopped the alarm. He had managed to sleep, but still felt exhausted. The adrenalin and the transition must have taken their toll. He pushed himself up and staggered to the shower. He still had a splitting headache, and his body ached something awful. He stood under the shower a long time trying to clear his head and boost his energy. Perhaps he should postpone his flight to New York until tomorrow. No...

he could hopefully sleep on the plane and again when he got to his hotel in New York. Time was of the essence. He wanted to make sure he was back in Berkeley for the first rendezvous.

He'd wait until he got to New York before contacting Fred Hinson. He hoped it wouldn't be difficult to get in to see Doctor Hinson. He had skimmed the information Rose and Diane had provided on the hard drive to be given to Hinson before he left 2050. Some of the information he thought too advanced, but Rose thought it was essential that Hinson understood what was in store in the future and important technologies that would help the transition to clean energy. He was worried how Hinson would take the information. The climate modeling software was extremely advanced compared to what was available in 1990.

After his shower, he went in search of a restaurant. He didn't feel hungry, but thought some fuel and coffee would make him feel better. He found a small café not too far from campus. The cloudy weather was a welcome. He felt hot even though it was quite cold and wondered if he had a fever. At the café, the only vegan dish on the menu was oatmeal. It came with milk, and when he asked for soy or almond milk, the waitress looked at him like he was crazy.

"We don't have anything like that. We just got the nondairy creamer powder."

He drank numerous cups of coffee, but they didn't seem to perk him up much. He started back to the hotel, wondering how he would secure the capsule. If it was just sitting in the closet, the cleaning person might become curious. He could wrap it in a hotel sheet, but they would probably want to take it off. Might be worse than leaving it as it was. No, that wasn't a good idea. He turned around and headed toward town. He'd buy a dark colored blanket, a chain and a lock, wrap the capsule in the blanket, then chain and lock it. If he lost the capsule, he wouldn't be able to return until he got someone to make something similar, which might be extremely difficult in 1990, since graphene wasn't discovered yet. The forces of the Bridge were too strong for an exposed body.

12- DECEMBER 11, 1990

Arthur awoke in his New York hotel in a daze. He wasn't sure where he was until he got up and looked out the window. Had the time travel affected his brain or was it just exhaustion. He would need to be on his toes when he met with Hinson. All of a sudden, he had a frightening thought: what if Hinson was out of town and wouldn't be available. Rose had tried to determine if Hinson would be present during this time period. She found no information that he was gone, but no verification that he was present in New York this week of 1990. He glanced at his watch, 9:30 AM. He had gotten plenty of sleep. Why was he feeling so tired?

His airplane flight yesterday had gone off without incidence other than him wandering around the airport, looking for his boarding gate for quite a while. When he arrived at Kennedy Airport, it had taken him nearly an hour to orient himself and find the taxi line. It was as if he was stoned on marijuana and had difficulty remembering what he was doing and where he was going. By the time he got to his hotel, he was extremely exhausted, collapsing on the bed as soon as he reached his room and falling asleep within minutes. When he woke in the middle of the night, he disrobed and crawled back into bed.

In the morning after collecting his thoughts, he reluctantly stumbled into the bathroom and stared at the mirror, holding on to the wash basin. He appeared haggard and strung out as if he had been on an all-night drinking spree. Not the countenance he wanted to present to Hinson. Hopefully a shower would help. After the shower, feeling a little better, he telephoned the Goddard Institute and asked to speak with Fred Hinson, explaining to the receptionist he was a climate scientist from Sweden, who was in New York for a few days and wanted to meet with Mr. Hinson. Doctor Hinson was not available so Arthur left his name and his hotel telephone number.

He stretched back on the bed, stuffed some pillows behind his head, and turned on the TV. He lay there the entire day except for walks around the room and orders of room service meals, but there was no telephone call.

Around 6:00 PM he thought about going for a walk in Central Park. How late would Hinson think he could call? At 8:00 PM, he decided to give up on a walk in the park in the dark as well as a call from Doctor Hinson. Hopefully Hinson would call in the morning.

In the morning he rose with the sun, feeling a little better. He still had a headache, but his intense body ache had lessoned. He order a room service breakfast— orange juice, oatmeal, whole wheat toast, and a carafe of coffee. He watched TV most of the morning. At 11:00 AM the telephone rang.

He picked up on the second ring. "Arthur Brown."

"Mr. Brown, it is Fred Hinson returning your call. I understand you are a Swedish climate scientist and would like to meet."

"Yes, that is correct. I would greatly appreciate meeting with you."

"What is it you would like to discuss?"

"I have some climate modeling software and other climate information I think you would be interested in."

"I see. Yes, I would be interested in meeting you. I can't this afternoon. I thought I knew most climate scientists, but I have never heard your name."

"I like to stay out of the limelight. I assure you the information I have for you, you will find most interesting."

"Sounds intriguing. Could you come to the NASA Goddard Institute for Space Studies tomorrow morning say 10:00 AM?"

"Yes, that will be convenient."

"Great, I'll see you then. Just go to the front desk when you arrive. They'll call me. I'll meet you in the lobby and escort you to my office."

"Thank you, Doctor Hinson. I look forward to talking with you. Goodbye."

He had his meeting. He felt better. Another day to rest up would be good. He could now take his walk in Central Park and go shopping for a suit and tie.

Arthur arrived by taxi to the Goddard Space Institute, an older square building on the corner of Broadway and West 112th Street. He went to the front desk. "Hi, my name is Arthur Brown. I'm here to meet with Fred Hinson."

"Yes, Mr. Brown. Here is your visitor badge." She picked up the phone and announced his arrival. "Doctor Hinson will be right down."

"Thank you." Arthur clipped the badge to his grey suit and strolled around the lobby. He was too nervous to sit down. Every time the elevator dinged, he turned to look. When Fred Hinson exited the elevator wearing a tweed sport coat and blue trousers, he recognized him immediately from the pictures he had seen of him and hurried to greet him. Hinson was a stocky, trim gentleman with thinning blond hair and an engaging smile.

"Hello, Doctor Hinson," Arthur said, smiling brightly and extending his hand. "I am so pleased you agreed to meet with me."

Hinson shook Arthur's hand. "Glad to meet you, Mr. Brown. Is it Doctor Brown?"

"Yes it is."

"You don't sound Swedish."

"I studied many years in the US."

"I see. Follow me and we'll go to my office."

They got in the elevator and went to the top floor. Hinson led the way into his office, a large corner office with many windows, and indicated for Arthur to have a seat in one of the black leather chairs around an oak coffee table. Photographs of space rockets, telescopes, and vibrant galaxies were spaced around the room.

Once Hinson took his seat, Arthur smiled and began. "Doctor Hinson, I have a hard disk for you with climate simulation software and additional information I believe that will be very helpful. I read the speech you gave to Congress in 1988. Even though we climate scientists have alerted society to the possible dangers of global warming from fossil fuels, I believe we need to be much more forceful in identifying the future dangers that will happen unless we begin to reduce reliance on fossil fuels. We need to publicize more strongly what continued use of fossil fuels will do to the earth, and get governments to increase funding for alternate sources of energy like solar and wind as well as backup battery storage." He paused to take a deep breath in order to ascertain how Hinson was reacting to his words. Hinson was watching Arthur with apparent interest.

So far so good. "I believe that the United States needs to lead in this endeavor and get the rest of the countries of the world on board." Arthur took another breath and relaxed a little. He wondered if he was being too forceful. "The information on the hard disk I am providing will aid you in that endeavor. However, I must ask you to keep the origin of the information on the hard disk secret and only disseminate the information as if it was developed by you. You need to keep our meeting secret." He waited while Hinson processed Arthur's request for secrecy.

"Why would the information you want to give me need to be kept secret?"

"The information does not need to be kept secret. Just the origin of the information must be kept secret. Do you agree to keep the origin secret?"

Hinson frowned slightly before shifting in his seat. "Yes, I suppose."

"Good." Arthur slid the hard disk toward Hinson.

Hinson picked up and examined the hard disk. "I've never seen a hard disk like this. There is no indication of the manufacturer."

"Yes it's a propriety prototype that is not yet in full production and is not currently on sale."

"Where was it made? Who made it? Was it made in Sweden?"

"I am not at liberty to disclose the manufacturer. Yes, the disk was made in Sweden."

"That sounds rather mysterious. I don't understand this need for secrecy. Why give me this information if it's secret. This is most unusual. Can you summarize the information on the disk you think I will find important."

"The origin of the information is what needs to be kept secret. The actual information can be widely distributed by you and shared with other scientists. There is a vast storehouse of information on the hard disk, including advanced climate modeling software, advanced new technologies that will be helpful in reducing greenhouse gas emissions, various tax proposals for helping to decrease dependence on fossil fuels, and much more. The world needs to take serious the future climate warming from the use of fossil fuels and begin significantly reducing carbon emissions sooner rather than later while there's time before climate warming becomes more problematic." Arthur leaned forward and fixed his eyes strongly on Doctor Hinson. "Once you've had time to digest the information I'm providing, we can talk. I'll be in New York until Friday if you want to telephone with questions."

"This seems all rather strange. I must admit, I don't know what to say. Why give the information to me. Why not disseminate it yourself with the help of your associates."

"I understand why you might feel it's strange and unusual. Let's just say I and my associates believe you as an American have the best opportunity to use the information to make progress in getting the US and other countries to reduce the use of fossil fuels and begin the transition to clean solar and wind energy. We believe that the US must take the lead on reducing fossil fuel use to induce other countries to follow suit." Arthur stood. "I'm afraid I must take my leave. I have some others things to take care of today, so I'll say goodbye." He outstretched his hand. "Thank you so much for meeting with me, Doctor Hinson. It has been a great pleasure. I've been a fan of yours for a long time."

Fred Hinson, looking very quizzical, stood and grasped Arthur's hand. "Doctor Brown, thank you for coming in and for this hard disk. I will look at the information you have provided, and I'm sure I'll be in touch. I have your hotel number. Is your home address in Sweden and phone information on the disk?"

"Yes, it is."

"Great, I'll escort you back to the lobby."

Arthur left the Goddard Space Institute with relief and worry. He thought he had explained himself adequately, but not very well. Rose would have done a much better job. He needed a distraction. He hailed a cab and went to Central Park. Upon arrival at Central Park, he leisurely strolled across the park in the warm sunshine, reviewing his meeting with Hinson. He was surprised by the number of birds in the Park. Birds in 2050 were not nearly as plentiful. When he reached the other side of the park, he went into the Art Museum and spent hours perusing the art exhibits. Feeling somewhat calmed by the beauty and amazing expertise of the artists, he walked back across the Park to his room at the Excelsior Hotel.

He chastised himself for not having a better prepared speech for Doctor Hinson when they met. He expected that he might have come across as somewhat inept. In any case, Hinson would find the information on the disk very interesting, and Arthur was confident that Hinson would telephone him.

If Hinson asked to meet again, what should he do? He knew Hinson would want to know how he had obtained the information. He didn't have a reasonable explanation. Rose should have anticipated Hinson's reaction and should have worked up a prepared answer for Arthur that was more convincing than his futile attempt at explanation. Maybe he should only talk on the telephone with Hinson. It was much easier to remain aloof and not be intimidated on the telephone than in person. He settled back on the bed and began reading the novel he had bought near the park, but found it almost impossible to concentrate on the story.

At 5:00 pm the telephone rang. He stared at the phone a few seconds before answering, "Arthur Brown."

"Hello Doctor Brown, it's Fred Hinson. I skimmed some of the information on the hard disk, and I am amazed. The climate models are much more advanced than our models here at NASA. Who developed these models?"

"Associates of mine."

"What are their names?"

"I am not a liberty to divulge their names."

"The technology referenced about hydrogen use in cement, steel, and aluminum manufacturing is interesting and something I haven't seen before. And the solar panel and battery technology is amazing. I'm pleasantly surprised. Could you meet me tomorrow morning to go over some of this information?"

What should he say? If they met again in person, he might make some dumb or incriminating statement. "I'm sorry, meeting in the morning would be difficult. The information I gave you for the most part was developed by my Swedish colleagues. We have a somewhat secret institute devoted to climate warming."

"There's something strange about you and your hard disk of information, Doctor Brown. It's almost as if you're from the future." He laughed. "All kidding aside, I am excited about the information you have given me. Being able to discuss the information with you would be invaluable. Won't you reconsider meeting?"

Arthur was still apprehensive of an additional meeting. Hinson was already suspicious of him and his hard disk. However, maybe an additional face to face meeting would help solidify Hinson's support. "Ah... well... yes... I can rearrange my schedule and we can meet again tomorrow afternoon if that's acceptable."

"Excellent. Name the place and time, and I'll be there."

"Is there a coffee shop near you that you like?"

"Yes, there's one just up the block from the Institute."

"Oh yes, I remember seeing it. I'll meet you there at 4:00, if that's convenient?"

"Good, I'll see you then."

As soon as Arthur replaced the phone, he jumped up and started ambling around the room. He would need to be on his toes so as not to make any mistakes in the meeting with Hinson tomorrow. It was important to spur Hinson to become more vocal and more engaged in the fight to transition from fossil fuels. He needed to take another walk in the park to dissipate some of his anxiety. He'd have an early dinner after his walk and go early to bed.

In the morning when he awoke at 8:30, he felt considerably better. His headache was gone and his body ache was only slight. He took a long shower and after dressing walked down the stairs to the hotel restaurant for breakfast. After breakfast, he reviewed the information on the hard disk on his laptop in his room. He felt better about meeting again with Hinson. It was the right thing to do. After a late lunch at the hotel, he hailed a taxi and went to the coffee shop determined to present himself well.

"Ah, Doctor Hinson," Arthur said as he came up to Hinson's table. "Good to see you again."

Hinson stood and shook hands. "Thank you for coming. I've printed out some of the information I want to discuss." Hinson set some pages in front of Arthur. "I would like to meet with the scientists responsible for this technology."

Arthur picked up the pages and ruffled through them. "I'm afraid that will not be possible." He was quite disturbed that Hinson had printed out information from the hard disk, but realized that it was natural for Hinson to do so.

"Why not? I'm quite willing to travel to Sweden to meet with them."

"I must reiterate that you must keep the origin of this information secret as I explained was necessary before I gave you the hard disk. You agreed to keep the origin of the information secret. You may not show this information directly to anyone else. You can discuss the information as theoretical, but cannot show the printed information to anyone. You can rewrite the information in your own vernacular and disseminate it, but please do not print out the information directly." Arthur studied Hinson. The look on Hinson's face was classic denial of what he was hearing. "You agreed to the secrecy."

"I know, but a lot of the information is revolutionary and needs to be disseminated."

It suddenly dawned on Arthur that the release of the new technologies all at once would be disruptive and could place Hinson in danger. Why hadn't he or Rose thought about this? He leaned forward. "Yes, of course they need to be disseminated, but you need to disseminate the information carefully a little bit at a time, so as not to draw undo interest. Disseminating this innovative information to the world all at once could lead to difficulties." He leaned back and relaxed some. "Treat the information as if you developed it, but release it sparingly."

"It would be unethical to claim that I developed the information?"

"We have provided the information for your own use freely with no strings attached."

"This is most unusual. I can't take credit for something I did not develop."

"We are reassigning our rights to you. Climate warming is an existential threat to life on earth. Proper incremental action on reducing the use of carbon fuels is essential and needs to begin in earnest now. A tax on carbon at the source with the majority of the proceeds returned to the populace would be a great method to reduce fossil fuel use as explained in detail in the information provided. Prices on almost everything would rise and would be a regressive tax on lower income people, hence the need to distribute the proceeds of the tax to the populace. I realize that at present this would be most difficult, but planting the seed now will hopefully allow a future carbon tax to be instituted."

Arthur was pleased with Doctor Hinson's nod of agreement. "Otherwise a carbon tax would be extremely unpopular. Our group would like to aid you in your endeavor to disseminate information of the dangers of climate warming in order to convince the populace that actions need to be taken. To this end, I have established a bank account in your name at the Chase Manhattan Bank in the amount of four hundred thousand dollars to be used by you to propagate the importance of reducing the use of fossil fuels and mitigate climate warming." He had planned to mail the bank account information to Hinson in order to avoid trying to explain the origin of the money, but decided to go ahead and give him the information on the account now.

"What? This is crazy."

"We believe you are the best person to lead the fight to reduce the use of fossil fuel and transition to clean solar, wind, and hydrogen energy. Of course we expect you to include other climate scientist around the world in this endeavor."

"I don't know what to say. I've never encountered someone like you. It defies explanation."

"Yes indeed. That's an excellent way to describe the situation. It defies explanation. Perhaps, I am from the future as you alluded to." Arthur laughed. "I understand why you would question how the information provided was obtained. Our Institute has been working on climate solutions for many years. We have wealthy people backing our research, who want to remain anonymous. I and my colleagues have chosen you to lead the way because of your stellar reputation and willingness to speak out. We want to encourage you, support you to be even more vocal, and induce you to get other scientists to join you."

"I don't know what to say. I'm only one person."

"Yes, but you are a scientist of great esteem and fortitude. We believe that you can lead a climate movement. We have great confidence in your enthusiasm and ability."

Arthur scooted his chair back. "I'm afraid I must be on my way. I'm on a tight schedule today. Here's the information on the bank account." Arthur placed the envelope on the table and stood up. "It has been a great pleasure to meet you, Doctor Hinson." He shook hands with Hinson. "I don't expect I'll see you again. Best of luck. Goodbye."

Hinson remained standing, looking dumbfounded as Arthur walked away and left the coffee shop.

Arthur quickly hailed a taxi and returned to his hotel. He called the airline and made a plane reservation to Oakland for the morning. He had completed the mission with Hinson and was excited to find out what reduction in greenhouse gas emissions his meeting with Doctor Hinson and the Doctor's subsequent work and activism had changed the climate situation in 2050—a climate that had already reached a global mean temperature increase of 2.5° C, where carbon had reached 450 parts per million in the atmosphere, and the situation was on the verge of irreversible tipping points that would spell future disaster and elimination of most of the life on the planet. He hoped his time travel endeavor would jump start the reduction in fossil fuels, and that Hinson would lead an international movement for clean energy. He expected he would know immediately upon his return to 2050 what the alternate timeline had produced in the intervening 60 years.

13- DECEMBER 15, 1990

Arthur awoke when the telephone rang. "Hello."

"Your 7:00 o'clock wakeup call, Mr. Brown."

"Thank you." He felt as if he had gotten hardly any sleep as his alarm was beeping. He was glad he had requested a wakeup call in addition to the alarm. He would have slept through the alarm. He vaguely remembered his dream of talking to Doctor Hinson. In the dream, Arthur could not stop himself from floating away from Hinson while Hinson kept asking Arthur to repeat his statement. He sat upright, clasping his head, feeling drained. What did he expect? Traveling 60 years back in time was undoubtedly a severe stress on the mind and body.

He rolled out of bed and staggered to the bathroom. He had plenty of time. His flight back to Oakland was at 11:00. He showered, shaved, wrapped a towel around his waist, shuffled back into the room, and started laying out his underwear, shirt, and suit when there was a loud knock on his door. Had Hinson come to his hotel? He could understand Hinson's curiosity about him, but wasn't looking forward to speaking with him again. Of course it could be someone at the wrong room.

He went to the door, kept the chain engaged, and cracked the door. Two men in suits were at the door.

"Yes, can I help you?"

"Are you Arthur Brown?"

"Yes."

"We need to speak to you." The man held up an identity badge. "FBI."

Christ, what the hell was this. "I just finished showering. May I get dressed?"

"Sure we'll wait inside while you dress. Open up."

Arthur hesitated before removing the chain. He had no choice but to let them in. As he removed the chain, the two men pushed past him, knocking him back slightly. One sat on the bed, and the other sat in the chair.

"Go ahead Mr. Brown," one said. "Get dressed, and we can talk."

"What's this about?"

"Your visit to Doctor Hinson," the agent announced smugly. "I'm Agent Dawson and my compatriot is Agent Fonner."

Shit... why would the FBI want to talk to him just because he met with Hinson? This didn't bode well. Arthur scooped up his underclothes, trousers, and shirt and went into the bathroom. "I'll just be a minute." He closed the door part way and quickly dressed, making sure they were not searching his room. If they found his futuristic laptop, the shit would hit the fan. He stepped back into the room as soon as he was dressed.

"Your modesty is refreshing," Agent Dawson said sarcastically.

Arthur remained standing. He didn't like the demeanor of these FBI Agents one bit. "What would you like to know about my meeting with Doctor Hinson?"

"Why did you meet with Doctor Hinson?"

"I'm a climate scientist from Sweden. I wanted to confer with Doctor Hinson. He is a renowned climate scientist. I wanted to discuss the increase in global mean temperature with him and get his take on mitigating the effects of increased warming."

"You're Swedish?" Agent Dawson frowned. "You don't have an accent."

"I studied some years in your country."

"Why have you paid cash for your room and flight here?"

"I like to deal in cash. It's a fetish of mine."

"Fetish?" Dawson stretched his forehead and pursed his lips. "Hmm, did you hear that Fonner?"

"I'm in a bit of a hurry. I have a plane to catch. Is there something particular you would like to know?"

"We just wanted to find out more about you. We have no record of a Swedish climate scientist named Brown. That's not even a Swedish name."

"My parents were originally from England and settled in Sweden where I was born." He was digging himself a hole. If they checked his story, he could be in real trouble. "I prefer to do my climate research unaffiliated with any organization. I'm working on a book about climate."

"I see." Agent Dawson stood and nodded to the other Agent, who also stood. "We'll let you get on with your morning, Mr. Brown. We like to know who Doctor Hinson meets and what the Doctor is up to." He raised his eyebrows with a grin. "You see, Doctor Hinson has been quite vocal about global warming. Many think he's an alarmist— if you get my drift."

"We had a harmless conversation about global warming. There was nothing sinister discussed."

"That's good, Mr. Brown," Agent Dawson said. He motioned to Fonner, who joined Dawson. They went to the door. As Dawson was stepping out of the door, he turned back. "Have a pleasant trip to Oakland, Mr. Brown. Nice talking to you."

As the door closed, Arthur slipped quietly to the door and put his ear against it. He heard Fonner quietly say, "There's something fishy about that guy."

Dawson replied, "Yeah, we'll notify Oakland to keep an eye on him."

Damn, this was terrible. He never thought he would end up being watched by the FBI. Hinson's climate activism must have initiated FBI surveillance. How did they know he was flying to Oakland? Did they know he had a hotel room in Berkeley? Jesus, what if they searched his hotel room and found the capsule? Surely they would need a search warrant for a search. He hadn't done anything to justify a search warrant. A tail on him though could be harmful and could possibly interfere or stop his rendezvous. He'd need to ditch anyone following him after he arrived in Oakland.

Arthur finished dressing and went out in search of a restaurant. He found a small Mexican restaurant and ordered a bean and potato burrito with no cheese, whole wheat toast, and coffee. No one seemed to be following him. He relaxed a little. He ran through various scenarios he could use in Oakland to escape from the terminal without being followed. He thought that leaving the luggage he had purchased and quickly leaving the terminal in Oakland might be a strategy. He needed to change back into his jeans, shirt, and insulated jacket. The suit would be too easy to follow. If he walked away quickly from the airport and hid for several hours before taking a taxi to Berkeley, he might be able to ditch any FBI waiting at the Oakland Airport.

As soon as Arthur deplaned in Oakland, he rushed through the terminal, not seeing anyone he thought was following him, and went down the escalator to the outside, abandoning his checked luggage with his suit and other clothes. He walked briskly away from the terminal into the parking garage and hid in a toilet. Luckily no one tried to use the toilet. He sat there for two hours, trying to read the novel in the dim light, then walked out, and back to the taxi stand. He saw no one paying him undue attention as he stood in line for a taxi.

After taking a taxi to Oakland Chinatown, he selected a restaurant to kill some time. He ordered Kung Pao with tofu and green tea, then leaned back and took a deep breath. His hands were quivering. He was confident no one was following him, but was still extremely nervous. He hadn't expected his time in 1990 would be full of intrigue. His nervousness interfered with the enjoyment of his tasty meal and gave him indigestion. As he took his time finishing his pot of tea, he decided he wouldn't return to his hotel room in Berkeley to retrieve the capsule until the last minute in case they had figured out where he was staying.

He'd get another room at a different hotel and only return to his Berkeley room for the capsule Sunday night. Hopefully, if they were watching his Berkeley hotel, they would give up when he didn't return. Then he would break into the laboratory at the Physics Building and await what he hoped was the Einstein-Rosen Bridge back to the future.

He stayed in the Oakland hotel in Chinatown until it was dark Sunday night. He walked away from the hotel and hailed a taxi driving down the street. He was confident no one had followed him from the Oakland hotel. He had the taxi drop him at the University in Berkeley where he went to the student union and waited until 11:00 PM. He walked to his hotel and stood outside across the street, surveying the area for any suspicious cars a few minutes, but saw nothing dubious. He went into the hotel and to the stairs. No one in the lobby paid him any attention. He entered his room and went to the closet where the capsule stood wrapped and locked in the dark blanket. He unlocked the chain, removed the blanket and checked the contents of the capsule. Everything was just as he left it. He donned his backpack, grasped the handle of the capsule, and looked out into the corridor. All clear.

He hurried down the hall to the stairs, descended, and walked briskly from the hotel. After he arrived at the University, he walked leisurely to the Physics Building. He went past the entrance and stopped a short distance away, watching the outside. When he saw no one in the vicinity, he quickly walked back to the entrance, slipped inside, then descended the stairs to the laboratory. He jimmied the door with the small pry bar he had purchased and entered the laboratory. He switched on his flashlight and searched for the spot he had marked on the floor of the exact position of his arrival in the capsule. He donned the special suit, connected the oxygen pack, secured his helmet and entered the capsule, lying back to await the Einstein-Rosen Bridge formation and hopefully his travel back to 2050.

14- DECEMBER 16, 2050

Rose and Diane arrived at the Physics building at 11:00 PM. Diane knocked on the door. "It's going to be okay, Rose."

Simon opened the door. "We're pretty well set. Come on down. We'll begin initiation in about fifteen minutes. I've made some coffee."

Rose and Diane followed Simon down the stairs. Seeing the huge enclosure made Rose shutter slightly. She wondered how Arthur had ever convinced her he should travel back in time. She was extremely worried that something would or had gone wrong. She was so glad that Diane was by her side. What if for some reason, they could not produce the Einstein-Rosen Bridge, or Arthur didn't make the rendezvous, or the Bridge wasn't capable of bringing him back? They didn't have any real confirmation that he even travelled to 1990. What if he had just disappeared into nothingness?

Rose and Diane sat down at one of the tables in the break room while Simon fetched both mugs of coffee. Violet came in and joined the three at the table.

"How are you two feeling?" Violet asked brightly, obviously very excited. "I know you're worried Rose. Don't be. We successfully retrieved the cat. Everything is going to be okay. We'll bring Arthur back."

Simon glanced at Violet with a look that Rose suspected was to get Violet to tone it down. She believed Violet was as nervous and apprehensive as she was, but tried to mask it with her enthusiasm.

Simon glanced at the wall clock. "Okay we should take our places." "I've set out chairs behind Violet for you two." He nodded to Diane and Rose.

Violet jumped up. "All right, let's get this show on the road."

Diane took Rose's hand and helped her up. They followed Simon and Violet to the chairs. Billy and Harold were standing near the big screens.

"The helium is ready," Billy said. "Harold and I will standby the pumps and power panel." Billy placed his hand on Simon's shoulder. "All the equipment has been tested and is working properly. We'll leave you guys to start her up. Good luck." Billy and Harold walked to the back of the enclosure.

Simon and Violet swiveled back to look at Rose and Diane. "All right, here we go," Simon said.

"Hold on to your seats," Violet added and turned back to her key board. "Initiating Phase 1."

Rose was sweating as the electric current reached maximum in the enclosure and the electromagnets seemed to vibrate, their hum nearly deafening.

"Stage four holding, Bridge initialization beginning," Simon excitedly announced over the din.

"Bridge is intact and holding... yes, capsule retrieval beginning,"

After several seconds Violet jumped up. "He's made it... he's made it."

Rose pushed herself up from her chair and started for the enclosure. Simon leapt from his chair and grabbed Rose. "No Rose. We have to wait and de-energize the Bridge and enclosure."

Rose encapsulated in Simon's arms went limp and almost fell to the ground, but managed to regain her balance. She turned to Violet. "How do you know he's here, Violet?"

"Violet is stating what the software indicates. We won't know for sure until we can open the enclosure." Simon escorted Rose back to her chair.

Rose bit her lip in consternation. "Arthur has returned," she said softly to herself, hoping vocalizing it would help to make it so.

Diane stood behind Rose and wrapped her arms around her. "It's okay Rose. We've got to wait. Just hold on."

Violet was rapidly typing on her keyboard. "Bridge is deactivating and enclosure is cooling. Another few minutes and we can open the enclosure."

Rose grabbed Diane's arms and pressed them to her. The twenty minutes of waiting was the longest twenty minutes Rose had ever experienced.

"All right, inside temperature down to 45° C," Violet announced. "Simon open the hatch. Let's see what we've got."

The three followed Simon to the hatch as he slipped on the furnace gloves. He turned the sealing wheel quickly and opened the hatch. "The capsule is inside. My God, he's made it." Simon stepped through the hatch and hoisted the capsule, carrying it outside and setting it down. He opened the capsule. Arthur lay inside motionless.

Rose stood rigid, staring down at Arthur. "Why isn't he moving? What's happened?"

Simon knelt and checked Arthur's pulse at his throat. "There's a weak heartbeat. I don't think the adrenalin was administered. He checked the pouch. "Adrenalin is still full."

"I'll get a hypo of adrenalin," Violet shouted. "Bring the capsule to the break room where its cooler." She raced away from the enclosure while the rest carried the capsule to the break room and laid the capsule on a table.

Violet was ready with the hypodermic needle of adrenalin. She cut open the suit, exposing his arm, stabbed the hypodermic needle into his arm vein and helped Simon remove Arthur's helmet. She felt his neck pulse. "Heart rate is increasing. Let's lift him out."

They laid Arthur on another table. "Should we slap him and try and wake him," Rose asked, her face white with anxiety.

"No," Violet said. "The cat was in a coma for several days and it took weeks for it to fully recover. He needs to come out of the coma in his own time."

"Should we take him to the hospital?" Rose asked as she slumped into a chair, her tears running down her cheeks. She felt as if her heart would stop.

Violet grabbed Simon's arm and pulled him to the side. "Taking him to the hospital is not a good idea," she said softly. "We need to get him home, get a saline drip into him to counteract any dehydration. If we wakes up delirious, no telling what he might say."

"We're not medical professionals," Simon replied. "I think we need to get him to the hospital."

Violet dropped her head. "Okay, maybe you're right" She turned back to group huddled around Arthur. "Who's got a car?"

"I drove mine here," Diane said. "Let's carry him out."

"Billy and Harold come give us a hand carrying Arthur to a car," Violet shouted.

Billy and Harold rounded the enclosure at a run. The three men and Violet grabbed Arthur and carried him out of the breakroom as Diane proceeded the group up the stairs.

Rose pulled herself up from the table and followed the group. She kept telling herself that Arthur was back, and he would recover. Yes, he will recover. He has to.

Arthur lay in his hospital bed still in a coma as Rose was sitting by his bed, watching his breathing. He had been in the hospital three days with no improvement. She should have stopped him. Traveling back in time.... How crazy. She should have known that it could damage him. What if he doesn't regain consciousness? What would she do?

When Rose looked at the climate numbers soon after Arthur's arrival, she sensed that the percentage of carbon in the atmosphere had decreased and the number of coal fired generating stations in service in the developing world was smaller, but it was only a vague feeling. Arthur to her amazement may have actually affected the future. Perhaps Hinson had used the information Arthur had given him to jump start the phase out of fossil fuels. The amount of CO_2 was at 430 ppm, but she couldn't remember what they had been before Arthur had left. It was as if her memory had changed.

She wondered if now there would be enough impetus to keep the level from advancing much further. Diane had run the simulation with the current figures. The continued use of fossil fuels would still need to be curtailed if they were to avoid 2° or 3° C. Methane hydrates were only just beginning to break down in the warming Artic Ocean. When she perused the current scientific papers on climate change all data reflected the current greenhouse gases. All literature on CO_2 in the atmosphere had instantly changed as if the circumstances prior to Arthur's travel had disappeared and there was a new reality. How was this possible?

Rose wondered about other effects caused by Arthur's travel. Changing the future was serious business, and she worried that his travel may have initiated other unknown aspects. If Arthur had died on his travel to 1990, would she no longer be pregnant?

As she held Arthur's hand and talked to him about how much she loved him and needed him, she suddenly felt a twitch in his hand. She stood and leaned over him. His eyelids were flickering. She pressed the call button. The nurse came in immediately.

"I felt movement in his hand," Rose said. "And look, his eyelids are flickering."

The nurse took his arm and checked his pulse even though the monitor showed a heart rate of 55. "I think he's reviving," the nurse said.

All of a sudden Arthur's entire body began twitching and his heart rate jumped to 160. He opened his eyes wide and screamed.

"What happening?" Rose shouted. "He's having a seizure." She began crying profusely. "Arthur... Arthur."

The nurse pressed the code button and grasped Arthur trying to control his twitching body. Soon several nurses rushed in with the crash cart and helped hold Arthur. Gradually the twitching subsided, and Arthur opened his eyes wide looking around frantically, his face stretched until he recognized Rose and then laid back, relaxing his rigid body.

"Where am I," Arthur asked reaching out for Rose.

Rose grasped his hand and used her other hand to caress his face. "You're in the Berkeley hospital."

"What's the date?"

"December 20, 2050."

Arthur exhaled forcefully. "The 20th… my god, I made it. Oh, Rose, you are the most beautiful person I have ever seen."

Rose bent down and hugged and kissed Arthur. "You had us all so worried." She kissed him again. "Welcome back. I love you so much." She started crying with happiness.

When Diane and Simon walked into the hospital room, Diane, upon seeing Arthur sitting up in bed, rushed to the bedside. "Oh, Arthur," Diane exclaimed, giving Arthur a hug and a kiss on the cheek. "I'm so happy you're out of the coma."

"It's good to be conscious."

"When can you go home?" Simon asked, grasping Arthur's hand.

"They said probably tomorrow," Rose said.

"I'm ready now. Is someone going to tell me if I was successful? Rose has been stonewalling. I need to know if the agony I experienced was worth it."

Simon glanced at Rose. Rose nodded. "Okay Professor, yes, we think you were relatively successful. That's all we are going to say until you're home. Okay."

"What do you mean, think?"

"As Violet explained to me," Rose said. "If you changed anything, we won't know because we are in the alternate future. We only know what the current situation is and the history of the altered time line. We have no memory of the before past. Perhaps you are the only one, who would know for sure if anything changed."

"Yes...yes." Arthur held up both hands. "You're right. I hadn't thought of it that way. Of course.... Simon, we did it. Thanks for your help."

"Hey man, I am blown away. You are the man."

"Has Violet been here," Arthur asked as he turned to Rose.

"Oh yes. Every day, multiple times."

"She'll be here shortly," Simon said. "She telephoned me and began crying on the phone. So get ready."

"Yeah, I know what you mean. So you two, how's married life?"

"Couldn't be better," Simon replied.

"What couldn't be better," Violet said as she hurried into the room. "Boss, you look tired. Oh it's so unbelievable. You did it. You actually did it. I've been so worried." She stepped up and hugged Arthur. "I'm sorry I said you looked tired. You look great. Better than I expected. Oh, that's a dumb thing to say."

"We know what you mean, Violet. Glad you could come."

"Wild horses couldn't have stopped me. Oh Boss, I'm so happy to see your eyes open." Violet hugged him again."

"Okay Violet, I'm happy to see you too. I'm happy to see all of you. The return journey was extremely painful. Much worse than the trip out."

"I think we should be careful what we say," Simon said. "There's people about."

"Right," Arthur said. "What a journey. I'm so happy to be back." He slumped back on the bed and closed his eyes briefly. "I'm fading and I think I'll try to sleep." He raised his hand to his forehead and moaned softly. "I thank you all for bringing me back. Thank you...thank you." He closed his eyes and slipped into sleep.

Violet hugged everybody. "I'll take off. See you all soon. Rest up, boss. We can't wait to hear you story. God, I feel so great that he's back." She turned. "Adios amigos. Catch you later." She bounded out of the room, waving as she went.

"If she got anymore exuberant, I'm afraid she'd pass out," Rose said.

"She's got a lot of energy," Diane added.

"Maybe we should have sent her." Simon grabbed Diane's hand and pulled her to him. "She probably would have come back bouncing." He hooked his arm in Rose's. "Let's go out and get something to eat and celebrate Arthur's return. It's a great day."

15- DECEMBER 25, 2050

When Rose heard the doorbell ring, she asked Simon to get the door. "Yeah I've got it," Simon replied. When he opened the door, Violet came prancing in.

"Merry Christmas, Simon," Violet heralded as she hugged Simon. "I've brought a superb bottle of Sauvignon Blanc. I thought of bringing Champs, but I figured you'd already have plenty. Where's our hero?"

Rose came out to greet Violet in her green silk dress, wiping her hands on her apron and hugging Violet. "Merry Christmas, Violet. Thanks for coming."

"I wouldn't have missed it for the world."

"Arthur's on the couch," Rose said as she accepted the bottle of wine. "He's still a little weak, but don't tell him I said so."

"Hey it's to be expected." Violet rushed into the living room and flew into Arthur as soon as he stood, hugging him tightly. "Merry Christmas, Boss, or should I say, Time Traveling Wizard."

"Arthur will do," Arthur said. "Merry Christmas, Violet. You look festive."

Violet was wearing a bright green dress with a split up the side, a thick garnet necklace, and a red Santa hat. Rose thought she looked stunning. Violet had applied makeup, and Rose could see that Arthur was surprised at how alluring Violet looked with her kissable dark red lips.

Diane stood up from her chair and gave Violet a hug and held her at arm's length. "Damn girl, you look wonderful."

"Thanks, I thought I should dress up for the occasion."

Billy rose and gave Violet a hug, wishing her a Merry Christmas. Harold stood back and wished Violet a Merry Christmas.

"Hey, Harold, you're not getting off that easy. Come give me a hug, handsome."

Harold turned bright red and advanced to receive his hug.

"We are all here," Rose said as she handed Violet a flute of campaign. "Here's to health, happiness, and love." They all repeated the toast. "Okay let's move to the dining room. Dinner is almost ready."

Everyone took their seat around the dining table. Rose soon came in with a large tray, loaded with a vegan roast, two types of stuffing, a pan of roasted vegetables: gold potatoes, carrots, sweet potatoes, and parsnips, as well as a dish of green beans with shaved almonds, and a pitcher of vegan gravy. She set the dishes on the table. "Dig in and pass them around."

"Smells wonderful," Arthur said. "Thanks for cooking, Rose."

"Here's to Rose," Diane said raising her glass, "an accomplished cook, beautiful person, loyal friend, and amazing climate scientist."

"Hear, hear," Violet said, raising her glass.

"Hear, hear," the rest pronounced.

Blushing, Rose raised her glass. "Thank you and cheers."

After dinner they returned to the living room. "Okay, Arthur," Violet said emphasizing Arthur. We've all been dying to hear the complete story of your adventures in the past." Violet looked around the room. "So, Time Traveling Wizard, let's hear it."

"Okay, I'll try my best. After I arrived in the past— that's a statement you'll not hear very often— I was unconscious in the capsule for about thirty minutes." He took a deep breath and paused momentarily after the group's laughter. "The automatic infusion of adrenalin worked, and I slowly became conscious. I felt like I'd been squashed through a straw. My entire body ached and everything was a blur. The graphene capsule that you made to look like a bass fiddle case, Billy, worked well. I can't imagine what would have happened to me if I wasn't in the capsule. After a time, I was able to move my limbs and slowly climbed out of the capsule. The Physics Lab was dark and when I checked the hall no one was around. I removed the transition flight suit to my street clothes and walked into the hallway with the capsule. As I continued down the hallway, I saw a notice on the bulletin board for a concert December 15, 1990. This perked me up somewhat, knowing for sure I had arrived as planned."

He related the rest of the story, frequently stopping to take a drink. When he finished everyone looked like they had been administered a small electric shock.

"That's the most amazing story, I've ever heard," Violet exclaimed. "Man, you made a narrow escape. The fucking FBI. Excuse my language. Jesus, I'm so glad you made it. You're pretty good at this clandestine stuff. Wow, what a journey. You changed time. How totally unbelievable." She raised her glass. "Here's to the most amazing person on the planet."

"I am so blessed that I could be a part of this amazing feat," Simon added. "As Violet said, you are the most amazing person on the planet. Thank you, Arthur."

"Okay, enough with the adulation," Arthur said. "Thank you all for your help. I couldn't have done it without every one of you."

Arthur walked into the laboratory December 31st. Simon and Violet were at their keyboards. Billy and Harold were wiping down the enclosure with long dusters. "Hey you guys. Glad to be back at work. Convalescing is not my scene."

"Welcome back, Boss," Violet called. "2051 is going to be a good year."

"That's right. It is New Year's Eve. Thank you all for coming in on a Saturday."

"So, Boss, what now?" Violet asked. "Should we plan on sending someone else back to the past? I would volunteer."

"No. We're going to have to show our sponsors what we have built, but we can't show them how far we have progressed. We'll have to archive the software and replace it with something that is not as advanced and could only produce the beginning of an Einstein-Rosen Bridge that cannot actually stabilize. Plus, we need to remove the additional power cables to the electromagnets and to the capacitors. We can leave the helium bypasses."

"Jesus, Boss, why?"

"No one outside our circle can know what we did. What we achieved in the wrong hands could be catastrophic for life on this planet. I thought about dissembling the Project, but we may need it in the future. I know we only changed the greenhouse emissions a small amount. I've been reading up on the 60 year history since 1990. Apparently, I'm the only person that knows what was changed. And even my memory of the previous past is fading. You all experienced a new timeline. I have spent my time convalescing writing down the climate statistics that I can remember that were in effect before I left. I did change the future as far a climate warming is concerned a fair bit, but not enough to stop us from reaching 2° and possibly 3° C if business continues as it is."

Arthur watched the group, thinking his announcement was disturbing to them. It couldn't be helped. "I know this is not what you all wanted to hear. Hopefully the better situation that my travels induced will allow the climate scientist to get governments to be more proactive. We'll leave that to the likes of Rose, Diane, and their brethren. Our need is to make our sponsors, when they come, believe we are making progress, and the vast sum of money they have provided has been well spent. We need to convince them that we are making reasonable advances in scientific knowledge." He shuffled his feet and exhaled. "Okay let's get to it."

"When are our sponsors coming?" Violet asked.

"They are chomping at the bit, so it needs to be soon. I hope we can be ready to invite them next week. Any other questions?" No one asked anything. "Good. Violet, I'm going to need your help with my office computer. Please come with me."

Violet followed Arthur into his office. "I took $900,000 from the Project to purchase gold for my journey. I need to spread that money amongst our expenses, so that no one can find out where the money actually went. Can you work on that?"

"Sure boss. $900,000… how did you change so much into gold without creating suspicion?"

"I went to many gold coin establishments in multiple cities. I needed quite a large amount since gold is worth a lot more now than it was worth in 1990."

"Cooking the books should be relatively easy." Violet gave Arthur a shove as she laughed. "Won't take me too long to work my magic."

"I haven't sent any progress and economic reports out since early December. Our sponsors have been used to weekly reports. I used my illness to explain the delay. The hospital stay stalled them, but also made them worry about my ability to carry on the Project. They must have somehow accessed my hospital records even though that would be against the law. Their questions about my health revealed to me that they knew a lot more about my hospital stay than they should have." He paused to watch Violet type rapidly accessing screens in fast succession. He shook his head in amazement at Violet's computer skills. "Rose told me that she saw the same man, who was not on the hospital staff, several times outside my room. I also need you to check the security of my work computer to see if anyone tried to hack into it to download some of my files."

"Jesus, you think they would do that."

"I have no idea, but I wouldn't put it past them. When you've finished checking, I'll archive my secret files onto a portable hard disk. They are encrypted, but I imagine they would try to overcome the encryption if they did hack in and copied them. We will also need to archive the Bridge software onto hard disks and replace the Bridge program with an inferior program that could only begin to form an Einstein Rosen Bridge." He came closer and placed a hand on her shoulder. "If I am ever relieved from head of this

Project, you will have to make sure my replacement is never able to reconstitute what we were able to do."

"Boss, you're scaring me."

"Good. Because I'm very scared as well."

Arthur arrived at the lab January 6th with a group of four men and a woman. The group followed Arthur down the stairs. He threw out his arm toward Violet and Simon as they were sitting at their terminals. "These two, Violet and Simon, are our computer specialists." He turned back to the group. "These people are from the Department of Energy: John Bowman, Christopher Simms, Jerry Buckner, Josh Frampton, and Mary Houseman is from the University, you may have seen her on campus." He moved toward Billy. "These two men, Billy and Harold, are our mechanical engineers." Everyone shook hands. "Let's go in the breakroom and I'll explain the demonstration we'd like to show you." He turned to Billy and Harold. "If you two would get the panel and pumps ready. We will be back out quickly for the demonstration."

When everyone was seated in the breakroom, Arthur went to the white board and began drawing a diagram of the inside of the enclosure structure. "Forgive my crude drawing skills." He added to the schematic a whirling cloud of gas. "Once we power up the enclosure we need to use the electrical power and the electromagnets to create the swirling ionized atmosphere at tremendous velocity that would then form an Einstein-Rosen Bridge. To date we have not been successful, but have been close so to speak. We just can't seem to stabilize anything we begin to form. We surmise that the electrical power needs to be significantly stronger and have been working on ways to improve the intensity. That's it in a nut shell. Any questions?"

"I have one," John Bowman said. "Isn't the electrical power available from the Oakland Fusion Generating Station of sufficient magnitude?"

"In theory, yes, it should be. I have a feeling we aren't utilizing the electrical power in the right way. Anyone else have a question." He looked around the room, but no one else spoke up. "Okay let's run the Project Demonstration and see what we develop." He gestured for them to follow him and hurried from the breakroom.

Violet and Simon took their seats at their terminals. The rest of the group took their seats in the chairs behind Arthur as he stood behind Simon and Rose.

"Billy," Arthur shouted, "are we ready to go?"

"Everything's ready on our end," Billy called back.

"All right, Violet begin initiation."

Violet typed on her keyboard and brought up the schematic on the big screen. Simon initiated the screen with the parameters.

"Ladies and gentleman here we go," Arthur said. "It's going to get hot in here. You'll want to take off your jackets as the temperature rises." He looked back at his audience, smiled, and nodded. "Okay, Violet let's go."

"Initiating Phase one. Helium circulating. Power ramping up."

"Parameters are rising," Simon announced. "All within range."

When they reached phase four, everyone was sweating. "What have we got, Violet?

"Looks like the swirling gases are trying to form something but they keep breaking apart. The program cannot stabilize the formation."

"Keep going," Arthur said.

After thirty minutes as the room got hotter and hotter, Simon turned to Arthur. "Enclosure temperature exceeding 500° C."

"Okay that's it, begin to shut her down." Arthur turned to the seated group. "Sorry, I had hoped we could have formed the beginning of a Bridge." He took out his handkerchief and wiped his face. "Let's go back to the breakroom. It should be a little cooler in there."

The group hurried into the breakroom. It was a little cooler, but not much.

"What do you think your next steps will be?" John Bowman asked after everyone had settled.

"Well, that's an excellent question," Arthur replied. "I and my team will go through the specifics that were recorded from this demonstration and past attempts and put our heads together. I have a niggling feeling that we need to supply electrical power in possibly different ways to the enclosure. I think there's enough electrical power as you had suggested, John. We just need to apply it differently to the enclosure. Have you any insights John?"

"Not off hand. Maybe applying electrical power in more locations on the enclosure might be helpful."

"Yes, that's a very good idea, John. Anyone else have any suggestions?"

"Well, besides getting some better air conditioners— that was a joke— perhaps another cable from Oakland would be helpful if you think you need more power," Jerry Buckner said.

"Yeah, maybe so," Arthur answered. "The cost would be significant. California Power Company would need to approve the additional cable, and they would have to install it. Their work costs top dollar. I will look into it, though. Anyone else."

"I don't have any suggestions," Mary Houseman said, "but I want to thank you for the demonstration. I found the demonstration fascinating. The work your team has accomplished is amazing. I am so happy to see your wormhole enclosure in operation. I must admit when I get your reports and see the expenditures, I find myself wondering if the expense is worth it. I never thought you would ever be able to form a wormhole. I hope you don't mind me calling it that, but I am sure even if you're don't succeed you are learning valuable scientific information. Is not that so?"

"Oh yes, Mary, you are entirely correct. I am so thankful for all of your continued support. If we ever do succeed in forming a stabilized Einstein-Rosen Bridge, the implications of our experiment will be profound."

"Let's give Arthur and his team a round of applause for this fascinating demonstration, and all the hard work he and his team have done. I am suitably impressed." Mary led the group in a round of applause.

"Thank you. You are most kind. Now, I expect you all would like to get out of the laboratory and in proper air-conditioned spaces. Shall we adjourn?"

"Sounds good," Bowman said and got up. Arthur led the group up the stairs.

"Thanks for coming," Violet called. "See you next time."

16- FEBRUARY 19, 2060

Rose was at the dining room table in her silk print, green robe going over her notes when she heard the front door. She jumped up and went to greet Arthur.

Arthur stopped walking and smiled widely in surprise as he contemplated the alluring presence hurrying toward him. "You're back," he said as he folded her in his arms. "How was Russia?"

"Terrible, they're just paying lip service to reducing gas fired power plants. The Artic is almost ice free."

"Damn, that doesn't sound good. I know it's depressing. It's almost as if my excursion in the past was useless."

"No, definitely not useless. You gained us essentially about ten years. We're now about where we were before you left in 2050 judging from the notes you wrote down about the climate conditions in 2050 that you remembered after your return before your memory faded."

"So what does that mean?"

"We are back to 450 parts per million of CO_2 and the global mean temperature has increased to over 2° C from the 1950 baseline. Progress in the ten years since your travel has been made in the US in reducing the use of fossil fuel use although not significantly.

China, India, Australia, South Africa, and others have made some progress, but they are still burning coal."

"Damn, our son, John, is still going to encounter a very difficult world when he's grown. The world should have been down to zero carbon years ago."

"Yes, I know. I trying my best to get other countries to shift to clean energy."

"What you are doing is so important. Me, I'm basically standing still. We're not making any scientific achievements at the Project. I've demonstrated fleeting Einstein-Rosen Bridges to our sponsors to try to keep them funding the Project, but I believe they are losing patience with the Project, and I believe my team is losing enthusiasm as well." He sat down and gripped the table. "I myself am losing patience. Continuing the Project is essentially useless. My excursion did not accomplish what we had hoped. I should have gone back to a later time when the effects of climate warming were more advanced. The information could have been used more extensively and more substantial progress would have been made."

"Perhaps." Rose pulled Arthur to her. "You can't do anything about that now."

No he couldn't, but maybe he could do something more substantial if he reconstituted the Bridge and travelled again. Something he had been considering for some time. Suddenly it dawned on him that the house was too quiet. "Where's John?"

John, their nine year old son, was good friends with Simon's and Diane's son, Josh, who was six months younger than John, and Shelia, their four year old daughter.

"He's still over at Diane's playing with Josh. When I called to arrange to pick him up, he wanted to stay for dinner with them. I had a nice long soak in the bath instead."

"Did you and Diane plan this so we could be alone?"

"Now why would you think that?"

"Because I was greeted by an alluring woman in a sensuous, diaphanous, silk robe."

"Aren't you happy that we have some time alone?"

"Ecstatic." He lifted her up and carried her up the stairs into the bedroom.

"Such a strong specimen."

"I'll give you specimen." He tossed her on the bed and undid her robe. "Well what do we have here? It's a long, lanky, sexy woman." He quickly removed his clothes, joined her on the bed, and embraced her strongly.

His chest against hers felt so warm, spiking her desire. Several weeks in Russia had driven her desire to lofty heights. Their love making was torrid as he took her repeatedly to shuttering climaxes.

As they lay back spent. Rose rolled up and looked into his hazel eyes. "You are so handsome. Where would I be without you? You are such a gentle, sweet man. You wouldn't believe how aggressive some of the Russians were toward me."

"Oh, I can imagine. A beautiful woman like you.... Let's just say, you are irresistible to me." He pulled her to him and kissed her. "What else did you learn in Russia?"

"I verified that they're shuttering all their coal fired plants. Their electrical energy production has more than doubled since they've become a big cryptocurrency storage haven. Hence their need to keep the gas fired electrical generating."

"That's not good. China has a lot of cryptocurrency storage too, don't they?"

"Yes indeed. They're still using their coal fired generating plants. They are the world leader in solar and wind generation, but still are the country with the highest greenhouse gas emissions. Of course they have over 2 billion people. They don't seem to be much interested in family planning anymore. Their recent takeover of Mongolia with its newly discovered reserves of oil, gas, and precious metals has hardly caused an international stir. They are the new planet powerhouse. I suppose I should try and meet with their government at some point. The UN has been after me to set up another trip to China to get them to phase out completely their use of coal. The last time I went to China someone accompanied me wherever I went. Even when I left my hotel room to go to the dining room, I was followed. The trip was basically a waste of time."

"Too bad. They need to do more if we're going to prevent reaching 3° C. I'm tempted to ramp up the Einstein-Rosen Bridge again and go back again to see if I can't make more of a difference."

"Don't you even think about it? You were nearly killed in 2050."

Several days later, Arthur was sitting in his office in front of his computer, contemplating the prospects of reconstituting the Bridge. His sponsors were undoubtedly distraught with his inability to produce a stable Einstein-Rosen Bridge. They had forced him to hire Randolph Muncher, a physicist from the Energy Department, to help with the Project. Arthur was sure he was a plant to spy on the Project. He suspected that in the near future they were going to turn the Project over to Randolph or were going to shut it down. Fortunately, Randolph wasn't in the same league as Arthur and would never be able to figure out the steps necessary to make the enclosure capable of forming the Bridge.

His thoughts were interrupted when Violet knocked on his open door. "Hey, Boss, got a minute."

"Sure, Violet, come on in and have a seat."

"You need to get rid of that asshole Randolph."

"I know you don't like him. I can't say I like him much myself, but we are stuck with him. Energy wants him here."

"He's a damn spy. He's always asking me questions and wanting to look at the software. He doesn't even know how to properly code. He suggested changes that would have caused the enclosure to overheat." She leaned forward gritting her teeth almost coming out of her seat. "He's a damn idiot."

"I'm sorry, Violet, we have to put up with him."

"Well then, I want to file a sexual harassment claim against him."

"What the hell." Arthur stretched his face in surprise as he stiffened. "Violet, this is serious. If you go through with this, the University will investigate. If this is a false accusation, I could lose you, Rose."

"It's not a false accusation although there were no witnesses. Simon could handle my job."

Arthur squeezed his hands together in an attempt to dissipate his frustration. "Please close the door." Violet got up and closed the office door. "Thanks. Perhaps Simon could handle your job as you say now that we have the code for forming the Bridge that your work made possible. I would never have been able to accomplish what we did without you. I don't know if I could carry on with the Project without you, Violet."

"Well thanks, Boss. It's nice to know I'm valued."

"You are so much more than just valued. So what was this sexual harassment?"

"Muncher came up behind me in the break room and placed his hand on my shoulders and got very close, his crotch touched my bottom and his lips were a fraction from my neck."

"Shit, that's terrible. I'm so sorry."

"He's lucky that I didn't tear his balls off." She scowled. "I stomped on his foot instead."

"Good." Arthur placed his hands together and focused intently on Violet. "Climate warming is again increasing alarmingly. The world hasn't done near enough to eliminate fossil fuel use. We should have gone completely to clean energy by now. My time travel did not produce the results we had hoped."

"It did make a significant difference."

"Yes, but not enough. I think I went back too far. In 1990, the effects of climate warming weren't very pronounced. The fossil fuel industry had too much power back then and were able to foil Doctor Hinson from making much progress. I don't think we will be allowed to continue this Project for much longer. The Energy Department, I think, believes we'll never produce an Einstein-Rosen Bridge. I imagine Muncher has promoted this idea. I think we have a diminishing window to re-establish the Project and send me back in time to get the world to begin the transition from fossil fuels more energetically."

He wasn't going to tell her he thought that Doctor Hinson was murdered. He had read Hinson's biographical information before travelling. Hinson's biographical information after Arthur returned suspiciously showed Hinson dying much earlier in a one car accident. From the news reports the accident seemed to have been improperly investigated. Had the fossil fuel consortium arranged to have him killed? Were the FBI involved?

"What about Randolph?"

"I have some ideas about working around Mr. Muncher. As you say, he is an idiot, which will help us keep him in the dark about what we are doing. We'll have to do most of the retrofit work on the weekends. I won't be able to do this without you, Violet. Can you let the sexual harassment slide? I'll have a talk with him and tell him that I noticed that he has been invading your personal space and ask him to stop it."

"Of course, Boss. Oh, this sounds exciting. Would you consider sending me back?"

"Violet, the forces on the body are extreme. I have a son, who I want to have a future in a livable earth. Plus, Rose is pregnant again. That's a secret. She hasn't even told me, but I can tell the signs. Time travel as you saw can be devastating and could result in death. I couldn't allow you to be in such danger."

"But, Boss, I could handle it. I know I could."

"Sorry Violet, it's out of the question."

"Okay." She dropped her head and sighed before lifting it and smiling. "I probably wouldn't be able to present the information as well as you anyway. Yeah, forget the sexual harassment. When do we start the retrofit?"

"Let me talk to Randolph first. Maybe he'll quit when I ask him to give you more space, and we can do the work more out in the open."

"Fat chance of that. I think your talk won't even faze the idiot."

"We'll see. Thanks, Violet." He stood. "Let's go back out into the lab." He and Violet walked out of the office, and he went in search of Randolph. He found him by the power panel talking to Billy."

"Randolph, can I have a word."

"Sure, Doctor Brown."

"Let's go to my office." After both walked into the office, Arthur shut the door. "Have a seat. I've noticed that you and Violet aren't getting on so well. I've observed you getting closer to her than she likes. She's very sensitive about her personal space. I would hate to lose her. Could you give her more space? Not get so close when talking to her?"

"Well... I don't think I've been invading her space. I'm just trying to understand some of software routines she's written. Has she complained?"

"No she hasn't. Violet is a sensitive person, who doesn't like people getting too close to her. It's something I recognized early on working with her. It's not a big deal, but I'm sure you can easily give her more space. Don't you agree?"

"Yes of course I can. Between you and me, I think she's a kind of prima donna, but she sure can write code. I've never encountered anyone like her."

"Great, thanks for your consideration. You can go back to what you were doing."

"I was having Billy show me the power panel. Its design is different than most power panels. How did you come up with the configuration?"

"Billy designed the power panel. He's an amazing mechanical and electrical engineer." Arthur stood and walked around his desk to shake hands with Randolph. "Thanks for your understanding." He escorted Randolph from his office.

When Randolph disappeared behind the enclosure, Arthur approached Violet. "I think we're good," he whispered. "Can you come in on Saturday?"

"Yeah, Boss. We're going to start?"

"Yes, just you and I to begin. Let's keep this between you and me for now."

"Will do."

Arthur left work early. He wanted to be ready to surprise Rose when she came back from work with dinner and a present. He stopped off at a jeweler and bought a simple ruby necklace. He made his red Thai curry that he knew she loved, chilled the wine, and awaited her arrival.

Arthur jumped when he felt a hand on his shoulder and opened his eyes. There stood his beautiful wife. He hadn't realized he had fallen asleep.

"Sorry I'm so late" Rose said. "I was on the phone with the UN giving them an update on Russia and telling them we need to get China to do more. Umm, I smell something good." Rose picked up the wrapped present on the coffee table. "What's this?"

"A gift for my wonderful wife."

"What's the occasion?"

"You know… but you've been keeping it from me."

Rose tilted her head to the side. "How did you know?" She sat down and punched his arm. "You bugger. It was supposed to be a surprise."

"It is a phenomenal surprise."

"The reason I'm late home is actually because I went to the doctor to confirm what I suspected or should say knew. Yes, I'm pregnant and it's your fault. You were supposed to get a vasectomy. We talked about not having any more children given what the future will be when our kids are grown."

"Aren't you happy?"

"Of course I'm happy, Doctor Brown."

"Well good, Doctor Manning. Go ahead and open your present."

She raised her eye brows and tore open the wrapping. When she opened the case her eyes widened and her smile was positively glowing. "Oh, Arthur, it's beautiful. You shouldn't have."

"I most certainly should. This is a monumental event you've got there." He placed his hand on her stomach.

She kissed him. "Thank you. You're happy too, aren't you?"

"Couldn't be happier."

"How did you know?"

"I'm psychic, don't you know?" He laughed. "I read the signs. I keep track of those beautiful breasts of yours and other things like your menstrual cycle."

"I see. I have a spy in my midst."

"Spy? I'm offended. I'm just a sensitive observer."

"Oh, I love my sensitive observer." She hugged him to her. "So what have you got cooking, Daddy."

"Red Thai curry."

"Oooo, my favorite." She should have known he would notice and figure out she was pregnant. She was surprised he let her go to Russia. Would he have known before she left? Maybe he wasn't sure until she came back.

"I'll go put the rice on and bring you a glass of lemonade. Just sit back and relax, Mama."

17- FEBRUARY 20, 2060

When Arthur entered the lab Saturday morning, all the lights were on. Violet was at her terminal as he slowly descended the stairs, yawning. He had gotten up before sunrise and was in bad need of another coffee. "Good morning, Violet. How long have you been here?"

"Long enough to get the coffee going."

"Oh good." He started for the breakroom.

Violet followed him. "Where are the hard disks with the archived programs?"

"Hold your horses, I need another cup of coffee. They're in a safe in my office. Let me get this cup in me, and we'll go retrieve them." He poured his cup of coffee and sat down.

"Safe? I haven't seen a safe in your office."

"Good. It's hidden."

After he finished his coffee, he stood up. "Okay, let's get to it." He went into his office, grabbed a screw driver from his desk, and opened the closet. He unscrewed the four screws holding a hook in the closet and pushed a button hidden underneath. A panel slid open in the back of the closet. There stood a large safe. He punched some numbers and letters into the keypad and opened the safe. He took out several hard disks and handed them to Violet. "There you go.

Reinstall the programs and we'll have a look." He rubbed the back of neck as he looked upward. "I need another coffee. Rose and I celebrated her pregnancy until the wee hours. Actually, I was the one who celebrated too much with the wine. She was imbibing lemonade."

Violet had already turned her back and was hurrying to the computer terminals. "This shouldn't take too long. That was cool how you rigged up the hiding space for the safe."

"Billy made the secret closet," Arthur called.

When Violet came back in to the breakroom, Arthur was finishing the last of his coffee and had perused the paper. "All set, Boss. Everything looks good."

"Great, let's have a look." Arthur strolled to Simon's terminal, entered his password, and brought up the program. He scrolled through the code while Violet watched on the big screen. "You write beautiful code, Violet. Yeah, it all seems to be here. Okay you can go, but you need to change your password. Billy should be here in an hour or so and I don't want him to see you here. I think Randolph may have seen your password when you logged on. You need to make it much longer— 'hotstuff' won't do."

"How do you know my password?"

"I've got eyes."

"Why don't you want Billy to see me here? I could help with the cables."

"You're a nosy one, aren't you?" He laughed. "I haven't told Billy what we're planning. I've just suggested reinstalling the additional cables to the structure, electromagnets, and capacitor bank so we can have another demonstration and begin to form a fleeting Bridge for our sponsors to keep them funding the Project."

"You don't trust Billy?"

"Yes I do. Muncher has been interrogating Billy a lot lately. Billy might inadvertently say something that would make Muncher suspicious. I'm probably being overly cautious."

"What about Simon? He'll know the programs have been reinstalled when he comes in on Monday."

"Rose and I are having dinner with Diane and Simon tonight. I'll fill him in on what we have done."

"Are you going to tell him you're planning to travel again?"

"Not yet. I'll just tell him we reinstalled the software just for simulations and possible improvements."

"I don't think Simon will believe that explanation. I wouldn't."

"Hmmm, you're probably right. I guess I'll have to tell Rose today before we go over and then tell Simon the whole plan. Rose is going to be hopping mad." He rubbed the back of his head. "I should have thought this out better."

"I don't envy you. Rose is going to be livid. Then you've got to go to dinner. Lord, you are going to have quite a night." She shook her head. "Okay, I'll change my password and be on my way. Good luck."

"Good morning, Arthur," Billy called as soon as he came through the lab door.

"Good morning, Billy. Thanks for coming in on Saturday."

"No problem," Billy said as he descended the stairs. "I agree reinstalling all the cables will be lot easier without Muncher hovering over me. I don't mean to be rude, but I don't like Muncher much."

"Well, I'd have to agree with you. He's a pain, but Energy wants him here."

"So what's the real reason you're having me reinstall the previous cables to the, structure, electromagnets, and capacitor bank on a Saturday? Are we going to send something back in time again?"

"Oh, Billy, I should have known you'd wouldn't be fooled by my explanation. I trust you explicitly. Don't think I don't. I just thought I would wait to tell you in case Muncher was overly curious about the cables and harangued you."

"Let the idiot harangue away. I can handle him."

Arthur placed his hand on Billy's shoulder. "I'm sure you can. Violet was here earlier and reinstalled the programs. I want to go back in time again and try to get governments to make the transition off fossil fuels more forcefully. I think I went back too early to 1990 before most people were aware of climate change."

"Yes, that might have been the case. Won't it be dangerous? The last trip put you in the hospital."

"Of course, but I think it will be worth it. The world should have been totally off fossil fuel 10 years ago. We are on a course toward a 3° C increase in global mean temperature and possibly more. I want my kids to grow up in a livable world."

"Yes, I'm with you, Arthur. I've got grandkids. You can totally rely on me and Harold. I know he's young, but he's totally trustworthy."

"Yes, of course. You can fill him in. I'm going to tell Simon the plan tonight."

"Does Rose know?"

"No, I've got to tell her this afternoon before we go to dinner tonight at Simon's. I can help you with the cables though."

"Don't worry, Arthur. I won't need any help. Go ahead and take off. I'll have everything installed in a jiffy. Good luck with Rose. She's not going to like it."

"You're telling me," Arthur said with a frown. "Okay, I'll lock up my office and take off. Thanks Billy."

Arthur walked slowly toward his house after leaving campus, going over in his mind how he was going to tell Rose. The day was heating up and he was sweating. When he passed the coffee shop, he turned around and went inside. He'd have an iced lemonade to fortify himself. Not that it would help much, but it was a delay from the barrage he knew was waiting for him once he told Rose what he wanted to do.

Rose spent her Saturday morning relaxing on the sofa, reading the paper, and playing with John. She was happy to be back home. John was a beautiful, dark haired, little boy, who looked so much like her. She had hoped for an outing to the ocean today and was disappointed when Arthur announced he needed to go into work. She pouted briefly, but John had soon cheered her up. She was happy that Arthur was overjoyed about her pregnancy. She had needlessly worried how he would react to it.

After the birth of John, they had agreed to have no more children in light of the coming climate catastrophe. She should have known Arthur would be happy with her pregnancy despite their agreement. He adored John and was an ideal father. Of course the future of the rapidly warming planet was not what her children and the children of the world deserved. Why couldn't governments come together on a worldwide plan to decrease warming? The technology and the money to do so was readily available.

When John heard the front door, he jumped up and exclaimed, "Dad's home." He smiled at Rose before running to greet Arthur.

Arthur walked into the living room carrying John on his shoulders. "Look who I found lurking in our hallway. Where do you think he came from?"

"Dad, it's John, your son, silly."

"Oh yes that's right." He lowered John to the floor and went to Rose. "John, look what we have here. It's a strange woman on our couch. Where did she come from?"

"It's, Mom, Dad. Have you lost your mind?"

"Oh… maybe I have. Can you help me find it?"

"Dad, what has happened to you?"

"I'm just joking with you, Son." Arthur bent and gave Rose a kiss. "How was your morning?"

"Great except for a little nausea, but not too bad yet. What happened at work?"

"I had Violet and Billy make some changes without Randolph snooping around." He sat down next to Rose. "I think we have time to go to the Eucalyptus Park for a picnic. I know you wanted to go to the seaside. We'll go next week if you like. We've got dinner at Diane's and Simon's. A trip to the seaside might have been too much. Besides they're still working on the ocean retaining wall, and the area will be congested."

Rose thought Arthur was acting uncharacteristic. He seemed on edge, but was masking it with feigned enthusiasm. She wondered what was going on. "Okay, I'll go pack a picnic."

"John and I will come help. I'll make the humus sandwiches and you, my lovely wife, can make the coleslaw and fruit salad. I'll just go and arrange for a taxi."

Rose knew that Arthur was very suspicious of Randolph Muncher and worried that the Energy Department wanted to replace him with Muncher. What Arthur had accomplished with the Project was beyond her understanding— something out of science fiction. It was a shame that the world did not recognize him for his genius.

"We've got 30 minutes to pack the picnic and change clothes," Arthur said, pushing John gently toward the kitchen. "Come on, John, let's get the picnic assembly line in gear. You put the bread in the toaster and I'll' be ready with the humus, lettuce, cucumber, and red pepper."

"It's a little windy out," Rose said. "You need to take a jacket, John, just in case."

"It's already over 70," Arthur said. "It is windy, but shouldn't be too bad in the Grove."

When they returned home from the Eucalyptus Grove, Rose sent John to take a bath. Arthur poured Rose a glass of lemonade and asked her to sit down. She complied wondering what he was going to say.

"Rose, as you well know climate warming is continuing unabated. Climate refugees are everywhere. Things in the future look dire. I want to do something about it."

Rose immediately suspected what the something would be. That's why he went to the lab today. He's reconstituting the Bridge. "No… no, you're not going back in time again. You almost died. I won't allow it. I'm pregnant for god's sake."

"What are we going to do then for our children? We can't stay here in Berkeley. It will get too hot. Shall we go to Canada? I think you and I, as scientists, would be welcome."

"This is our home. We're both professors with important jobs. I don't want to leave. I'm trying my best to mitigate the warming. You think I like traveling to Russia speaking with their government officials, who eye me like a slab of meat."

"I know you are trying your upmost to end the use of fossil fuels. We have to face facts. The governments of the world are not doing enough. You know what's in store better than me. Sea levels rising, life threating heat waves, more climate refugees. Antarctica, the Arctic, and Greenland are melting faster than predicted. Methane hydrates are bubbling up." He tried to embrace her, but she pushed him away.

Why did it have to be him? She saw the logic in traveling back again, — the forces against change were formidable. She doubted he could initiate any greater change with a brief trip than he had last time. The information on the dangers of climate warming were apparent to most people, but the will to force governments to change wasn't strong enough. She thought the risks outweighed the benefits his travel back in time might induce.

"If I went back to 2025 with the information and technology we can offer, I believe I could make a significant difference." Arthur threw his hands out to emphasize his statement and tried again to hug Rose, who stepped back with a scowl. "Harris was elected President in 2024, and although a consummate politician, she was supremely aware what climate warming was doing to the planet. The IPCC dire report came out in draft form in 2021. Unprecedented heat waves swept the world, and forest fires were rampant around the world. News stories predicting the dire future because of climate warming were prevalent. Unfortunately, Harris and other world leaders were not able to make the progress on reducing fossil fuels and ramping up clean energy that they should have. The capitalists and oligarchists were successful in stifling major progress. 2025 would be an ideal time for me to go back and try one more time to get scientist to speak out and get the populace behind them to force governments to eliminate fossil fuels and champion clean energy. In 2025 the SARS-Covid-2 pandemic had mostly burned out in Western countries, but was still present in many developing countries. 2025 would be an opportune time to go back— 1990 was too soon. You know that." He stepped again toward Rose, and she reluctantly allowed him to hug her. "I can't sit by and see the future for our children be destroyed without doing something when

I know in my heart I can make things better for them. Can't you see that?"

Rose pulled away. "What if you can't induce the changes you hope for? Is risking your life and not seeing your children grow up worth another trip?"

"I didn't die, did I? I'll come back... bruised, battered, and crushed, but alive. I'll recover like before."

"How can you know that? It's a terrible risk. Why can't you send someone else? I bet Violet would be willing to go. She's younger and single."

"Can you see Violet meeting with climate scientists and presenting the information? It wouldn't be a good idea. Besides, Violet is important to the Project. She needs to stay and insure that I can be brought back. She understands the software. She wrote most of the programs."

"You or Simon could do her job. You designed the damn programs."

"You're not being realistic."

"Your last trip only resulted in delaying climate warming ten years. Ten years of reducing climate warming is not enough. It's not worth the risk."

"I believe that I can do so much more in 2025 and hopefully advance the phase out of fossil fuels all together by 2050. It's worth a try I believe. This is probably our last chance. The Energy Department, I suspect, has already decided to replace me and put Randolph in charge, which would mean the end of the Project. I have a fleeting window to travel back."

"I thought you said your technology could be used for space travel."

"Yes, it probably could, but to what end. What would space travel do for the climate? Nothing. If the world continues on as it is, life on this planet will end. There's no other planet that would support life within a distance that an Einstein-Rosen Bridge could access." He took a breath and squared his shoulders. "I've never been a proponent for space travel. Sure there have been scientific advances as a result of research for space travel, but not many that have helped people."

"I don't care what you say. I'm against you doing this." Rose got up, her reddened face contracted. "You can go to Simon's on your own. I don't want to listen anymore about this stupid plan of yours." Rose stormed off up the stairs and slammed the bedroom door.

Arthur rang the doorbell, shifting his feet as he and John waited. When the door swung open, Arthur extended the bottle of wine. "Rose isn't feeling well and asked me to offer her regrets at not being able to come."

"Oh, I'm sorry," Simon said. "Will she be okay? What's the problem?"

"Well, it's a welcome surprise not really a problem. I'll tell you and Diane together."

Simon rubbed John's head. "Hey little buddy. How's it going?"

"Fine, Mr. Johnson. Where's Josh?"

Josh, Simon's and Diane's 8 year old son, and Sheila, their 4 year old daughter, came running in and hugged Arthur.

"Hey, you two gremlins," Arthur said. "Good to see you again. You're both looking well."

"Hey, Josh and Sheila," John said.

"Come on, John," Josh demanded. "Let's go to my room." The two boys ran off with Sheila running after them.

"Diane is in the kitchen," Simon said before leading Arthur through the dining room where the table was elegantly set with a lime green table cloth, beautiful red and green flowered plates, red candles, and crystal glasses. Landscape photographs dotted the walls.

"Good evening, Diane," Arthur said as he approached. "Table looks nice."

Diane turned around from the stove in her form-fitting, red dress and gave Arthur a hug and kiss on the cheek. "What's wrong with Rose?"

"Nothing's wrong. It's actually great news. She's pregnant."

"Oh, how wonderful. How long have you known?"

"I suspected a possibility before she went to Russia. When she came back I was sure. She admitted it tonight after she went to the doctor today."

"I'm gonna give her a call and see how she is," Diane said.

"She's extremely angry. It's probably better to wait until tomorrow to talk to her."

"Angry? About what?"

"I'll tell you later." He approached the stove. "Umm, smells good."

"You guys sit down at the table," Diane said. "It should be ready in a minute."

Simon and Arthur walked to the dining table and took their seats. Diane brought the rice and Jerk Tofu with spring peas, collard greens, and red and green peppers."

"Ahh, Jerk Tofu," Arthur said with enthusiasm. "One of my favorites."

Diane handed him the rice. "Go ahead and start. The kids are eating on the back porch. I didn't want them disrupting our meal." She raised her glass. "Congratulations on the new addition to your family. I'm so happy for you and Rose."

"Thank you."

"Yes, congratulations," Simon added.

After the dinner they moved to the living room and settled around the coffee table with their drinks.

"This is an excellent brandy," Arthur said, holding up his glass.

"Yeah, it's made locally. Expensive but so smooth."

"I've waited long enough," Diane said. "Why's Rose angry? What did you do? You should know that pregnant women are overly emotional."

"I told Rose that I wanted to reconstitute the Bridge and travel back to get our government to do more on mitigating climate warming and get other countries on board much more aggressively," Arthur announced.

"Oh no," Diane said. "No wonder she is angry. You almost died last time."

"I didn't even come close to dying. It's hell on the body, but survivable." Arthur looked to Simon hoping for some agreement. Simon just stared back at him. "I had Violet reload the Einstein-Rosen Bridge software, and Billy reinstall the additional cables today when Muncher wasn't around."

"I don't know that another trip back will do much," Diane said. "Your last trip really wasn't that successful. Why risk doing again?"

"You know the answer full well. Climate warming is still out of control. We've already exceeded 2° C. Next will be 3° C, then on to 4°. We should have been down to zero emissions years ago. Rose told me the hydrates are bubbling again on the Artic shelf and the Arctic Ocean was ice free."

"Maybe Rose and Diane have a point," Simon said. "What do you hope to do?" Simon glanced at Diane before focusing again on Arthur. "The information and money you gave Hinson in 1990 didn't accomplish near what we expected. It helped but not enough."

"I think I went back too early. Hinson tried to initiate fossil fuel elimination, but the power of the fossil fuel industry was too strong in 1990 and most of the populace didn't understand climate warming yet. The effects of the warming were hardly noticeable to people." He took a drink of brandy. "Hinson's life was cut short, and I believe he wasn't able to use the information we gave him as he would have liked. I never told you this, but I believe the fossil fuel industry or the government were responsible for the accident that killed Doctor Hinson. A lot of the technology we gave him never was instituted."

"Jesus, that's horrible," Diane exclaimed. "You think your trip resulted in his early death?"

"Yes, I'm convinced it did, and I am supremely sorry."

"It could have been just a freak accident," Simon said.

"Perhaps, in any case, I think if I go back to 2025, I can have a bigger impact. The need to reduce fossil fuels was often in the news, and there was some progress, but not nearly enough."

"I don't blame Rose for being angry one bit," Diane said. "Seems to me many things could go wrong, and you could end up stuck in the past. You might put other lives at risk. Rose is at a very fragile time. You should at least wait until she gives birth. Better yet give up on the travel completely."

"I believe that the Project will be turned over to Muncher soon, which will mean the eventual end of it."

"The sponsors must know that Muncher is a lightweight compared to you," Simon said.

"He's good at bullshiting and sucking up. Plus, he's the cousin of the Secretary of Energy. They have no real inkling of his lack of ability."

"Oh… no wonder he prances around like he's the heir apparent," Simon said.

"What did Rose say when you told her?" Diane asked.

"She lambasted me. She's adamant against the trip." Arthur shook his head. "I probably should have done a better job of explaining why I thought I should do this. I sprang it on her. I should have gradually introduced the idea. I'm probably over anxious, but I'm convinced we have a limited opportunity to use the Bridge again." He focused on Diane. "Diane, will you help me convince Rose that I should do this?"

Diane expelled her breath forcibly. "I don't know if I agree it is a good idea."

Diane understood full well why Arthur would want to travel to the past again. His argument was logical, and she wondered if he did go to 2025 if he could accomplish what was needed. The moneyed interests had been strong in 2025. She never understood why governments had not come together and done what scientists were telling them for years what they needed to do. They were willing to make their profits and ignore what was obvious even though they must have known they were dooming their offspring to a terrible world.

"Do you want your kids growing up in a world that is 3° to 4° C warmer?" Arthur said more forcefully then he intended. "We all know full well what that would mean. We've already have over 300 million climate refugees and an ocean rise of over 2 feet and were only over a 2° C increase."

"He came back alive last time and fully recovered," Simon said. "I'm on board. I want a future for my children and all the children of the world. I'd be willing to go with you."

"What are you saying, Simon," Diane shouted, stretching her face. "You want to risk your life too."

She couldn't countenance Simon going with Arthur. Racism was still being fanned by Republicans and their white supremacist supporters in 2025. She thought Simon would be more of a hindrance. She was proud that he was willing to risk his life along with Arthur. They had sure formed a bond working together.

"I think trying to get the world working to reduce emissions more strongly in 2025 would be valuable for the future," Simon said. "I'm ready to do all I can for the future for Josh and Sheila."

"Lord Almighty," Diane exclaimed. "You wouldn't take Simon with you, would you?"

"No, I would need him in the lab to insure that I was brought back." Arthur thought though it would nice to have someone to help him on the journey. Violet had wanted to go. Would she be a help or hindrance? Could Simon run the programs without Violet? He was confident that the Bridge could send two people as well as one.

"That's a relief," Diane said, looking daggers at Simon.

"I'll need you and Rose to help provide the climate information and technology that I'll need to disseminate and who I should talk to in 2025. I want to talk to multiple climate scientist and activists. I don't want to rely on just one person to disseminate the information. I will need to stay longer and travel to other countries."

"How long were you thinking of staying?" Simon asked.

"I don't know yet." Arthur looked up at the ceiling and blew out air between his puckered lips, then focused intently on Diane. "I need you, Diane, to quickly convince Rose to come on board and help compile the information I'll need to disseminate." He patted Diane's hand. "I'd liked to go in two or three weeks." He turned to Simon. "Once Muncher sees what Billy has done with the cables, he'll be full of questions. I had Violet change her password and make it much more difficult to hack her terminal. Simon, you will have to do the same. I wouldn't put it past Muncher coming in at night and trying to access the programs to ascertain why we added the other power cables. It's essential that he can't access the programs."

Yeah," Simon said. "He's certainly a pain in the butt. Last week I wanted to kill the nosey shit." Simon raised his glass. "Here's to another trip in time and great success."

Arthur raised his glass. "Yes indeed."

Diane reluctantly raised her glass but remained silent. She agreed that what Arthur and Simon were saying made sense. She wasn't, however, pleased about them wanting her to try to convince Rose. Rose had a fiery temper and was her boss. She would have to be very diplomatic. Not one of her strong suits. Oh well, it had to be done.

18- MARCH 16, 2060

"I'm so happy, Boss, that you are taking me with you," Violet said. "Don't worry, I will obey your every command and not speak out of turn." She stood in her flight suit, clutching her helmet, shuffling her weight from one foot to the other, her graphene capsule at her feet. "This is going to be so cool."

"Okay, Violet, just relax," Arthur said as he held Rose's hand. "Violet, you have to get out of the habit of calling me boss."

"No problem, Doctor Brown."

"It's going to be okay, Rose," Arthur said and hugged Rose to him.

"You promise."

"Yes, I promise," Arthur said and kissed Rose.

"Do you have to stay so long?"

"I want to try my utmost to initiate meaningful change. This is our last chance." He walked behind Simon and placed a hand on his shoulder. "You've got this, Simon."

"Yes, I'll be fine. No worries. Go ahead we're ready."

Billy slapped Arthur gently on the back. "Don't worry. We'll send you on your way and retrieve you successfully."

"I never doubted it."

Arthur and Violet opened the hatch to the enclosure and went inside with their capsules. They set them in the center of the enclosure, pulled on their helmets, adjusted the oxygen, and climbed inside the capsules.

"Here we go," Simon announced.

"We're ready and able, Simon," Violet said enthusiastically. "Send us to 2025. Look out past here we come."

"Stage four holding," Simon called. "Bridge initiation beginning." Simon took a deep breath. "You guys still conscious."

"Barely," Arthur replied into his headset with a moan.

"Still here," Violet said. "Ready for takeoff."

Simon laughed. "Bon voyage." Simon punched the keys. "Good luck in 2025. Bridge is forming and everything looks good." He held his breath as he tapped the last of the instructions. "They're away." He exhaled strongly and looked back at Diane. Rose was crying softly as Diane hugged her. "They're coming back, Rose. I can feel it."

"I sure hope so." Rose replied weakly. She felt hollowed out as she took a series of shuttering breaths. She wondered how she would cope for the weeks they would be gone.

Simon shut down the system and they waited for the structure to cool. "Down to 40°," he announced. "Go ahead, Billy open the hatch."

"Structure empty," Billy called. "This thing amazes me every time. Wishing them great success."

"Amen," Simon added. "Go ahead, Diane, take Rose back to our place, I'll be along shortly."

Rose followed Diane into the apartment, feeling as if part of her had left as well. She would have to try act normal for John, who was told that Arthur had gone to Washington for a conference. Diane paid and thanked the sitter while Rose ventured into Josh's room where he and John with the help or hindrance more likely from Sheila were building a tall building block tower.

"Hi, Mom," John said. "We need a ladder so we can make the tower higher."

"I think that's plenty high enough. Get your stuff, and let's go home. It's way past your bedtime."

"Wow, that's a nice tower," Diane sad as she entered the room. "Josh you and Sheila, get in bed. I'll walk Rose and John out and be back for a quick story. Say good night to John and Rose."

"Goodnight," Josh called followed by Sheila.

"Good night," John said before taking Rose's hand. "It was fun staying up."

Rose lay in bed staring at the ceiling as her heart thumped in her head. She had worked hard coming up with the climate information and people Arthur needed to talk to. She was glad that Violet had gone with him. Violet had a photographic memory and would be able to recall the information she and Diane had compiled easily. This would be a big help to Arthur.

She tried to stifle the tears rolling down her cheeks. Tears wouldn't help. She knew Arthur was right. The present climate warming was going to take off with the feedback loops that the ocean warming, thawing permafrost, and methane hydrates would cause. It was obvious to anyone with any sense. In some ways, she felt her failure to convince the US and other governments of the importance of totally eliminating fossil fuels had led to Arthur's trip back in time. She hoped Arthur and Violet could convince the people they were going to meet to do what was needed to stop the pending climate catastrophe. Why did it have to be her husband, who needed to save life on planet earth? She knew the answer. She had married a genius. What did she expect? His genius had been what had drawn her to him in the first place. She rolled over and scrunched her pillow. "Arthur, I love you more than words can say. You come back to us. Please... please come back."

As Arthur was gaining consciousness, he heard Violet's weak voice. "God, this is horrible."

Arthur opened his capsule to the dark room. He tried to rise but couldn't get his body to respond. "You okay, Violet?"

"Hell no, I can hardly move and my headache is the worst I've ever experienced. I can't get this damn thing open."

"Just lie back a few minutes. Let your body adjust." He was able to get an arm outside his capsule and push himself up into a sitting position. He turned off his oxygen and removed his helmet. He switched on his flash light and shined it on Violet's capsule.

"Ah, let there be light. Thanks." Violet opened her capsule and slowly sat up. She turned off her oxygen and removed her helmet. "Are we really in 2025?"

"I believe so."

"Damn, that was the most pain I've ever encountered. How long is this headache going to last?"

"Couple of hours or so. You won't feel normal for several days. Take it nice and slow getting out of your capsule."

"Normal? After this, I don't think I'll ever feel normal again."

When Arthur slowly pulled himself from the capsule, he was surprised to see Violet standing next to him.

Her face was bright red and the grimace on her face said it all. "Jesus, I wouldn't want to experience that every day."

"Go ahead and check the hallway. Make sure nobody is around. We left at 10:30. It's now 11:15. We were out about 45 minutes. A little longer than last time. The adrenalin works well, but gives you an intense headache."

Violet went to the door of the laboratory and looked up and down the hall. "Coast is clear, Doctor Brown."

"Excellent, go ahead, take off your flight suit, and don your back pack."

When they both were in street clothes, they left the laboratory and headed for the stairs carrying their capsules.

"Look Doctor, the flyer on the bulletin board is for a lecture tomorrow March 17, 2025. How cool is that. Oh man, I'm pumped." She laughed. "This is so unbelievable."

"It is totally amazing, I must admit."

"You're the man, Doc."

Arthur led them to the wooded area of the campus to await the morning. A few hours after the sunrise they went into town.

"I'm surprised that walking around with these large capsules doesn't cause more of a stir," Violet said as they walked across the campus. "It's cool how Billy made them look like bass fiddle cases."

"Yes, it was a great idea of Billy's. He's such an astute man and great fabricator. I was surprised last trip how people ignored the capsule."

When they arrived in town, the first thing they did was change a quantity of gold for cash before heading to a rental storage business and procuring a rental unit for the capsules, thinking the rental unit would be more secure than a hotel room. Then they went to a hotel and obtained one room, deciding that it would be better if they were together in case they ran into trouble.

Violet slumped down on a bed in the hotel room as soon as Arthur closed the door. "I'm wacked but wide awake."

"The adrenalin will soon wane, and you should be able to sleep," Arthur said. "Tomorrow we'll call Victor Ramada at Scripps Institute and make an appointment to meet with him."

"Can't wait to talk to the King of Soot. Then it's off to MIT to meet Joyce Salmon, right, then Mike Oppender at Princeton."

"Yeah, why did you call Victor the King of Soot?"

"He's famous for his study of brown clouds and their effect on the monsoon seasons in India. He's rather conservative about the dangers of climate warming and believes the effects of continued warming are not as dire as many scientists predict. He may not be that welcoming. Joyce Salmon on the other hand has been very critical of the lack of progress on reducing the use of fossil fuels. Her papers predict a difficult world without major reduction in fossil fuel use. She is famous for her work about the dangers of hydrofluorocarbons and their effect on the ozone blanket as well as the dangers of methane and nitrous oxide. They'll both be good to talk to, but Ramada may not be very welcoming. When are we going to Russia?"

"We'll have to play that by ear. It will be cold in Moscow. Sergey Viskov might be difficult to get in to talk to. He's out of favor with the government and may be isolated." Arthur moaned as he stretched. "Phew, I starting to feel the effects of the adrenalin dissipating. I'm feeling sleepy. I'll get ready for bed unless you want to go first."

"Doc, go for it. Age before beauty." She laughed. "I'm probably wrong about the beauty. You're quite beautiful, Doc, in more ways than one."

"Thanks. I'll say the same about you, but in your case, it is actually true."

"Doctor Ramada, it is a pleasure to meet you. This is my colleague, Violet Drummer." They shook hands. "Thanks for agreeing to see us."

Doctor Ramada was a short thin man, with a receding hair line and a warm smile. "I've met Doctor Swenson from Sweden, but I haven't heard your name before, Doctor Brown."

"Yes, I'm out of the country a lot, and I like to keep a low profile." Arthur watched Doctor Ramada a few seconds to see how he took his statement. "I have some research information for you that my group has compiled." Arthur rose and handed Ramada the memory stick. "There's some advanced modeling software, advanced battery technology, and other new technologies that I'm sure you will find interesting." He paused to gather his thoughts. "Our impetus in meeting you is to get your help in eliminating fossil fuels. Since you are of Indian descent, I was hoping you might be able to help to convince India to shutter its existing coal fired power plants and stop the planned building of new coal fired plants. As you are aware unless drastic steps are taken to do so, climate difficulties could reach catastrophic conditions."

"I'm not sure I agree. Europe and the US are responsible for most of the CO2 in the atmosphere. India should be entitled to develop it industries and provide work for its citizens. I believe the climate situation is not nearly as bad as many climate scientists portend. In any case, I have very little influence in India."

"I believe climate warming has already caused problems," Arthur said surprised by Ramada's statement. "Intense hurricanes and cyclones, extreme temperatures unheard of before, rising oceans, recurring forest fires. We believe more direct actions by climate scientists like yourself is needed. Scientific papers are all well and good." He looked toward Violet, hoping she would chime in. Violet remained staring at Ramada, her brow creased. "Just look what Greta, a teenager, has been able to accomplish.

Change comes from the people. We have to get the people to understand what is happening and what the future will be. I'm not advocating doomsday type information, but information on what can be accomplished with concerted actions. We need to force politicians to institute the changes needed. That is why we are visiting climate scientists and advocates around the world."

"What you are advocating seems contrary to your proclivity to keep a low profile. Not that I disagree with anything you've said, but as I said I believe the future effects of climate warming are not as bad as you profess. I'm willing though to look through the information you have provided. I'm not ready to get out there more, as you seem to be advocating, but I understand your position."

"Great, please review the information on the memory stick." Arthur was disappointed in Ramada. How could a climate scientist not believe the future situation was dire? Maybe the man was funded by the fossil fuel industry. He wished Rose had chosen a more informed and sympathetic scientist as their first visit. From Violet's face, he could tell that Violet was ready to strangle Ramada.

Arthur stood up "Here is my card with my cell phone information. If you have any questions, please don't hesitate to call me." Violet stood up, looking acerbically at Ramada. Arthur went to Violet and placed his hand on her shoulder, hoping to calm her. "We'll leave you to it. Thanks again for seeing us." They shook hands. Arthur and Violet left.

"You don't have to remain silent, Violet, in the interviews. How did you think that went?"

"I was letting you lay the ground work. You've done this before, not me. I don't see Doctor Ramada getting out there much. I think he's a fucking asshole. Probably sucking at the teat of the fossil fuel industry."

"I agree, but I wouldn't have stated it so strongly. Thanks for remaining calm."

"I wasn't calm at all. If I had been on my own, I might have done some damage to the idiot."

"Yes, it wasn't a pleasant interview. Sorry that Rose even picked him to talk to."

"Maybe she thought our talk would get him on board. As you said, India needs to shutter its coal electric generation."

"Yes, she probably did. Maybe the information we provided will have some good influence." He inhaled strongly. "After we meet with Doctor Salmon at MIT, I think we should try and meet with Bill Macer, head of 350.org. He's good at publicity and might be more able to disseminate the new technology we are providing."

"Maybe we should meet with someone at Harvard while we're in Cambridge. There's Professor Bob Staver. He's an economist working on climate change. Economics are extremely important for making the changes necessary."

"Yes, indeed. Countries need to institute significant carbon taxes that act as real economic deterrents to burning fossil fuels. If we could get the US to pass such a tax soon with the proceeds returned to the populace, it would help immensely as we know. The current 2025 carbon taxes and the trading of carbon credits are useless. The sensible carbon tax that the US Congress passed in 2040 helped immensely. If we could induce an earlier institution of that form of carbon tax, it would have profound effects." Arthur stopped when they were outside and sat down on a bench. Violet joined him. "Nice day, not too hot yet. It's a beautiful campus here. Let's get a room in town. I'm rather exhausted. I need some more rest before we fly to Boston."

"Doc, it's 9:30," Violet said as she gently shook Arthur. "Don't we need to make plane reservations?"

"Oh, Violet," Arthur said, rubbing his eyes, "where are we?"

"San Diego. I've been up about an hour. I felt the same way when I woke up, wondering where in the hell I was. I thought jet lag was bad, but time travel puts a whole new face on lag." She laughed. "Here's a cup of coffee."

"Oh thanks. Go ahead, call for plane reservations this afternoon to Boston. Late afternoon, please. Use the cell phone we bought."

After Violet made the plane reservations, the phone rang. Violet handed the phone to Arthur. "Arthur Brown. Yes, Doctor Ramada, how can I help you?" Arthur scrunched his face as he listened. "Yes, the battery technology is cutting edge. Yes, sodium battery prototypes have been produced by my colleagues in Sweden. No, the technology is not proprietary." He turned to Violet and made a face. "We are providing this technology freely for any one's use. Yes, it is could be considered revolutionary." Arthur repeatedly shook his head as he continued to listen. "I see. No, I wasn't aware that the company you mention was working on the sodium battery. Yes, any company could start manufacturing the glass sodium batteries using the schematics and information provided." He rolled his eyes. "I'm sorry, we will not be able to meet with you again. We have other plans for today. We are flying to meet Joyce Salmon and Bob Saver in Cambridge. No, that will not be possible. I have to go, Doctor Ramada. It was a pleasure meeting you. Goodbye."

Arthur hung up. "We need to check out immediately."

"Why, what's up?"

"I'm not sure, but I think Ramada is going to report us to the authorities."

"Why would he do that?"

"He thinks we stole propriety information on the sodium batteries."

"Oh shit. I haven't taken a shower. I smell like old socks."

"No time. We need to hurry."

They dressed, gathered their belongings, slipped on their back packs, and headed to the lobby.

"Let's get some breakfast," Violet said heading for the restaurant after they checked out.

Arthur grabbed her arm and pulled her closer. "No," he whispered. "Those two men in the suits, who just came in, might be the authorities. Stay nice and calm. Let's amble around the lobby and then go to the restrooms. Hide in a stall. Wait thirty minutes then meet me outside around the corner to the north."

"Holy shit, you aren't kidding," Violet said her eyes wide. "Damn, okay."

Arthur heard their flight called and shook Violet. She opened her eyes and stared at Arthur. "Come on we need to board," Arthur said, patting her shoulder.

"Okay... driving here was exhausting." Violet frowned. "I haven't driven a car in years. Lucky you, got to sleep on the drive to LA."

"Yes, thanks for driving."

"I'm totally knackered. Give me a hand."

"You can sleep on the plane," Arthur said as he helped Violet up.

"You really think Ramada called the authorities? I don't like this clandestine stuff. You sure it's necessary?"

"I'm not willing to find out if it is or isn't. Ramada has called me several more times. We'll have to get another phone and new number."

"You haven't left the phone on, have you?"

"No, I looked at it in San Diego and then turned it off and removed the chip."

"Hey, you're good at this cloak and dagger stuff. Good thinking on bringing additional identities. Who are we using now?"

"The same we used for renting the car— Arthur Simpson and Violet Remy."

"Shouldn't we use the ones with different first names?"

"We'll use those next time. We don't want to run out of identities."

"You cancelled the tickets from San Diego, didn't you?"

"Yes, I called them from a pay phone here."

"It would be nice if we had a credit card. Putting down cash deposits at the rental places is a drag. The airlines don't like us paying cash either."

"Too easy to keep track of our movements. We wouldn't be able to change our identities at will."

Violet looked at Arthur askance, then smiled and stuck out her tongue. "I was just saying it would be nice. I know we can't have one."

19- MARCH 19, 2025

"I didn't see anyone following us," Violet said as they left the Boston airport. The sun was shining and only a few clouds were drifting by. "At least the weather's nice. There's the car rental bus. Are we going to Cambridge or staying here?"

"Let's drive to Cambridge," Arthur responded. "Let's try Budget Rental this time."

"You mean I'll drive to Cambridge. There's no us in driving."

"I'm sorry. You may not have driven in years, but I haven't driven in over five years. It'll be much safer if you do the driving."

"I agree, Doc. Not to worry. It's all good."

"Doctor Salmon, thanks for meeting with us on such short notice," Arthur said. "This is my colleague, Violet Remy."

They all shook hands. Violet stared at Joyce Salmon for a time. Doctor Salmon was an attractive tall and full bodied woman with auburn hair and large brown eyes, dressed in a deep violet pant suit. She returned Violet's stare, causing Violet to smile and blush. Arthur was surprised by the interest passing between Doctor Salmon and Violet.

"Please have a seat," Joyce said, briefly glancing at Arthur before returning her gaze to Violet. "You want to discuss climate actions and new technology I understand."

Arthur nodded to Violet. "Yes, Doctor Salmon," Violet said. "We have compiled some information on this memory stick that I believe you will find most interesting." Violet stood and handed Doctor Salmon the memory stick, smiling brightly, focusing her deep blue eyes on the attractive and shapely scientist. "When you have a chance, please review the information. There is advanced climate projection software, new hydrogen fuel cell technology, battery technology, and other innovations we have developed as well as studies on economic policies we believe would be invaluable in reducing emissions."

"Thank you. I would be happy to review the information. Can I offer you tea or coffee?"

"No, we are good," Arthur replied. "We are on a tight schedule. We are meeting Doctor Saver this afternoon."

"I see. You are making the rounds here in Cambridge."

"Yes, we are trying to meet with as many prominent climate scientists and advocates as we can in our short time in the US," Violet said.

"You said on the phone you are based in Sweden. I love going to Sweden. It's such a beautiful country, and the people are so friendly."

"Yes, well, we like it, but the multitude of landscapes and wide open spaces of your country are true wonders," Arthur said. "We wish we had more time to enjoy your country."

"Yes, I wish I got around more myself. My ex-spouse often said I worked too much."

"Please review the information we have provided," Arthur said as he stood, handing her his card that they had printed at the hotel. "Give us a call if you have any questions." He turned to Violet, who was still sitting and watching Salmon intensely.

Violet rose and, moving closer, offered her hand to Doctor Salmon. "I like your suit. It's a lovely color."

"Why thank you. Yes, it is a lovely violet. My favorite. Like your name." Doctor Salmon held Violet's hand for an extended moment and smiled, opening her eyes wide. "Are you staying in Cambridge this evening?"

"Yes," Violet answered quickly.

"If you don't have other plan, I could join you for dinner this evening. I'm free. I know a great restaurant. And after I've perused your information, we can discuss it."

Violet glanced at Arthur and answered before Arthur could speak. "That would be lovely. Thank you. Where shall we meet?"

"How about we meet at the restaurant at 8:00. That's not too late is it? The restaurant is called Samuel's."

"Eight would be fine," Violet said. "We'll see you then."

When they stepped outside, Arthur looked at Violet. "Why did you agree to meet for dinner? She might find the information hard to believe like Ramada."

"She won't. I can't believe how welcoming and sophisticated she is? I dig her. She and I are alike in many ways."

"How do you know?"

"Don't worry, I know."

Arthur and Violet entered Samuel's restaurant after parking the car. Arthur was wearing his sport jacket he had purchased in San Diego and jeans. Violet was wearing a new red satin hip hugging dress she had purchased in the afternoon after they had talked to Professor Saver at Harvard. The maître d' almost stumbled over himself he was so taken by Violet's appearance as he led the two to Doctor Salmon's table.

Doctor Salmon, wearing a cream dress with printed small wild violet flowers and a low cut V-neck that revealed her impressive cleavage, stood up as soon as Violet approached the table. She extended her hand, her face bright as she studied Violet. "Good evening. Glad you were able to make it."

Violet seized Doctor Salmon's hand and slipped close to give her a kiss on the cheek. "I like your dress. It suits you wonderfully." She stepped back and smiled, raising her eyebrows and moistening her lips.

Salmon surprised by Violet's kiss blushed. "Thank you, I chose it for the wild violets. You are gorgeous in that sleek dress. Goes well with your hair."

"Thank you."

After Violet stepped back, Arthur shook hands with Salmon and everyone took their seat. He was stunned by the overt interest Salmon was showing Violet. Violet had been correct. She and Salmon were of the same persuasion.

"I scanned the information you provided, but didn't have time to go much into the detail," Doctor Salmon said. "There is an immense amount of information on the memory stick that will be helpful. I am honored that you chose to talk to me. I wish many of the economic ideas you purported could be implemented. I'm afraid the political will to do so is lacking."

"Yes," Violet said. "We believe that greater involvement by climate scientist like yourself would be helpful in publicizing the importance of taking bold action on climate."

"I must admit that I'm not very vocal about the dangers of fossil fuel emissions other than the papers I publish. If we could eliminate the influence or should I say money the fossil fuel companies lavish on legislators, I believe a lot more legislative action could be implemented to help reduce fossil fuel use. The value of fossil fuel assets still in the ground is immense. Getting companies to write off those assets and keep it in the ground is a difficult battle. I agree totally that more has to be done to drastically reduce the use of fossil fuels. We can't even get rid of tax subsidies for fossil fuels. Elimination of the oil depletion tax subsidy would result in over 12 billion in additional taxes oil companies in the US would have to pay." Salmon laughed and smiled at Violet. "I'm running on, we should order."

"Well said Doctor Salmon. I agree totally." Violet opened her menu. "Not a lot of vegan choices. What do you normally get?"

"I suspected you would be vegan," Salmon said. "I'm afraid veganism is just starting to take off in Cambridge. I am almost vegan. Living in Boston I grew up eating scads of fish, lobster, and crab. I don't eat fish any more. The pollutants in the ocean and the terrible over fishing is destroying the ocean not to mention the rising temperature and acidity." She paused and looked at Violet a few seconds. "I normally get the Mushroom Wellington here. It is delicious and the polenta with walnuts is a good compliment along with the sautéed broccoli."

"Sounds yummy. Thanks, that's what I'll order. What are you thinking of ordering, Arthur?"

Arthur looked up from his menu. "I'm leaning toward the Thai red curry with tofu. Have you had it here, Doctor Salmon?"

"Please call me Joyce. Doctor Salmon sounds much too formal. Yes, I've had the red curry, and it is delicious here. Shall we get a bottle of wine?"

"Yes that would be lovely," Violet replied. "How about a white wine. What would you recommend?"

"I like the Italian Pinot Grigio, Santa Christina, that they have, but I'm open to any other one."

Violet glanced at Arthur, widening her eyes and protruding her lower lip, raising both hands above the table, palms up.

"Santa Christina works for me," Arthur said.

"Great, Santa Christina it is," Violet announced.

Joyce raised her hand to signal the waiter standing nearby. Everyone placed their order and the waiter departed.

"How did your meeting go with Professor Saver?" Joyce asked.

Violet looked to Arthur. "It went well," Arthur said. "Doctor Saver also believes a key to reducing the use of fossil fuel is a significant tax on carbon at the source of extraction with most of the proceeds being distributed to the people so it doesn't end up being a regressive tax. He didn't have any suggestions on how to get such a tax implemented. The Democratic versus Republican split in Congress and the fossil fuel campaign cash as you alluded to is a difficult hurdle to overcome."

"Ah, here's our wine," Joyce said.

The waiter went to Arthur with the bottle of wine. Arthur motioned the waiter toward Salmon. "The lady should have the honors. It was her suggestion."

"That's nice," Joyce said after taking a sip of the wine. "Yes, we'll take it."

When their food arrived, Violet leaned over to smell her dish. "Smells yummy. Bon appétit." She took a bite. "Oh, Joyce, great suggestion. This is delicious. The pastry melts in your mouth and the mushrooms with the tasty sauce is superb."

"The red curry is very nice too," Arthur added.

"Glad you are enjoying the food. This is my favorite restaurant."

"Have you lived in Cambridge long," Violet asked.

"I grew up in Boston as I said. I went to graduate school at MIT and have been here ever since. I like the academic atmosphere of the town. Our Climate Science Department is very good and has received international recognition. I think what you two are doing is so important. The US in not making the kind of progress we need. Sometimes I feel so despondent."

"Yes, we need to ramp up the production of clean energy and drastically reduce the use of fossil fuels," Violet said. "We hope our visits will prompt people to become more active."

"Your visit has certainly made me feel that I need to do more. Are you meeting with government officials?"

"We do not have any US government officials on our list to meet," Arthur said. He was buoyed by the obvious interest Joyce portrayed in their cause. "Our thinking is to get more scientists to speak out and hopefully the people will respond and force governments to take notice."

"Fossil fuel companies have essentially bought government representatives in the US," Violet said. "We need a ground swell of people clamoring for the government to provide the funding incentives and mechanisms to encourage the development of clean energy, and force fossil fuel companies to stop exploration and abandon their reserves. The fossil fuel companies know full well what the burning of fossil fuels is doing to the world."

"Yes indeed, Violet," Joyce said, staring wide eyed at Violet. "Getting companies to abandon their reserves is a tall order, but I couldn't agree more."

"I'm glad we were able to have dinner together," Arthur said. He felt they had made a great convert. "This is so enjoyable."

After dinner, Joyce excused herself and went to the restroom. As soon as Joyce was out of earshot, Violet leaned toward Arthur. "Why don't you, make up an excuse to leave, and I'll stay."

"What's going on?"

"If you are not here, I bet she'll invite me back to her place." Violet winked. "What do you say?"

"We are on a tight schedule and mission, Violet. What do you hope to accomplish?"

"I believe I can get Joyce to be even more active and engaged to help our mission. Of course I hope to have fun in the process."

"I've never seen this side of you. I'm at a loss for words." He wondered if Violet's assertiveness was a result of time travel.

"Good... just do as I ask. How about saying you need to get back to the hotel to prepare for a conference call to Sweden."

"Okay. When will you be back to the hotel?"

"In the morning, I hope... or maybe sooner if things don't work out as I plan."

"All right, I'll wait for you at the hotel before making any further meeting or travel plans."

When Joyce returned and was seated, she asked, "Do you want desert, tea, or coffee?"

"Joyce, thank you for the lovely dinner and your interesting company," Arthur said. "I need to take off and prepare for a conference call. You stay, Violet, and have a coffee and dessert. I know Violet likes her desserts." Arthur stood. "I'll see you later, Violet. Both of you enjoy the rest of the evening." Arthur smiled at Joyce, who was surprised by his announcement and looked toward Violet.

"Thanks, Arthur," Violet said. "Catch you later."

"It was a pleasure talking with you, Doctor Simpson," Joyce said as she stood and shook hands with Arthur. She remained standing momentarily as she watched Arthur depart, then she resumed her seat and smiled demurely. "Anything on the desert menu look enticing?"

"Oh yeah, I'll have a raspberry sorbet, coffee, and a ruby port."

"Hmm, that's sounds good. I'll get the same."

20- MARCH 21, 2025

Violet, smiling from ear to ear, entered the hotel room late morning while Arthur was working on his laptop. "Good morning, Doc."

"And a good morning to you. How was your night?"

"Wow, it was fantastic. We had such a good time. We laughed ourselves crazy." She plopped down on the bed. She had thoroughly enjoyed her time with Joyce. Their love making had sent her to such heights of pleasure. She had never experienced such satisfying love. Of course it was only one night, but what a night. She would remember it fondly forever and was hoping she could have another night with Joyce before they went to Princeton. "Joyce had a lot of questions about the sodium battery and the advanced hydrogen fuel cells. Seems to be a big deal to everybody."

"Yes, I knew some of the advanced technologies would create controversy. I was of two minds about not including the information. In the end, I thought it would significantly help with converting transportation to electric and might get the US to jump ahead in production of electric vehicles and trucks. Still I think the most important measure we need to emphasize is a proper carbon tax. I was disappointed with our meeting with Professor Saver.

He agreed with us, but there was something about him… some underlying hesitancy toward us."

"Joyce and I talked about him. She knows him and his wife well. He's rather conservative. She's going to work on him and hopefully get him to be more proactive and vocal, especially about a meaningful carbon tax. She's pumped, man. I think she will get a lot of scientists to be more proactive. She's incredibly smart." She felt her lips and fondly remembered Joyce's full lips on hers— wonderful kisses.

"That's great. I haven't phoned Bill Macer yet. It was fortunate that Saver had Macer's cell phone. I'll call Doctor Oppender at Princeton and try to get an appointment for Monday. We can drive there and spend the weekend or stay here tonight and Saturday and drive up Sunday. Are you okay to drive there? It will take probably 5 hours of so. I checked on trains. There's a train to New York where we'd need to change to a train to Princeton."

"Since we have the car, we might as well just drive there. I vote to stay here tonight and Saturday. We can hook up with Joyce again."

"That's fine with me. I enjoyed talking to her, but if you want to be alone with her, I'll understand."

"Make your calls. Maybe we can meet Macer this weekend. Where is he?"

"He lives in upper New York State, but I have no idea where he is now. He travels extensively according to Saver."

"I'll go take a bath and relax while you make the calls."

Violet strolled out of the bathroom wrapped in a towel. Arthur watched her cross to her bed and was surprised when she dropped the towel and started sorting through her clothes.

"I can give you some privacy, Violet."

"Hey Doc, no need. I'm not shy. Does the naked female body excite you?" She danced around, laughing. "I'm sure you're very familiar with the female body."

Yes of course he was familiar with the female body. He remembered the first time he and Rose slept together and how wonderful he felt caressing the smooth shapely body of Rose. He was missing Rose terribly, and Violet's naked lanky body reminded him what he was missing. He was happy that Violet had an enjoyable liaison with Joyce. He had always known she was gay and often felt sorry that she didn't have a partner to share her life. It was ironic that she found someone she really connected to 35 years in the past.

"Very funny," Arthur said. "Your antics just cause me to miss Rose even more."

"Sorry, Doc. I miss Rose myself. She's such a wonderful and incredibly beautiful woman in more ways than can be told."

"Yeah, that she is." He rose from his bed and walked to the window to gaze out a few minutes, thinking about Rose and his son before turning back to Violet. "I talked to Macer and he's in New York City for a television interview. He agreed to meet with us on Sunday 4:00 PM at his hotel. We've got an appointment with Oppender Monday morning."

"Excellent arrangements." She donned her jeans and orange blouse. "I'll call Joyce and see if she's free for dinner tonight. Looks like a nice sunny day. Let's go for walk. We're both in need of some exercise."

The cell phone rang. "Hello," Arthur said. "Oh yes, she's right here." He turned to Violet. "It's for you. I think it's Joyce."

Violet's face lit up as she moved to take the phone. "Hello... really." Violet scrunched her face as she continued to listen. "Uh oh, damn, we were hoping to have dinner again with you. We'll have to leave. I'm sorry. Shit... thanks. Okay, bye."

"What did she say?"

"Saver called her today. He was questioned by the FBI and was very upset at being questioned. He asked Joyce if she knew where we were staying."

"Did she tell him?"

"No, she told them that she thought we had left Cambridge, but didn't know where we were going."

"Did Saver give the FBI Joyce's name? Did we mention Oppender to Saver?"

Violet lowered her head momentarily. "No, Saver said he hadn't given Joyce's name to the FBI, but you had mentioned Doctor Salmon to Ramada. I expect Ramada has already mentioned Salmon to the FBI. However, you didn't mention Oppender to Ramada or Saver."

"You're sure?"

"Definitely."

"Damn, I bet Ramada is behind this. Pack up, we better take off and drive to New York. We'll be harder to trace in the city."

"What about the car? They could trace it. It's got GPS."

"You're right. We'll leave it here and take a taxi to the train station. Okay we have to change our identities again. I wish we had never talked to Ramada. I don't understand why he's after us."

"It's the sodium battery. He and the FBI must think we stole the technology."

"How can we steal technology that doesn't exist yet? I mean they already have the lithium ion battery and quite suitable electric cars. In Norway, 100 percent of the new cars sold are electric. The sodium battery lasts longer and is cheaper to make, but I don't see it as that revolutionary to cause so much fuss." He massaged his chin. "Ramada must have some connection to a company involved in battery research. This has got to be about money."

At the train station, they bought their tickets and took a seat to await the train. "I was so looking forward to another night with Joyce," Violet said, rubbing her neck.

"I know. I sure wish we hadn't visited Ramada. What a jerk."

"For sure, Doc. A total asshole. Ah, here's the train. Looks like we made another escape. What will we do if the FBI catches us?"

"We'll stay calm and answer their questions. I don't think we've done anything that is seriously against the law. We have used false identities, but not for nefarious reasons. I don't believe they would arrest us or hold us for very long, but I certainly hope we don't have to find out. I'll call the car rental, tell them where the car is, and have them take our cash deposit as payment for retrieving the car."

"Doc, I think you're too trusting. If we're caught, they could keep us a long time. We could miss our Bridge rendezvous."

"Don't even think like that," Arthur replied. He knew she was right. They had to stay one step ahead, or they could be stuck in the past, which would have drastic consequences.

They boarded the train and took their seats. "The FBI may have a picture and file on you from your travel in 1990," Violet said.

"I was 33 then— I'd be 68 now. I doubt they could make the connection."

"If Saver gave you Macer's cell phone, then he'll know we want to meet with Macer. He may have told the FBI or called Macer."

"Yes we should postpone talking to Macer and go on to Princeton."

"Perhaps I could leave a memory stick for Macer at his hotel, then take off, and meet you in Princeton."

"No, we should stick together. We can mail him the memory stick or try to make a connection when we come back to the States. If they're looking for me, they'll be looking for you as well."

"We could remove the sodium battery info from the memory stick."

"Yeah, that might be a good idea although we already given it out to Ramada, Saver, and Joyce."

As they were sitting in their Princeton hotel, Violet telephoned Joyce using a new prepaid cell phone. "Hi Joyce, it's Violet. Sorry we had to take off so abruptly. Have you heard any more from Saver?" Violet looked abruptly at Arthur and frowned as she continued listening. "Oh, I'm sorry. Okay, we will. Thanks, bye."

"What did she say?"

"The FBI came to her house looking for us. They showed her a photograph of you and asked if that was the person she met with. She told them that it looked like the Arthur Simpson, a Swedish scientist, she met with on March 20th. The picture she said appeared to be a slightly younger photograph of you. Maybe it was the photograph from your file from 1990. They wanted any information she had received. She told them that she had talked about climate aspects with you, but had not received any written information."

"What about you?" Arthur asked.

"She told them you were accompanied by a younger woman and gave them a vague description, but they brought out a surveillance photograph. She said that they had gone through the security camera footage at the University."

"Damn, they'll have photos and will be looking for us both. They may find out we arrived in New York from the train station camera footage. We used the same identities to come here to Princeton. We should leave for Europe and skip meeting Oppender. We'll have to change identities again. We better change back to our real identities to fly so we don't run out of identities later." He got up from his bed and started pacing. "Are you sure the photograph they showed Joyce was a younger version of me?"

"That's what she said."

"Damn, if they're making a connection to 1990, we could be in unbelievable trouble. How would they try to understand a picture from 1990 when I was 33 with my picture now at 43 in 2025 when I should look 68? It can't be. They must have shown Joyce a photo from surveillance where the lighting made me look younger."

"You're probably right."

"Joyce didn't say anything about 1990, did she?"

"No...sorry that I jumped to the conclusion that it was a photo from 1990. Yeah, it couldn't be."

"We better hope so."

"I don't think it's wise to go back to New York to fly to Germany."

"No... you're right. Let's rent a car and drive to Philadelphia to fly out.

21- MARCH 22, 2025

"How long are we staying here," Violet asked as they entered their hotel room. "The FBI will eventually figure out we flew to Hamburg."

"Hopefully, we can fly out on Monday to Moscow after talking to Hans Strenner, the leading climate scientist here. Let's change identities when we talk to Strenner. I'll be Arthur Hansen and you'll be Violet...."

"Erlander," Violet answered. "You know Germany is doing fairly well with alternate energy. They are way ahead of the US. They've cut their greenhouse gas emissions over 50% since 1990, while the US has increased emissions since 1990. Germany expects to phase out coal next year. The US still has over 200 coal fired power plants that produce 18% of the electricity."

"You're right, but Germany still has high transportation emissions. Some of the technology we'll give Strenner should be helpful in reducing transportation emissions. Plus, the more climate scientists we can get to be proactive the better. As soon as we're settled, I'll call Strenner."

"It's Sunday. He won't be at the University."

"I have his home phone. It was listed. It will take the FBI a while to trace our movements and contact German authorities. If we meet Strenner Monday, we can fly out in the afternoon long before the FBI could probably alert German authorities."

"Okay, Doc. I think we should try to find some disguises to fool any cameras."

"I guess it can't hurt, but probably won't help that much. They'll have our passport photos when we flew in even though the names would be different."

"Can I call Joyce for an update?"

"Let's wait until tomorrow. We'll buy another prepaid phone and then ditch it before we fly."

"Russia is not a big emitter, but as you say the more climate scientist we engage the better. Too bad we can't get China on board. They're planning on building more coal fired plants. They have over 250 megawatts of coal plants in planning or development and are looking at even more in the future."

"China has the most sophisticated surveillance apparatus in the world. It would be extremely dangerous. We'd end up being detained and questioned."

"I know, but it is going to be a problem in the future. I just wish we could do something there."

"Getting Western climate scientists more proactive will help. China feels that they are within their rights to emit as much as they do, since historically the total CO_2 in the atmosphere came mostly from the US and Europe as Ramada said." He held up his hand when he saw Violet was ready to respond vehemently to his comment. "I know it's dead-end thinking, but they feel they have a point."

"Jesus, Doc. We've got to get China and India to stop these planned coal plants."

"My hope is that Russia can have an influence on China. One of the reasons to go there. Their emissions as you say are low. They have, however, tremendous oil and gas deposits that need to stay in the ground."

"Doctor Strenner, thank you for seeing us on such short notice." Arthur stepped forward and shook Strenner's hand. "This is my associate, Violet Erlander."

After Doctor Strenner shook hands with Violet, he indicated the chairs in front of his desk and moved around his desk to sit down. He was of average height and obviously liked to eat. His gray hair was long, and he had a trimmed goatee. He leaned back in his chair, smiling broadly at Violet. His office was cheery with its landscape paintings of country settings and bright sunlight from his large windows. "I thought I knew most of the Swedish climate scientists, but I've not heard your names before. You do know Doctor Swenson, I presume?"

"Of course," Arthur answered while still standing before stepping to the desk and presenting the memory stick. "This memory stick has our latest research for your perusal and use. None of the new technology is proprietary. There's new battery and hydrogen fuel cell technologies, climate forecasting information, and innovative fossil fuel taxation. I think you will find the information interesting." He sat down and glanced at Violet, who was sitting erect, somewhat disturbed by Strenner appraising stare.

Doctor Strenner accepted the memory stick and set it on his desk, still keeping his gaze focused on Violet. "Did you take the train here?"

"No we came from the US where we met with a number of climate scientists," Violet said quickly before Arthur could respond, hoping to stop Strenner's lewd stare. "We are visiting climate scientists in many countries to encourage them to be more proactive and providing important information and new technologies." Her explanation mitigated Strenner's stare, and Violet relaxed a little.

"I see. I'm pleased that you came to see me. I'm always interested in new technology. I wish we could raise our carbon tax as high as Sweden's. Ours is about half of yours. "

"Yes, we agree," Arthur said. "We believe realistic carbon taxes can do wonders on reducing CO_2 emissions. We have information on carbon taxing strategies on the memory stick as well."

"Are you affiliated with a University or do you work for the government?" Strenner asked, finally focusing on Arthur.

"No we are a private institute, privately funded."

"What is the name of the institute?"

"I am not at liberty to disclose that information."

"That sounds rather ominous. Why do you need to keep it secret?"

"The entities funding the Institute prefer to remain anonymous," Violet added.

"I say that is most unusual."

"Not really," Violet said. "As you know, the fossil fuel industries and countries with fossil fuel reserves are doing all they can to deter the movement toward eliminating fossil fuels and transitioning to total clean energy. The amount of money represented by fossil fuel reserves is immense. They certainly don't want to write off those reserves. Our Institute prefers to work in the background to hopefully avoid confrontations with the fossil fuel industries and their minions. We believe they are not above clandestine attacks."

"Attacks? I'm not aware of any attacks by fossil fuel industries."

"Well, let's just leave it at that," Arthur said. "Please review the information we have provided. If you have any questions, you can email your questions to me." Arthur handed Strenner his card. "I'm afraid we have other appointments and limited time." Arthur stood followed by Violet. "Thank you for seeing us."

Strenner stood and came around his desk to shake hands. "Thank you for coming, Doctor Hansen and Violet Erlander." He held Violet's hand a little too long to her liking before she pulled it from him, frowning at Arthur. "I'll review the information you have provided and hope to talk to you both in the future."

Violet rushed to the door to hide her animosity. Strenner obvious licentiousness was hard for her to tolerate. Arthur thanked Strenner again and followed Violet out.

When they were outside. Arthur stopped Violet with a hand to her shoulder. "Thanks for keeping your cool, Violet. Doctor Strenner was almost drooling at you."

"Yeah he's an obvious letch, but a top climate scientist. We need his help. I hope I didn't offend him."

"I'm sure you didn't. Let's go back to the hotel and check out."

"You look good with long hair and a mustache, Doc," Violet said before erupting in laughter as they walked from their hotel. The sun was out, but the clouds were often blocking the sun, and it was cold enough that they could see their breath.

"You look good as a blond."

"Why thank you. They say blonds have more fun."

"In your case, it may not apply."

Violet pushed Arthur in the side. "I think we're far enough from the hotel, and I haven't seen anyone paying us close attention. I'm hungry. Let's find a restaurant before taking a taxi to the airport. I don't want to eat at the airport. Food at airports is seldom vegan and often insipid." She pointed down the street.

"There's a Middle Eastern restaurant ahead. I bet they have falafel."

"Okay, I bet they do."

They walked into the restaurant and were shown to a table. "What happened to your mustache?"

"I can't eat with that thing and it makes my nose itch."

They each ordered the falafel plate. When the plates arrived, Violet bent over and inhaled the aroma. "Smells good and looks yummy." She cut a falafel ball in half, dipped it in the hot chili sauce and placed it in her mouth. "Oooo, that's hot chili. The falafel is nice and moist." She smiled as she chewed the other half of the falafel ball. "Nice music. Where's the belly dancers?" She laughed. "This hummus is good too."

"Yes, this restaurant was a good choice." Arthur glanced at his watch. "We should leave in at least an hour in case the traffic is bad getting to the airport."

"Okay, I'll make short work of this plate."

"Damn, I'm tired," Violet said as the taxi was taking them to the hotel after their flight. "It's already dark here. I need to lie down. All this traveling is wearing on me. You weren't kidding about it being cold here in Moscow." She hunched her arms around her. "This jacket is not very warm. I'll need to buy a sweater here."

At the hotel they checked in and started for the elevators. "I hope our room is warmer than this lobby," Violet exclaimed as she quickened her pace.

"I'm sure it will be."

As soon as they entered the room, Violet dropped her backpack and climbed into bed, gathering the coverlet around her. "Ah, that's better. Can you turn the heat up?"

Arthur walked around the room. "I don't see a thermostat." He sat down on his bed. "When you are warm, let's go to the hotel restaurant."

"Oh yes, I'm starving, but I need a while to stop shivering."

After about fifteen minutes, Violet climbed out of bed and went into the bathroom. When she came out, she was wearing her blond wig. "I'm ready."

"They have our passports," Arthur said. "They know what we look like."

"My hair's a mess, and I don't feel like fixing it. This wig also keeps me warm."

They took the elevator to the lobby and walked into the restaurant. As soon as they were seated, Violet asked for hot tea. The hostess said she would send the waiter over. Violet frowned and opened the menu. "Shit, they don't have anything vegan."

"Yes, I see that. We can get some sides of vegetables, potatoes, and black bread. The soups will have meat stock."

"That sucks." Violet said, furrowing her forehead. "Oh well. We can hopefully find a better restaurant for breakfast."

"I'll call Kiskov in the morning. If we can get into see him tomorrow, we can fly to Sweden later in the afternoon or evening. I'd like to meet with Doctor Swenson."

"I didn't think we were going to Sweden. They're judged the most sustainable country in Europe. Are you going to tell Swenson we're Swedish?"

"No, I'll say we're from the States. Sweden might be able to take advantage of the new technology more quickly and get other countries using the technology."

"What about our Swedish passports?"

"We'll use them at the airport. They'll pass muster. Swenson won't need to see them. There's another person I'd like to find in Stockholm if I can, Lucas Nilsson. He's a friend of my father, who went to college with my dad at Berkeley. He's Swedish and might be able to get our Swedish identities codified so to speak."

"Codified?"

"Yes, I met him when he came to visit us in January of this year— 2025 that is— when I was eight. I believe he is a computer hacker now and not adverse to illegal hacking. He might be able to register our births in Sweden so if we were apprehended by the FBI, and if they check with the Swedish authorities, we will be real Swedes."

"You remember somebody well enough when you were eight to be able to induce him to hack into the Swedish birth records and add us in. If he met you this January when you were eight, what the hell is going to think when he sees you at 43?"

"I'll have to tell him the truth, convince him we are from 2060, and hope he will support what we are doing."

"Jesus, Doc, he'll think you're some kind of nut."

"We'll see. I think it's worth a try. He and my Dad were great friends. I felt there was a real bond between them. If he blows us off, then we carry on."

"He could turn us in."

"I don't think so."

"Okay, I hope you find Lucas and can convince him. I wouldn't bet much on your probability of success, but it would be nice to be registered as real people if the authorities catch up to us."

"As they say— nothing ventured, nothing gained."

"Where are we going after Sweden?"

"I was thinking back to the States via Canada."

"How are we going to get into the US? We'd probably be apprehended when we cross the border?"

"I hope we can smuggle ourselves into the US without going through border security."

"How?"

"I don't know yet. Perhaps we can sneak across the border in Maine in a wooded area or someplace like that. We have to get back into the States if we are going to make our retrieval date. I'd still like to meet with Macer and Oppender. Once in the US we'll have to travel by car back to Berkeley. Any public transportation would be risky. There's undoubtedly a bulletin out for our detention and turn over to the FBI. Our rendezvous with the Bridge is April 12th at midnight. We have plenty of time to visit more people and still make the rendezvous."

Arthur walked out of the bathroom after his morning shower. He noticed Violet was awake but still hunkering down in her bed. He moved to her bed. "Violet, I talked to Kiskov," he said, giving her a shake. "We have a meeting this afternoon at three. He said he only recently has been allowed visitors. They had him under a kind of house arrest because of his public statements about climate warming and the need to transition to clean energy." He rustled Violet again. "Come on, let's get going. We are lucky we can get in to see him. It took forever to get through to his office telephone."

"I'm not getting out of bed until it warms up in here. I can't believe there's no way to adjust the room temperature. We picked the wrong hotel. It looks gloomy outside as well."

"Any other complaints?"

"Yes, I need something wholesome to eat."

"I did some research. If we ask for fasting food, we should be able to get vegan food even if it's not on the menu. When you're ready, we can try it at the hotel restaurant."

"Okay, I'll get up." Violet swung out of bed and quickly donned her clothes before striding to the bathroom. When she came out of the bathroom, she stood near the door to the hallway. "Don't just sit there. Come on, let's go eat."

At the hotel restaurant, Arthur explained that they wanted fasting food. They were each brought a bowl of potatoes, cauliflower, and mushrooms.

"This isn't half bad," Violet said after she took a bite of the dish. "All right, Doc, way to go. This toast is tasty too."

"Yes, this should hold us for a while."

"Do you really think we will change future climate projections very much with our information and visits?" Violet pursed her lips. "Russia only emits about 1600 megatons of CO_2 compared to the US's 4,500 megatons. China emits 10,000 megatons. But as you say looking at cumulative emissions with Europe at 520 billion tons and the US at 410 billion tons, China has a ways to go with their cumulative emissions of 220 billion tons. There is not much Russia can do in the big scheme."

"Yes, but they have influence around the world," Arthur said. "If they keep most of their reserves in the ground that would be fantastic. In any case, every bit helps." Arthur finished his food and leaned back. "My last travel to 1990 resulted in a reduction in greenhouse gases. This trip has to have an impact.

Hopefully much more than my last trip. Otherwise... well you know full well what will be in store for us, our children, and their children if we are not successful."

"Welcome to the Moscow Institute of Physics and Technology," Doctor Kiskov said, as Arthur and Violet were shown into the office. "Please have a seat. Too bad it is so gloomy today, but I suppose you are used to this kind of weather." He gave a quick laugh. "It's much the same in Sweden, is it not?" He was a tall muscular man with red hair and brown eyes that seemed to wander as if he couldn't focus long on one spot.

"Yes it is."

"You want to talk about climate I understand."

"Yes." Arthur approached the desk and held out the memory stick. "We have some information for your review that I believe you will find interesting—climate models, battery and fuel cell technology. Have a look and if you have any questions you can email me." He handed Kiskov his card.

"Thank you. I will have a look." He studied the two. "I have not heard your names before. Are you at the KTH Institute of Technology?"

"No, we work at a private Institute. We often collaborate with KTH, but are not affiliated."

"I see," Kiskov replied. "I'm afraid the Russian government is not very concerned with climate warming. I try to get the government more involved." He shook his head. "But it is not easy. After my last house detention, I have to be very careful. Were you followed here?"

"I believe so. Two men in dark overcoats followed us soon after we left our hotel."

"Yes, they are watching me carefully. I am so glad we were able to meet." Kiskov got up and walked behind the two, which caused both Arthur and Violet to turn to watch Kiskov. "You may want to watch what you say." Kiskov said very softly, smiling sheepishly, and indicated with a nod of his head the cameras near the ceiling behind him.

He moved back to take a seat at his desk. "I am quite worried about the effects of global warming in Russia. I'm afraid that permafrost melting will be a big problem for us and the world in the future. Many Russians envision increased economic development with climate warming. You could say that most Russians are short sighted about global warming. Amazingly, Russia has reduced its greenhouse gas emissions, but not significantly. We still have 25 coal electric generating stations. There is not a plan as yet to shutter any of the plants. Wild fires in Siberia have been a problem and will probably get much worse. Most are just allowed to burn since they are remote, and access is nearly impossible."

"We believe the best way to foster the elimination of fossil fuels use is with a significant carbon tax,"

Arthur said. "The information we have provided has carbon tax pricing programs as well."

"Getting the Russian government to tax carbon is virtually impossible. We have less than a thousand electric vehicles on the road in Russia. They are mostly a novelty status symbol for some of the wealthy. Fossil fuel is our biggest export. We have a long way to go."

"Yes, we know," Arthur said. "We are glad that you are a leading advocate for alternative forms of energy. That is the chief reason we wanted to talk with you and provide you the information. Thank you for your work on climate." Arthur nodded to Violet. "We will take our leave. We have a plane to catch." They both stood.

"Thank you for coming. I will faithfully review the information you have provided, and I hope to be in touch in the future." He escorted them to the door of his office. "Have a pleasant trip."

They walked down the corridor and down the steps to the lobby where the two men in dark overcoats followed them out to the street.

"If I was Kiskov, I'd get the hell out of Russia," Violet whispered as they walked back to their hotel.

"He may feel the same, but cannot leave. His willingness to speak out is commendable. I wonder if he will be chastened for his outspokenness in our interview."

"I'd put money on it."

22- MARCH 26, 2025

"I've talked to Lucas on the phone," Arthur announced as he re-entered their Stockholm hotel room. "I called him from the coffee house down the street in case he called the authorities. After some lengthy discussion, he has agreed to meet with us. I've told him to bring a laptop. I'll give him the memory stick and show him my laptop to try to convince him that we are actually from 2060."

"Where and when are we meeting him?" Violet asked.

"Today 4:00 PM at the train station. He wanted to meet where there'd be crowds in case it was a trap. He's wanted by the authorities in Sweden for his hacking. He's apparently a quite famous hacker here."

"Why are we not meeting with Swenson first? What if you can't convince Lucas, and we have to hightail out of Sweden? Wouldn't be wise to see Swenson first?"

"Perhaps, but I've got a good feeling about Lucas."

"Okay, Doc. What should my roll be? Would it be better if I stay at the hotel?"

"No, I think information coming from both of us will be more persuasive. Let me lay the ground work, and then join in whenever you feel it is appropriate. I'm sure together we have a good chance of convincing him we're from 2060. My futuristic laptop will be a big aid."

Arthur recognized Lucas as he sat on a bench in the train station. "Okay, he's over there." Arthur nodded his head toward the man sitting alone. "We can do this, Violet."

"Yes, indeed," Violet returned, thinking this was a crazy idea, but would never go against Arthur. His intuition was uncanny. How he recognized Lucas amongst all these people was a feat in itself.

"Lucas Nilsson, I presume," Arthur said as he approached the man."

Lucas stood and shook hands with Arthur. Arthur turned to Violet. "Lucas this is my associate and phenomenal computer scientist, Violet Drummer. Let's sit."

Lucas, still staring at Violet, looked away and nodded before sitting back down. Arthur sat down on one side of Lucas, and Violet sat down on the opposite side.

"Thanks for meeting with us. I suspect you think we might be pulling a sting operation on you or are completely crazy. However, I assure you I am Arthur Brown, who you met earlier this year when you visited my father, Frank, in Berkeley when I was eight years old. To help convince you we are actually time travelers from 2060, I have brought my laptop." Arthur removed his laptop from his backpack and handed it to Lucas. "Have a look. The password is 'Einstein8Relativity'."

Lucas hesitated to accept the laptop. He glanced at Violet, who nodded, then with a frown of apprehension, reached out for the laptop. He turned it over examining the bottom before slowly opening it up and typing the password. As he brought up the file explorer his face went slack. He looked up at Arthur, then turned to Violet, his face contorted in thought. He opened additional files, shaking his head. He appeared totally overwhelmed, his face flush as he continued to open and close files.

When he stopped searching the files on the laptop, he stared at Arthur. "How is this possible? How did you get here? Are you truly little Arthur Brown... well, not little anymore?" He kept shaking his head.

"It's true," Violet said, placing her hand on Lucas's shoulder, causing Lucas to stare into Violet's deep blue eyes, obviously mesmerized by the situation. "Arthur produced an Einstein-Rosen Bridge, a Wormhole, which has allowed us to travel back in time. I know this seems impossible. It would be in 2025. Just as the laptop you are looking at would be impossible in 2025. You can see that the laptop is extremely advanced compared to computers today in 2025. Even if we faked the file origination dates and the time clock, we couldn't have obtained a computer with this computing speed and advanced software." She slipped her hand down his back and rubbed slowly. "I realize you are finding this very hard to comprehend. I sympathize with you. It is totally bizarre, but actually true."

"What do you want from me?" Lucas asked as he turned back to Arthur.

"We are hoping that you can hack the birth records here in Stockholm and add recorded births for Violet and I. We had a run in with the FBI in the US. We have forged Swedish passports that are undetectable and will pass muster anywhere. They were accepted when we flew here from Moscow and everywhere else we have used them. If we are apprehended by the FBI, and, if they check to see if we are who we are purporting to be, we want them to find the birth records. Thus they would have no reason to arrest us for using false identities. Would you be able to hack the birth records?"

"I could, but why should I do it? What's your purpose here?"

"Climate warming in 2060 has surpassed the mean global temperature of 2°C and is on its way to 3°C, which will be very detrimental for life," Arthur said. "There has been a sea rise of over 2 feet and there are over 300 million climate refugees, mostly from the tropics and low lying areas that are homeless. There is continued fossil fuel use that will devastate the planet. We are traveling around the world in 2025, visiting climate scientists and advocates, providing them advanced technologies that will be an aid in the transition to complete clean energy. We are encouraging them to be more active and vocal in fighting for the elimination of fossil fuels now in 2025 when real meaningful reduction in the use of fossil fuels can have an immense impact on the future. I don't want my children to grow up in a world plagued by a climate catastrophe."

Lucas looked from Arthur to Violet not saying a word. Violet wondered what he was thinking. He focused on Violet. "Is what he's saying true?"

"Yes, it is completely true," Violet said. She leaned toward Lucas and opened her eyes wide. "Climate warming in 2060 has reached an alarming level. The populace of earth know that fossil fuel use is killing life, but the forces of money and the fossil fuel industries still have a lot of power in 2060. They are still trying their utmost to utilize their oil and gas reserves, knowing full well what it doing to life."

Lucas closed his eyes and rubbed his temples softly with his hands. Slowly he opened his eyes and looked first at Violet and then at Arthur. "Okay, Arthur Brown, I'll do it."

"Thanks, Lucas. I have something for you. Arthur handed him a wad of Swedish Krona."

"That's not necessary. I'm happy to help." He did though accept the money. "How did you at the age of eight remember me so well?"

Violet laughed. "The things Arthur can do are totaling amazing. He's a true genius."

"I'll say. How's your father doing in 2060? He's such a great guy. We had fun together in college. I really enjoyed seeing him this year. I also enjoyed visiting the western US. Such dramatic landscapes."

"He and my Mom are getting forgetful, but doing well. They're retired and enjoying their retirement in Berkeley. Violet and I are free tonight. Would you like to join us for dinner?"

"Yeah, for sure. You wouldn't by any chance be willing to give me your laptop."

"No, I'm sorry. We will need it, and it could cause quite a stir if it was found, but I can give you a memory stick with the information we are giving the climate scientists we are visiting. It may be of some use to a clever guy like you."

23- MARCH 28, 2025

"I'm glad Joyce suggested we meet with Richard Pellet here," Violet said after they cleared passport control in Toronto and began walking leisurely toward the exit. "It would be a shame to come here and not talk to a climate scientist. Canada is still mining tar sands, and their electrical generation is mostly fossil fuels. If the Canadian government became more proactive, it would hopefully encourage the US to do the same. As you've said, the more climate scientists we encourage to get out and be more vocal the better. It was a real coup getting Lucas to add us to the birth rolls. I don't know how you came up with the idea." She shook her head. "I can hardly believe we actually convinced him we were from 2060."

"I think you were instrumental in helping to convince him. You made quite an impression on him. During dinner, he could hardly keep his eyes off you."

"I liked him. There is a big difference between an admiring look like Lucas exhibited compared to the lascivious look that Doctor Strenner gave me. I don't mind being admired, but lasciviousness makes my blood boil. Lucas was very amusing when he got going. He sure liked hacking corporations and the government to shake things up. He may be able to use the information on the memory stick to rile things up."

"Yeah, he may."

"You still think crossing legally into the US now that we are real persons, so to speak, is too dangerous?"

"I don't think we should risk it. If we don't make it back to 2060, all we've done will have been in vain. I want to thank you Violet for accompanying me here to the past. You have been an immeasurable help. You certainly brought Doctor Salmon to our side and helped enormously with Lucas." He rubbed her shoulder. "Your recall memory has been amazing as always, and your moral support is invaluable. If I had had to meet all these scientists on my own... while evading the FBI, I don't know if I could have done it. I thank you so much."

"Doc, don't go maudlin on me." She gave Arthur a shove. "This has been an adventure of a lifetime. It is I, who should thank you." She really was having a phenomenal experience that was hard for her to believe was even happening. She wondered what her life would have been like if she had not taken the job with Arthur. She could think of no other pursuit that would have been so exciting and all consuming.

Once outside the terminal, Arthur and Violet got in line at the taxi stand. "I've been thinking about how we're going to get back into the US," Arthur said. "I had thought of walking across in a remote forested area, but that is risky. I have no idea what kind of surveillance Canada and the US employs for the remote boundaries. If we had an advocate, who could smuggle us across in their car that would be the safest."

"You think Pellet would know someone who would do that?"

"Not really. The only person I can think of who might be willing to help us is you know who."

Violet grabbed Arthur's arm, her eyes wide. "Joyce?" She shook her head. "Arthur... I don't know if that's a good idea. It would be very risky for her."

"Maybe not. The times I have crossed into Canada with my parents no one bothered to search the car. When we crossed north of Glacier Park, there was a kiosk with one agent, who looked at our passports, asked why we were visiting Canada, then stamped our passports, and we drove off. Nobody even looked in the car. When we drove back from Vancouver on the US side, an agent looked into the car asked if we had any fruit purchased in Canada and then stamped our passports. I think someone like Joyce would breeze through the border with no problem."

Violet frowned. "How long ago was that?"

"Yes, it was a while ago. I was six."

"You know border security became much tighter after the Covid-19 pandemic, not to mention international terrorism." She frowned. "I suppose you expect me to ask her?"

"It would be better coming from you, but if you don't want to ask her, then I'm quite willing to ask."

"I'll think about it." She knew Arthur was probably right. There was no one besides Joyce, who would be willing to smuggle them back into the US. Even so, she did not like the idea of putting Joyce is such danger. They had already significantly disrupted Joyce's life. Joyce seemed to like the excitement somewhat that helping them entailed. It would certainly be wonderful if Joyce came and got them.

"Pellet was an interesting guy," Violet said as they entered their hotel room. "He's was very enthusiastic about being more proactive. I liked him. His research on the warming ocean effects on ice flows was ground breaking. I think he's going to take the bull by the horns and really get vocal. I bet he's a pretty good public speaker too."

They had spent the previous day resting after their rather nonstop travels from Germany, to Russia to Sweden and had met with Pellet the following morning.

"He's already emailed me with questions," Arthur said. "He was very interested in the hydrogen fuel cell technology for larger transport. Joyce was spot on about us needing to talk to him."

"Speaking of Joyce, I called her from the University. She's coming tomorrow to get us."

"Violet, you are amazing. Good idea calling from the University. Unless they've recording her phone, the authorities will have no idea we called or that we're in Canada. Does she think she's been followed or surveilled in any way?"

"No, she's made sure that no one has been following her." Violet laughed. "She said she has never looked so much in the rear view mirror in her life. I asked her to leave her cell phone at home and buy a burner phone for the trip."

"Good thinking. Well, let's go out and celebrate. Toronto is a pleasant city. They must have some vegan restaurants."

"Oh yeah, I already picked out a good one. Supposed to be a vegan paradise."

"Great let's get ready and go."

Even though Joyce had accepted Violet request to drive to Toronto and smuggle them back into the US, she was having second thoughts. There was something very strange about Violet and Arthur. The technology on the memory stick they had given her was so advanced. Some of the technologies she had no knowledge that any entity was working on. She doubted that a private Swedish Institute could have developed such technologies and climate projection software. She wondered if they were working for the Swedish Defense Department. Maybe the Swedes had hacked the US Defense Department and had stolen the technologies as Ramada had intimated. She decided that she would drive to Canada as she had agreed, but when she got there she would get to the bottom of how they had managed to obtain the many technologies.

She left Cambridge as the sun was rising. She thought about Violet and how much she adored her. Her admiration for Violet was what led her to make the journey. Was she putting herself in danger? If she confronted them in Toronto could they become violent? She believed Violet really cared about her. She wasn't sure about Arthur although he seemed a mild mannered, extremely intelligent person. She was sure there was something they weren't telling her, and she vowed that she'd get to the bottom of it.

The journey was long. She stopped at rest areas, and filled the gas tank on her hybrid when it was just getting low or to use the toilets and take a rest. She stopped in Syracuse for lunch. She was glad of the longer rest. She hadn't driven such a long distance for some time. She enjoyed her Chinese tofu dinner with almonds and snow peas. She laughed to herself. If Violet was with her, the dinner would have been much more fun. She had to admit she had such fun with Violet and missed her. She had never felt this way for another person. She had married her long divorced husband more out of a sense of duty than any real desire. She believed she had an actual and tantalizing affection for Violet. Violet made her feel so wonderful.

When she reached the Canadian border, she started sweating profusely. She told herself to relax. By going into Canada, she wasn't doing anything wrong. She shouldn't be so worried, but couldn't stop her apprehension. She wasn't cut out for intrigue, but had to admit it was exciting.

"She should be here by now," Violet said, pacing back and forth in their hotel room. "She said she was going to leave in the morning. It's going to be dark soon."

"Relax, it's quite a drive— more than eight hours if you include lunch breaks and border crossing. She'll be exhausted by the drive. I've booked her a room across the hall." Arthur handed Violet the electronic pass key. "Do you want to take her to the restaurant we went to last night that you thought was so great? Or, there's a Thai place within walking distance."

"Let's walk to the Thai restaurant. I'm sure she'll be glad to be out of the car."

As soon as there was a knock on their door, Violet jumped up from the bed she had finally settled on and was at the door in a flash. When Joyce stepped into the room, Violet hugged and kissed her. "I am so glad to see and hold you, Joyce."

"I'm pleased to see you as well," Joyce answered, holding Violet at arm's length so she could gaze into her face. "You seem a little on edge."

"I was worried about you."

"It was a long drive. I haven't done a sustained drive like that in a long time. I had no problems." Joyce let go of Violet and approached Arthur. "Arthur, nice to see you as well. I trust your travels have been rewarding." She gave Arthur a quick hug.

Arthur relished the physical contact and breathed in her subtle perfume. The first hug since he had left 2060. He thought of Rose and how much he was missing her. "Yes, I sincerely hope we have persuaded those we have seen to increase their activities. Hopefully it will be helpful on getting governments to make the expenditures and pass legislation needed to progress to total clean renewable energy."

"I'm sure you have. The new technologies you have provided should be very helpful as well, although it has created quite a stir. Ramada called me a few days ago wanting to know if I've heard from you again. Kind of made me quite paranoid. I can understand why he and the FBI are so intent on finding you. I found some of the information you gave me remarkable and somewhat futuristic. The fact that your institute was able to develop so many amazing new technologies, I myself have found it difficult to comprehend. How were you and your associates able to do it?"

"Yes, I can understand why you would find it hard to believe our Institute could have developed so many new technologies," Arthur replied as he looked over Joyce's shoulder at Violet. He was surprised and worried by Joyce's statement. It seemed that Joyce had become suspicious of them. "We have quite a research facility and many bright scientist working for the Institute in conjunction with scientists around the world." He hoped that Violet could renew Joyce's trust in them.

"How was Doctor Pellet?" Joyce asked.

"A very wise and pleasant man," Arthur said. "I believe our visit will prompt him to get Canada more involved in clean energy."

"He was nice and very articulate," Violet added. "I bet you're tired. We've gotten you a room across the hall. You want to freshen up before we go to dinner." She believed she needed to get Joyce alone to solidify her willingness to help despite the many doubts that had surfaced.

"Yes, I'd love to shower and regroup. I must say I was nervous at the border. I must smell, I was sweating so. Of course they stamped my passport and waved me through with no problem. I've made sure nobody followed me here. I drove around Toronto a bit before coming here."

"Good, well, let's go to your room," Violet said with a big smile. "We'll come back and give you a knock when we're ready to go to dinner, Doc."

As soon as they were alone in their room, Violet grabbed Joyce kissing her and bumping her pelvis against her. "I missed you so much." She sensed a hesitancy in Joyce as Joyce returned her hug. Joyce's skepticism of the Swedish Institute was a problem. Could Joyce turn against them? She'd need to handle Joyce with kid gloves. If they lost Joyce's support, they would be in dire circumstances, and she could lose her first real love.

"I've missed you too," Joyce replied, keeping Violet at arm's length. "Not to be rude, but I've got to take a shower. I can't stand the smell of me."

"Of course, go for it. Can I join you?"

"By all means. I'd love you to scrub my back."

Joyce's reply had boosted her prospect of solidifying Joyce's support. "Oh, I'm an excellent scrubber." It was essential that she alleviate any qualms Joyce was having about her and Arthur.

They quickly disrobed and proceeded into the bathroom. Joyce adjusted the shower and stepped into the spray. Violet followed her in and began soaping up the wash cloth. She leisurely massaged Joyce's back with the wash cloth as Joyce cooed in satisfaction. Violet relaxed somewhat, hoping Joyce was still in their camp.

"You weren't kidding about your scrubbing expertise," Joyce said, slipping back against Violet. "So how was your trip?"

"It was good." Joyce's plump rump against her made her feel wonderful. "We flew from Philadelphia to Hamburg and met with Doctor Strenner. We thought flying from New York might be risky with the FBI on our tail. Doctor Strenner stared at me lasciviously, which bummed me out somewhat, but I was polite and, he was appreciative of us visiting him and giving him the memory stick. Moscow was colder than hell and food was terrible. Doctor Kiskov was interesting, and trying his utmost to get Russia to reduce fossil fuel use, but admitted he wasn't making much progress. Swenson in Stockholm was nice and very welcoming. You won't believe this, but Arthur got a friend of his Dad's to hack the Swedish birth records and add us. We're now on paper actual Swedish citizens."

Joyce abruptly turned to face Violet. "What do you mean?" She stared at Violet with a menacing red face. "You're not Swedish?"

"Shit... Oh... I'm sorry... I got carried away." Violet couldn't believe she had been so stupid. What the hell had she been thinking? "Sorry, Joyce. Damn... no, I'm not Swedish." She had made a terrible mistake blurting out about the birth records. "I'm an American. Sorry, I told you we were Swedish. I'm very sorry for lying to you." She reached out for Joyce as Joyce stumbled back, her face drawn.

"Why the subterfuge," Joyce almost shouted. She dropped her head and when she raised it again her facial expression changed to scrunched anger. "I must say I've had my doubts about you and Arthur. I've found it very hard to believe that the technologies, climate simulation programs, and all the other information on the memory stick was compiled by a secret Swedish Institute." She shook her head as tears began to form in the corner of her eyes. "I was of two minds if I should come and smuggle you into the US. My infatuation with you overrode my doubts about you." She wiped away her tears. "No wonder the FBI are after you. Maybe I should turn you in."

"Joyce, I will tell you the truth." Violet needed to be very careful. Convincing Joyce that they were time travelers from 2060 was her only choice to save their connection. "Let's finish our shower, and we can sit down. What I'm about to tell you, you will find difficult to believe, but I swear it will be the truth."

They finished showering. Violet could sense Joyce's hostility and realized her slip up could cost her Joyce's support and love unless she could convince her of the truth. She was very worried as they left the bathroom. She and Joyce silently dressed, then sat down on the bed. Joyce's concerned face spurred Violet's determination to convince Joyce of the truth. She didn't want to lose Joyce's help nor their mutual intimacy.

"Joyce, please listen to me. I love you, and will be completely truthful from now on. The reason for the subterfuge was because it will be very hard for you to believe what I'm going to tell you." She paused and rubbed Joyce's back. In response Joyce looked at Violet with a mixture of admiration and doubt. "Arthur and I are time travelers from 2060."

"Yeah, right. Do you take me for a fool?"

"No Joyce, I know you are a very intelligent and savvy climate scientist. Arthur is a quantum physicist and a real genius. He invented and built, at the University of California at Berkeley with funding from the US Energy Department and the University, a structure that with the gargantuan electrical power from a recently built Fusion Electrical Generating

Station in Oakland, he was able to produce inside the structure an Einstein-Rosen Bridge, a Wormhole." She paused and watched the consternation and doubt build on Joyce's furrowed face. She reached out and grasped Joyce's hand. "Arthur and I built computer programs that were able to establish travel to the past inside the wormhole. I wrote most of the computer programs for the Project with Arthur's direction."

Joyce withdrew her hand. "That is impossible. Why keep lying to me?"

"I know it sounds impossible. In 2025 it would be impossible. With AI and quantum computing, many amazing things are possible that could not be done in 2025. What I'm telling you is the absolute truth. I swear with all my heart."

Joyce seemed to relax somewhat. "Why would you do this?"

"To try and save life on this planet. In 2060 the global mean temperature is higher by 2.5° C, climate refugees are in the hundreds of millions, sea levels have risen over 2 feet, and still there are fossil fuel generating stations around the world. A 3°C increase is just around the bend, then 4° and on until life on the planet is no longer viable."

Violet moved closer to Joyce and grabbed her hand again. "Arthur first travelled back in the Einstein-Rosen Bridge to 1990 where he met with Fred Hinson at NASA and gave him the advanced climate software, technologies, economic programs and so forth on a hard disk. Upon Arthur's return to

2050, a small additional reduction in greenhouse gases had been accomplished in the alternate timeline from 1990, but from 2050 to 2060 fossil fuel use continued and what he accomplished was wiped out. He felt that he had gone back too far. In 1990 the effects of climate warming were only beginning to be felt. He also learned upon his return that Doctor Hinson's life was cut short by an auto accident before many of the technologies given to Hinson could be utilized. Arthur believes that the fossil fuel consortium had Hinson killed."

"What!" Joyce stiffened. "They killed Doctor Hinson? He was a hero of mine. His speech before congress in 1988 about climate was the first real public notice that fossil fuel use was detrimentally warming the planet."

"We don't know for sure that he was killed. Arthur remembered before he left 2050 that Hinson lived to be an older man, but there's no way to be sure. One of the things about time travel is that any changes in the past are immediately the reality in the future, and the people in the future are on the alternate time path and have no memory of the past before the changes. Only the time traveler has a brief memory of the past before the alternate time line, but their memory fades as they experience the alternate time line."

"I can't get my head around what you're telling me. It's too fantastical to be believed."

"I know, Joyce. It is fantastical, but true. Arthur wanted to try one more time to get people in the past to begin to eliminate fossil fuel use while it would have a major impact. Thus, his desire to come to 2025 when climate change was apparent and most intelligent people knew climate warming was detrimental. I wanted to come with Arthur to help convince scientists that they had to lead a revolution to start to eliminate fossil fuels in 2025 and beyond, so in 2060 things wouldn't be so dire, and we could save life on earth."

"You swear you are telling me the truth."

"Yes, I am being completely honest, and it's the absolute truth."

"My god, someone could do horrible things with time travel."

"Yes, indeed they could, but they could also do wonders. Time travel is an extremely delicate endeavor, but Arthur can be trusted to handle the travel with utmost caution. This will be the last trip. When we return, Arthur will destroy the programs and inputs to the structure that allowed the formation of the Bridge so that no one can ever use his Project to time travel again."

"Why would you destroy such an amazing achievement?"

"As you said people could do horrible things with time travel. The Department of Energy that has provided the bulk of funding for the Project is suspicious of Arthur and has forced Arthur to hire a physicist, who has been spying for the Department. Arthur believes they will take the Project away from him. To be safe we need to render the Project inoperable.”

“I see. So you and Arthur are going back to 2060?”

“Yes we have to, or what we did would not exist.”

“How can that be?”

“It’s the reality of time travel.”

“You mean I’m going to lose you.” Joyce scooted to Violet and embraced her. “When are you going back?”

“Our rendezvous is April 12th in Berkeley where we landed.”

“That doesn’t leave you much time. What if the FBI catch you?”

“That could be catastrophic if we are held for any length of time. We have two alternate dates a week apart for return travel, but that’s it. We can’t call home and arrange another rendezvous time.”

“I find it fantastical what you’ve told me, but I believe you. I can’t explain why I believe you. It must be because I love you.”

“How would you gauge your success so far?” Joyce asked looking toward Arthur as they were sitting in the Thai restaurant, enjoying their meal.

“Hard to say. Most of the scientists have been welcoming and were interested in the information we gave them. All except Ramada have written emails to me. I have no idea why Doctor Ramada contacted the

FBI about us. When he called me, he insinuated subtly that I may have stolen the sodium glass battery technology. Everyone seems quite taken with the battery technology."

"I should say so," Joyce said. "If companies can manufacture sodium batteries from your information, it will sharply reduce battery backup system costs. The fact that these types of batteries can be recharged almost indefinitely is monumental, plus the fact that sodium is prevalent around the world and can be easily sourced." She glanced at Violet, who smiled back nodding. Joyce shifted in her seat before sitting erect and leaning forward. "Violet has told me the truth," she said softly. "I didn't believe her at first, and I have a hard time believing what she told me even now."

Arthur's face went blank as he looked toward Violet.

"I had to tell her, Doc. I couldn't answer her questions. She knew things didn't add up. I had to tell her the truth."

Joyce reached across the table and grasped Arthur's hand. "Don't be mad at Violet. If she hadn't told me the truth, I might have been tempted to turn you in. The information on the memory stick about new technologies is unbelievable and so advanced. I couldn't believe that a private Swedish Institute could develop all those technologies. Plus the climate models are so exact."

"Now what?" Arthur asked, looking solemnly at Joyce.

"I hide you in my trunk, drive you across the border, and then back to Cambridge. You and Violet need to complete your mission. I will do all in my power to help you, and I will work tirelessly to raise awareness on the importance of stopping climate warming when you are gone. I completely understand why you and Violet have made this trip. Of course I will never understand how it was possible."

"I don't know what to say." Arthur took a hurried drink of wine. "Many previous advances in quantum physics and the availability of tremendous electrical energy has made it possible. I'm actually relieved that Violet told you. Trying to maintain our secrecy when you have been helping us so much was difficult for me. I feel as if a weight has been lifted from me."

"It took Violet a long time to convince me. If I didn't have such fond feelings for her, I probably wouldn't have believed her."

Arthur raised his glass. "Here's to Joyce Salmon, a most amazing climate scientist and wonderful person."

"Hear, hear," Violet added before taking a drink and rubbing Joyce's arm.

"You remind me of my wife," Arthur said. "You and she would get along great. She's a renowned climate scientist like yourself."

24- MARCH 31, 2025

"We're at the border," Joyce called out. "Stay silent and still."

Violet reached out in the dark to grasp Arthur's arm. She heard the border agent question Joyce and held her breath. When the car started moving again, Violet exhaled. She hoped that was it, and they were back in the US, home free. Well not home free. They had to travel across the country, and then travel 35 years back to the future. She thought Arthur had taken the news that she had revealed the truth to Joyce well. He was such an understanding man.

She was totally in love with Joyce, the first real love of her life. She had had sexual liaisons with other women back in the future, but none had captured her heart. Why she had to travel 35 years back in time to find someone who she really loved and felt so complete in her presence, she had no idea. What a strange destiny. Unfortunately, she would have to leave her new found love behind. Something she wasn't looking forward to.

She had always loved Arthur like the big brother she never had. Working with him and accompanying him here had been so incredible. She was still young. Surely back in the future she would find someone like Joyce. She had to go back didn't she? If she stayed, the work she had contributed would not exist. No, she had to return, but what if she came back and stayed? She needed to talk to Arthur about it.

Joyce pulled into her driveway and exhaled loudly. "We made it." She laughed. "I was worried the whole way, but to be honest the trip was quite exciting. Quite a change from my staid life." She looked back at Arthur in the back seat. "Let's go inside and relax."

"Wow, this is a great house," Violet exclaimed. "Compact, but feels so spacious. You have done a great job of decorating."

"Thank you, Violet. I'm comfortable here." Joyce smiled for a few seconds at Violet with obvious yearning before turning to Arthur. "I've made up the spare bedroom." With a nod of her head, she led them to the bedroom. "You can put your things in here." She pointed across the hall. "That's my bedroom."

Violet sauntered into Joyce's bedroom and collapsed onto the bed. "This bed feels good." Joyce and Arthur were watching from the doorway. She sat up and laughed. "You guys look much too serious. I think a glass of wine is just what we all need." Violet jumped up and pranced out of the bedroom, hooking her arm in Joyce's and pulling her to the kitchen. "Yes, Doctor Salmon, that's just what we need."

As they were sitting around the low table in the living room drinking wine, there was a knock on the front door. Joyce looked at both and hunched her shoulders. "I don't know who that could be."

"Be careful, we may have been followed," Arthur whispered

Joyce crept to the door to look out the peep hole, then came rushing back. "Two men in suits are at the door," she whispered. "Get your packs. Leave by the back door and climb over the back fence. My neighbors over there are gone for a week. She grabbed a key from the counter. "Here's the key to their house." She herded them toward the bedroom as she picked up their glasses. "I'll come over when the coast is clear. Leave the lights off."

When they had their packs, Arthur and Violet left the house, dashed across the yard, and scrambled over the fence. They went into the neighbor's house and sat down.

"Someone must have been watching Joyce's house," Arthur said. "Jesus, they got here fast. They had to be nearby."

"What in the hell are we going to do now?"

"When Joyce comes, we'll have to figure out a plan of escape. Maybe we can have Joyce meet us somewhere with her car and drive us to a car rental."

"Where are we going?"

"I'd still like to go to Princeton and meet with Oppender. We'll skip Macer. He's already trying to publicize the need to get off fossil fuels as much as he can."

"Joyce could drive us and join us in the meeting," Violet said. "Oppender knows her. Having her along might help."

"I don't know if that's such a good idea. We've compromised her enough already."

When the men left her house, Joyce hurried across her yard, climber over the fence and knocked on the back door of her neighbor's house.

Violet let her in. "Who was it?"

"FBI," Joyce said. "They came in and looked through the house."

"What did they say?" Violet took Joyce's hand.

"They said that they saw some other people enter my house." Joyce frowned. "I told them they were mistaken. When they couldn't find anything to verify that anyone besides me was present, they left."

"Somebody must have been watching your house," Arthur said. "I'm sorry we've gotten you involved, Joyce. Unfortunately, we will still need your help."

"Don't worry. I'll help all I can. I'm ready to do anything you need. Let's go back to my house, and I'll make something to eat. They are probably still watching the house, but the curtains are drawn. I doubt they'll think you came back."

"You may be right, but maybe Violet and I should get away from you as soon as possible. If they find us with you, it could get nasty for you. If you drive us to a car rental place in the morning, we can rent a car and take off. Get away from you so you can have your life back."

"I'm not so sure I want my life back. Helping you has been exciting. Now that I know the truth, I understand completely why you are doing what you are. It is important. Don't worry about me. Come on. If they do come back, you can escape out the back again."

Violet got up and grabbed her backpack. "Come on, Arthur. I need to have a glass of wine. My last one was abandoned down the drain. I'm starving as well." She turned to Joyce. "I'll help you make dinner."

"Very nice spaghetti, Joyce," Arthur said as they were sitting around the dining table, finishing the last of the meal."

"Hey, I helped too."

Arthur laughed. "And I thank you, Violet."

"You think renting a car in Cambridge will be a good idea?" Joyce asked. "The FBI might have a bulletin out about you two." Joyce sat upright and watched Arthur consider her statement. She thought she saw and inkling of agreement. "I could leave my car here to fool them, then rent a car and drive you to Princeton. We could go to the neighbor's early in the morning. I'll call a taxi, have them pick me up at the neighbor's house, and take me to the car rental. Then I'll come back and pick you up. What do you think?"

"Joyce, I hate to get you tangled up with us," Arthur said.

"I think Joyce's idea is a good one," Violet said. "The watchers will think she's still at home." Was she being selfish wanting Joyce along? "It might be risky for you or me to rent the car."

"Okay, I'm out voted," Arthur said. "Let's have any early night. Shall we get up around five and go to the neighbors. When does the car rental place open?"

"Let me check." Joyce retrieved her phone and pulled up the car rental agency. "It opens at 6."

"That's early, but great. It's still fairly dark then. I guess that will work well."

"Excellent," Violet said. "I'll help Joyce tidy up. I think this is a good plan."

When Joyce pulled the rental car in front of the neighbor's house, Arthur and Violet scampered to the car. No one seemed to be around, and Joyce drove off.

"Well done Joyce— excellent get away," Violet said energetically and massaged Joyce's shoulder.

Joyce glanced at Violet. She felt good about helping her and was looking forward to more nights with her. She realized she was putting herself in danger, but didn't think the authorities could do much to her if they caught them. It was a much different scenario for Violet and Arthur. If they were apprehended...well, she'd need to do everything in her power to make sure that didn't come about.

"Thanks, Joyce, you've been such a help," Arthur added. "Can you call Oppender in a while and make an appointment for tomorrow? Mention us as friends. Maybe a luncheon meeting. What do you think?"

"Yes, a luncheon meeting or an afternoon coffee meeting would be better away from the University."

"I like the way you think, Joyce," Arthur replied.

Joyce drove until she came to a rest area and pulled in. Everyone used the restroom. As they gathered around the car, Joyce telephoned Doctor Oppender. "Hello, Doctor Oppender, it's Joyce Salmon. I'm going to be in Princeton tomorrow and was wondering if you had time to meet and have lunch with me and some friends." She smiled at Violet as she listened. "Yes, I know the restaurant. One o'clock would be fine. See you then." She disconnected and winked at Violet. "Okay, we're on." Ever since she accepted that Arthur and Violet were from the future, she was in awe of them. They had risked their lives to save life. She was ready to risk her life in the endeavor as well.

Joyce and Violet slept in one room at the hotel in Princeton and Arthur in another. At 7:00 AM, Violet knocked on Arthur's door. He went to the door and looked out the peep hole to see Violet.

Violet swept into the room as soon as he opened the door, closing the door behind her. "You ready for breakfast, Doc."

"Yeah." Arthur rubbed his head and yawned. "Did you two have a good sleep?"

"Yes, we had a pleasant and relaxing sleep. Most enjoyable." Violet laughed and gently punched Arthur on the arm. "Come on, Doc. I've got a raging appetite. Joyce knows a restaurant we can walk to that serves vegan pancakes and has vegan sausages."

"Okay, let me finish dressing. I'll meet you in the lobby."

As soon as Joyce saw Arthur coming toward her, she stepped to him and gave him a hug. "Good morning, Arthur. Shall we be off? Violet can't wait. She said she's been dreaming of vegan pancakes."

"I don't doubt that. The restaurant sounds delightful. Lead on."

At the restaurant Violet ordered two stacks of pancakes, vegan sausage and vegan bacon. Arthur ordered the same.

"You guys must be hungry," Joyce said.

"This is the first proper vegan breakfast we've been able to get," Violet said with a bright smile. "It's been mostly oatmeal and toast so far. I like a big breakfast."

"You eat like a horse," Joyce said, "and yet you remain as thin as can be. How do you do it?"

"I've always been thin. I don't know why. As you say, I do like to eat."

"She's an enigma," Arthur said.

"That she is." Joyce rubbed Violet's back. "You up for a stroll around the University after we're finished eating?"

"Of course," Violet said. "Nothing like a leisurely stroll after a big meal."

When Doctor Oppender entered the restaurant, he looked over the occupants until he saw Joyce. He waved and maneuvered through the close tables.

Joyce, Arthur, and Violet stood. "Doctor Oppender, thanks for coming," Joyce said. "May I introduce Arthur Brown and Violet Drummer?" Everyone shook hands. "Have a seat, Doctor Oppender. Arthur and Violet are climate scientists from Sweden. They have been traveling around the US meeting with prominent climate scientists. They have some information they developed that I'm sure you will find most interesting. I found the technologies and carbon pricing methods they gave me very enlightening."

"I see."

"Doctor Oppender, here is the memory stick with the information," Arthur said. "At you leisure you can review the information. If you have questions, you can email me. Here is my card."

Oppender studied the card, then focused intently on Arthur. "Doctor Saver telephoned me asking if I had met an Arthur Freeman, a climate scientist from

Sweden. Are you and Doctor Freeman both traveling around meeting climate scientists?"

"This is a little embarrassing," Arthur responded. "I and Doctor Freeman are the same person. We had a misunderstanding with Doctor Ramada in San Diego. Consequently, we thought using a different name might be advisable with Doctor Saver."

Oppender frowned and looked to Joyce. "I don't understand."

Joyce sat erect. "You know how Doctor Ramada is. He's somewhat of a climate warming sceptic and receives funding from the oil giants. He is friends with Saver."

"Plus, he was not very welcoming and insinuated that we may have stolen some of the technologies we detailed in the information we gave him," Violet added. She was glad Joyce hadn't mentioned Ramada reporting them to the FBI.

"Ah, yes, Doctor Ramada can be rather difficult. He is not convinced that the projections of climate warming are accurate. The fossil fuel funding he receives has colored his opinions. I tolerate him but often prefer to keep him at a distance." Oppender turned to Joyce. "What is your interest in this, Doctor Salmon?"

"Oh, Arthur and Violet are friends of mine. I agreed to help them disseminate their information."

"That's great," Oppender said. "I often think I should be more forceful speaking about the terrible dangers of a warming planet. There are a lot more articles now days on the dangers of climate warming in the news, which is heartening, but the fossil fuel companies are employing every means to keep fossil fuels burning. Such as paying scientists like Ramada to promote their misinformation."

Oppender paused as he looked from Violet to Joyce. "Their green washing advertisements seem to be working. The general population are not nearly concerned enough with climate warming as they should be. The corporate lobbyists have pretty much bought off many of the politicians. If we could get a realistic carbon tax, it would make a big difference. I don't think we have to worry much about coal in this country. The market has pretty much taken care of that. Companies are shuttering the old plants and no new coal plants are planned. Coal plants are expensive compared to gas fired turbine plants. We shouldn't be building new natural gas generating stations in the US either. If we had a realistic carbon tax, they would be much more costly than wind and solar. Fossil fuel generating plants need to be phased out. Electricity from solar and wind is cheaper, and, although their manufacturing processes require scarce minerals and lots of energy, they should be the preferred method for energy generation."

"Well said, Doctor Oppender," Violet said. "Another action we are encouraging is for climate scientists like yourself to be more proactive in promoting a clean energy future. Climate peer reviewed papers and articles for mainstream press are all well and good, but to counteract the fossil fuel green washing and conservative legislator's acceptance of bogus science, we scientists need to be more vocal."

"I couldn't agree more. We need to combat the lobbyists and get the people informed on what is really going on."

"That we can all agree on." Joyce surveyed the group. "Shall we order? I'm quite famished." She signaled the waiter.

Violet and Joyce both ordered a seitan Ruben sandwich with fries, Arthur ordered a humus sandwich with a side salad, and Oppender choose a chicken sandwich with fries. They made small talk until the food arrived.

As soon as everyone was served, Violet dug into her sandwich. "Oh, this is delicious. What a great restaurant. Thanks Doctor Oppender for choosing such a great place."

"Yes, it is one of my favorites." He looked from Violet to Arthur. "What's Doctor Saver's interest in you two?" He focused intently on Arthur. "He asked me to call him if Doctor Freeman contacted me."

"Oh, he did," Joyce said. "He's a pain. We're not completely sure why he's getting involved. Saver called me as well wanting to know if Doctor Freeman contacted me. He and Ramada both, I believe, accept fossil fuel money. Consequently, Saver is rather conservative on climate change as well. Ramada and I don't get along well. He's a bit of a chauvinist. I imagine Ramada asked Saver if he knew who the

Swedish scientists were going to see after him. Ramada may have personal and monetary interests in having Arthur and Violet arrested. From what I understand Ramada is involved in a company working on battery technology. Among the information Doctor Brown has provided is a prototype for a glass sodium battery that Ramada thought Arthur stole."

"Stole?"

"I assure you, Doctor Oppender, nothing contained on the memory stick has been stolen," Arthur said. "The technologies were developed by our Institute and are given freely without patents. Nothing is proprietary."

"I'm glad to hear it. I've heard of research on sodium batteries, but not that anyone had been successful enough to produce and market the batteries. I can't wait to review your memory stick. If everything you are presenting is above board, then why is the FBI looking for you?"

Arthur abruptly looked up from his food frowning. "Did Saver say the FBI were looking for us?"

"Yes, he did," Oppender replied. "I'm concerned that if the FBI is looking for you that there is something you are not telling me. I don't want to get crosswise with the FBI."

"I think it is a big misunderstanding," Joyce interjected.

"Why then the avoidance in talking to the FBI?" Oppender asked.

"Who said we were avoiding the FBI?" Violet said. "We are not excited to talk to the FBI, but we've done nothing wrong. We are worried that fossil fuel money is behind the search for us. We don't relish being held and interrogated just because we are promoting more effective action on mitigating climate warming."

"That's understandable," Oppender said.

Violet grabbed Arthur's leg. Arthur looked toward Violet and saw her subtle eye flick toward the front door. Two men in suits were entering.

Arthur immediately stood and turned away from the door as he helped Violet up. "I'm afraid that Violet and I must leave," Arthur said softly. "Please excuse our abrupt departure, Doctor Oppender." He placed his hand on Joyce's shoulder. "Joyce, we'll go out the back and meet you later. Carry on with your meal. Don't look for us. We'll find you later." He and Violet made for the kitchen, slipped through the commotion in the kitchen as the staff prepared the meals, and went out the back door.

25- APRIL 1, 2025

Arthur watched the Princeton hotel from across the street. When he saw no one outside watching or anyone in a car watching, he whistled to Violet. Hearing the whistle, Violet went to a side door of the hotel and entered with her electronic key pass. She went up the stairs to their floor, cracking the door to the hallway. No one was in the hall. She hurried to Joyce's room and entered with her key.

"Damn, you scared me," Joyce said, sitting up in bed, her face stretched. "Did anyone see you?"

"I don't think so. Arthur was watching out in front and gave me the all clear signal."

"Is he coming in?"

"No, he thinks we should take the rental and leave you. You can take the train back." Violet laid down next to Joyce and pulled her into her arms, kissing her gently.

"Is that what you want to do too?" Joyce asked solemnly, her face drawn.

"No, I want you to come with us. I've never cared for anyone like a care for you, Joyce. I'm so totally in love with you."

"Oh, Violet, I love you too. Could you stay? Arthur could drive back to Berkeley on his own. You could live with me."

"I'd love nothing more. However, as I explained earlier if I don't return to 2060 the work I did would disappear with the new time line. I have to go back."

"This time travel is complicated. Could I go to the future with you?"

"Yes, you could, but you are more valuable to life if you stay and continue to get the world to recognize the dangers of climate warming and foster the changes that will mitigate the future warming that is on track to destroy most of the life on this planet."

"I'm only one person."

"You are a renowned and respected climate scientist. Your advocacy is invaluable." She kissed Joyce again. "I haven't talked to Arthur about this, but, if I could get Arthur to send me back after we return, then I could live here in the past and nothing prior to me coming back would be erased." She smiled brightly. "I could help you publicize the importance of transitioning from fossil fuel and work to avoid the problems that stopped societies from making the changes necessary to stop a runaway climate catastrophe."

"Would you do this?" Joyce stretched her face, opening her eyes wide. "What about your life in 2060— your work, your friends?"

"I would miss my friends. The Bridge will be dismantled so that it cannot be reestablished. There are detrimental forces in 2060 just like here in 2025 that could use the Bridge for perverse means. If Arthur agrees to send me back, I'll do it in a heartbeat.

I never felt a love like yours. I want to stay with you, Joyce."

Joyce grabbed Violet to her. "Oh Violet, that sounds so wonderful. Could it really happen?"

"Yes, I think so." Violet pulled away. "We'll see. For now we need to focus on our escape. What happened after we left the restaurant?"

"The FBI men, Agent Toliver and Agent Masset, took me to their office and questioned me. They wanted to know how I knew you and Arthur. I told them we were travelling together because I knew Doctor Oppender and wanted to introduce him to you. They wanted to know what I knew about you and the information you were offering. I told them that I first met you when you came to see me in Cambridge, and we discussed climate models, new technologies and carbon pricing methods. They wanted to know where you had gone to. They asked if I had been given a memory stick. I said I hadn't. I told them you had other travel plans and were on your way to meet other scientists."

"Sorry you were subjected to the third degree," Violet said. "Sounds like you acquitted yourself well, and they won't be looking for us in Princeton."

"It was intimidating, but I wasn't scared. Well maybe a little. They insinuated that I tried to give the FBI the slip. I denied it. I said my car was acting funny, and I rented a car and left early to make sure we arrived to meet Doctor Oppender on time."

"Did they mention that they saw us leaving when they entered the restaurant?"

"No, they had their backs to you, talking to the receptionist while you left."

"Did they take Oppender away too?"

"No, he left and went back to his office."

"I bet he told Saver about our planned meeting."

"Why would he do that?"

"Maybe Saver told Oppender that if he aided us he could be charged with assisting criminals," Violet said. "They could have questioned Oppender after interrogating you."

"So what do we do now?" Joyce asked

"Arthur and I need to be back to Berkeley before April 12th to get ready to be picked up by the Einstein-Rosen Bridge. You can return to Cambridge, or, if I can convince Arthur that it's okay for you to come with us, you can come and be there when I return from the future."

"Sounds like a fascinating adventure. What about the FBI?"

"We've given them the slip for now, but we still need to remain alert and vigilant. As I blurted out days ago, Arthur and I met with a friend of his father in Sweden, Lucas Nilsson, who Arthur met earlier this year in Berkeley when he was eight. We met him in the Stockholm train station. He wanted to be in a big public space in case it was a trap. Arthur and I convinced him we had actually time travelled from

2060. He believed us after some discussion and showing him Arthur's laptop from 2060. Can you believe it?"

"I can. You and Arthur can be very convincing."

"Lucas is a famous hacker. Arthur got him to hack Stockholm birth records and add Arthur and me to births there. So now we are actually legitimate Swedes."

"That is amazing."

"If I come back from 2060, I won't have to worry about being charged with entering the country illegally. I can even apply for permanent residency and eventually US citizenship."

"How wonderful. You know, the FBI said I should contact them if I see you again."

"They can't do anything to you. We haven't been charged with a crime, and I don't see how they can charge us with a serious crime even if they catch us other than using forged documents. But it will be best if they don't catch us." Violet held Joyce by the shoulders. "So what will it be? Back to Cambridge alone or with us to California?"

"I choose California."

"Great. Pack up and go down to the side door to the parking lot. I'll pull the car near the door and you can run out. Where are the keys to the car?"

"What about Arthur? He doesn't want me to come."

"He didn't want you to come for your own safety. Don't worry I'll convince him it's okay if you come."

Violet pulled the car near the side hotel door. Joyce ran out and jumped in the back seat.

"I hope you realize you may be putting yourself in danger," Arthur said.

"I know, and I don't care. They can't do much to me."

"Okay, I'm glad you're coming with us," Arthur said. "We need to make some distance tonight and then tomorrow we need to rent a different car."

"Good idea," Joyce said. "Has Violet told you about our plan?"

"I haven't." Violet preceded to tell Arthur about her desire to come back and remain in the past to help Joyce publicize the need to transition to clean energy.

"This is a big decision, Violet," Arthur said with solemnity. "I think you both should consider the ramifications. Once you're back in 2025, there's no coming back to the future. You'll be stuck permanently in 2025 and the subsequent years. When 2060 rolls around, you'll be an old lady."

"Yes, I understand completely."

"Okay, I will agree to send you back, Violet. That is, after we return to 2060, you still want to return. It's a serious and lasting decision. In any case, we need to keep the FBI at bay, or we both may be stuck permanently here in 2025."

"Have you heard about Jeff Grossman at UCLA?" Joyce asked to change the subject.

"No," Arthur replied.

"He's an up and coming climate scientist that would be good to talk to," Joyce said.

"I'm not sure we should expose ourselves any more than necessary. Violet and I have to— at all costs— return to the future. It is absolutely critical and essential."

"Let's stop here and rent another vehicle," Arthur said. They had driven all night with all three taking turns driving. Arthur had been nervous at first driving, but he soon remastered the skills. "Louisville, Kentucky."

Violet woke up in the back seat. "Louisville?" She rubbed her eyes. "What time is it?"

"Almost nine," Joyce said. "Did you sleep well?"

"I forgot how tiring driving at night is. I slept like a log."

"It sounded like someone was sawing that log," Joyce said.

"I don't snore," Violet snapped.

"You do when you're sleeping on your back," Arthur added.

"Damn, you learn something new every day," Violet responded, laughing.

Joyce directed Arthur to a car rental agency using her phone.

"Violet, why don't you rent the car with your Violet Remy ID? Nobody, should be looking for her."

"Okay... I could sure use a cup of coffee."

"They might have some inside," Joyce said.

"We'll park across the street and follow you in the rental," Arthur said. "After say a quarter mile, pull over and we'll abandon this car."

"Gotcha, Doc."

"If there's any trouble, come running out, and we'll take off."

"Okay."

After fifteen minutes, Violet drove out of the rental agency and Arthur followed. When Violet pulled to the curb, Arthur and Joyce joined her. Violet drove off.

"I'm so hungry. I don't know why we came to Kentucky. This is Republican territory. We'll play hell finding some vegan food."

"This is a fairly large city," Joyce said. "I have an app on my phone for vegetarian and vegan restaurants. I bet I can find a place with vegan food."

"Good, find us a place nearby. I'm ready to faint I'm so hungry."

"After you find a restaurant, you need to turn off your phone and remove the chip," Arthur said. "They've probably been tracking you by your phone. I didn't say anything sooner because they were undoubtedly tracking us by the car rental. They'll know we came to Louisville, but from here on after, we won't be trackable."

"I don't know how to remove the chip," Joyce said.

"After you find the restaurant give the phone to me," Violet said. "I'll disable it."

"That wasn't too bad," Violet said when they were back on the road. "A plant based burger and fries is not my usual breakfast fare, but it hit the spot."

"My oatmeal was pretty good," Joyce said. "I liked that they had almond milk. The coffee was good."

"Yeah, it was good coffee" Violet said. "I could hardly drink that weak stuff they had at the rental place." She glanced in the rearview mirror to make sure Arthur was still awake. "It's March 29th, Doc. We've got some time to kill before our rendezvous, April 12th. What shall we do?"

"I thought we'd do some sightseeing. I thought we'd spend a day in St. Louis. Maybe go up in the Arch. I've always wanted to do so, but never had the opportunity."

"That sounds cool," Violet said. "Have you seen the Arch, Joyce?"

"Only from a distance when I went there for a conference."

26- APRIL 3, 2025

"Wow, that was cool," Violet said as they strolled from the Arch Park down to the Mississippi River. "It was amazing how they connected the two pieces of the Arch so precisely."

"I felt a little claustrophobic in that elevator," Joyce said. "I find this wig rather uncomfortable. You think these disguises are necessary?"

"Hey, you look good with long black hair," Violet said. She was so happy that Joyce had agreed to come along. She felt so lucky. If she hadn't taken the job with Arthur, she would have never met Joyce. She didn't believe in fate, but it sure seemed strange what was happening. Something she could have never predicted. Life was so full of amazing interactions. The future of life on earth would be in her and Joyce's hands upon her return. Would they be up to the challenge?

"I don't know, Joyce, if it's necessary," Arthur said. "I don't like my wig either— makes me look absurd. I imagine the FBI has pictures of us at every FBI office, and police department. Better safe than sorry."

"What do you guys think about a paddle-wheel boat cruise tonight?" Violet asked. She knew Arthur was right. They needed to take every precaution, but they still needed to have fun. "I loved Mark Twain's stories about life on the Mississippi."

"Doesn't sound that appealing to me," Arthur said.

"Doc, don't be such a stick in the mud." Violet grabbed him from behind, laughing.

Joyce joined in the laughter. "Yeah, Doc."

"Don't you start, Joyce." Arthur hung his head. "Okay, I'm out voted again. You ladies are ganging up on me."

"You should be so lucky," Violet said. "Just kidding. Let's find an East Indian restaurant. I fancy a curry."

"Mmm, that sounds appealing." Joyce took Violet's hand.

The clouds were thickening as they drifted across the expanse of the vast, muddy Mississippi, occasionally hiding the sun briefly. The three strolled back to the main street and called a taxi on their prepaid phone to take them to the Indian restaurant.

"The two nights in St. Louis were fun," Violet said as they drove west out of the city. "I liked the paddle wheel boat dinner cruise, but mostly I liked visiting the Cahokia Mounds across the river. I hadn't heard about the ancient Native American civilization there. Must have been quite a site in its heyday." She looked back at Joyce in the back seat as Arthur drove. "Where to next?"

"You ladies can pick." Arthur said, looking at Joyce in the rearview mirror.

"I've always wanted to go to Santa Fe, New Mexico," Joyce said. "I've never really taken a vacation in the US. I've been so wrapped up in my work for so many years. I've only taken a few short vacations somewhere warm late fall or early spring— the Caribbean or Hawaii. The winters in Cambridge can get you down although they're not nearly as bad as they used to be with climate warming. I've been to quite a few of the large cities in the US on conferences. It's interesting and refreshing to see the countryside driving across this vast country."

"Yeah, Santa Fe sounds like an interesting destination," Arthur said. "My wife visited there on a conference and was enchanted by the city. We should stop somewhere in between. I don't want to sleep in the car again, and we've got plenty of time. You guys take a look at the map and tell me the way to go."

Violet and Joyce conferred. Joyce suggested Oklahoma City. Violet initially didn't like the destination. "It's the largest cattle shipping center in the US, and oil and gas are its biggest industries."

"It's about half way between St Louis and Albuquerque," Joyce said. "It's got a botanical garden in the center of the city. It's the largest city in Oklahoma. It's bound to have restaurants with vegan options."

"Sounds okay to me," Arthur said.

"All right then, it's about 500 miles," Violet announced. "Nothing much in between. I can practice my Okie accent when I get there."

Joyce laughed. "You are a joy to be with, Violet."

"See, I told you you'd enjoy Oklahoma City." Joyce pushed Violet as they strolled around the Myriad Botanical Gardens. "The Osteology Museum was fascinating."

"Who would have thought there'd be bones from around the world here in Oklahoma City?" Violet said. "Pretty amazing." She skipped ahead to the fountain in the lake as the sun slipped behind a cloud. When Joyce caught up, Violet put her arm around her. "I wasn't too high on the Cowboy Museum. Although their collection of native art was great. The trail of tears and other forced migrations to the Oklahoma Indian territory were horrible. Reading about it made me sick. Europeans sure thought they were the top of the human race and had no qualms about destroying the native population of this country."

"It was one of the largest genocides in history," Joyce said. "More so then the Nazi genocide of Jews and ethnic minorities. It was estimated before the European invasion there were 10 million Native Americans, and by 1900 there were three hundred thousand left. It boggles my mind to think about it."

"No shit," Violet added.

"If we had followed their wisdom about caring for the land, we wouldn't be headed to the climate catastrophe that we are," Arthur said.

"Wow, this is a great little city," Violet announced as they walked across the Santa Fe Plaza, surveying the few people walking or sitting on the benches, enjoying the warm sun, listening to the birds in the many trees. "I love the architecture. It seems to blend in with the land. The Native American jewelry the Natives were selling in front of the museum was beautiful. This is so great—the end of the Santa Fe Trail. Good choice, Joyce. Hey it rhymes—choice, Joyce."

Joyce laughed and shook her head. "Must have been quite an endeavor to work with this vixen," Joyce said to Arthur as she gave Violet a gentle shove.

"You have no idea," Arthur responded. "How about a drink. We could sit on the balcony up there and enjoy the Plaza for a time before we hit the road. The New Mexican food we had at the Shed was delicious. I like the chili here. Way different then the chili in California. Reminded me of Rose's chili enchiladas. Too bad they didn't have any vegan cheese." His talk of Rose made him homesick.

He wondered how Rose would take Violet's determination to return to Joyce. He understood why Violet wanted to return. Joyce was an amazing person and phenomenal climate scientist. Without her help, they may have ended up stranded in 2025. The repercussions of not returning would have been monumental. They weren't out of the woods yet though. They were down to their last fake identities. If somehow the FBI learned of their switched identify and detected the car they rented .... Well, they'd made it this far with no problem— another 1200 or so miles to go.

"My spinach enchilada would have been so much better with some vegan cheese for sure," Violet said.

As Arthur started toward the upstairs restaurant and bar on the corner, he caught a glimpse of a man he thought he had seen across the street when they had entered the Shed restaurant. "I'm not sure," Arthur said softly, pulling Violet and Joyce by the shoulders closer to him, "but there's a man walking behind us on the Plaza, who was across the street when we entered the restaurant. Don't turn around. Let's keep walking to the bar."

They went up the stairs and got a table on the balcony overlooking the Plaza. They all ordered margaritas. "Is that him in the tan sport coat?" Violet asked.

"Yes," Arthur answered. "He's glanced up at us, but is trying to act nonchalant. Now he's going into the store across the street."

"How could they have known we're here?" Joyce asked.

"I don't know." Arthur took a drink of his margarita before shaking his head. "Maybe it's nothing although the hairs on the back of my neck are bristling.”

“It makes no sense that anyone has caught up to us,” Violet said. “Nobody has been following us. There was nobody in Oklahoma City.”

“It could be the car we rented in Louisville,” Arthur suggested. “Somehow they may have made the connection with the car Joyce rented and left in Louisville and the one Violet rented. Using the Violet Remy identity could have allowed them to make the connection. It was probably not the best idea, but Violet and I have only one identity each that we haven’t used.”

“Shit, maybe so,” Violet said. “He can still see us from the shop window. He’ll know when we leave.”

“Yes he will.” Arthur looked around and leaned over the table. “Let’s not panic. Act normal and let’s enjoy our drinks. Violet, why don’t you leave and bring the car around.”

“Jesus, I haven’t finished my margarita.”

“I meant after you finished your drink.”

“I know Doc. I’m just pulling your leg.” Violet punched Arthur’s shoulder. “Let’s not start freaking out. When I leave, tan sport coat or a possible partner is going to follow me.”

“You’ll have a head start. Tan sport coat may stay put since we’ll remain on the balcony.” Arthur motioned to the waiter and paid the bill. “When we see the car, we’ll rush down and jump in. We’ll have to change cars at a rental agency soon, but we need to make some distance first."

"I should have used the Bridget Larson identity in Louisville." Violet took a large drink of her margarita. "I bet tan sport coat is not alone."

"I would imagine you're right." Arthur said. "He'll have a partner. I don't have any idea who the partner could be, but when you leave, we'll probably find out if there are any partners. You'll need to be quick."

"Speed is my middle name." Violet downed the rest of her margarita. "Okay, here I go."

When Violet left the building, a man on a park bench in a gray jacket rose quickly and started after Violet. "There's the partner," Joyce said.

"Yeah."

"What if the he stops Violet?"

"He'll not catch up to her."

Joyce and Arthur sat patiently nursing their drinks until they saw the car. "Let's go." He helped Joyce up and they hurried down the stairs, crossed the road, and jumped into the car. They saw the man in the tan sport coat come out of the shop, and the man, who had followed Violet, join him. As Violet sped away, both men took off at a run. The one in the tan sport coat was talking into his cellphone as he ran.

"Moab, I like the sound of it," Joyce announced as they wound down the road from the interstate. "It was great going over the mountains in Colorado. Long drive.” She placed her hand on Violet’s shoulder. “Gosh, Violet, you did most of the driving.”

“I’m not much for sitting still in a car. Driving keeps me engaged. I like this car we got in Grand Junction better than the one in Farmington. I’m so happy we haven’t been stopped by the police”

“The car changes have seemed to work,” Joyce said.

“Let’s hope,” Arthur said. “It was fortunate that I and Violet had the Samuel Johnson and Bridget Larson identities left. Changing vehicles in Farmington and again in Grand Junction will hopefully keep the authorities from tracking the vehicle rentals. We’ve got a couple of hours or so before sunset,” Arthur said. “Let’s drive through Arches Park. I made a hotel reservation so we don’t have to worry about the time. We need to relax and recharge tonight.”

“Sounds good, Doc,” Violet said.

Violet pulled the car into the Arches National Park and drove to the first formation parking area, and they all disembarked and started down the trail.

“It feels so good to walk,” Joyce said. “These red sandstone formation are amazing. The rich red and copper colors in this light are beautiful.”

“Wow, this is amazing, but there aren’t any arches,” Violet said.

“The arches are further along,” Arthur said. “You’ll see them, Violet. Don’t worry.”

"Great, I wonder why I never came out here before," Violet said. "How many times have you been here, Doc?"

"This is my second visit."

They completed the trail, got back into the car, and carried on deeper into the park. When they came upon the area with many arches, Violet parked the car and jumped out. "Look at that. That's incredible. I love it. Come on let's get closer."

Joyce laughed as she hurried to catch up with Violet. "Violet hold on, let me catch my breath."

Violet stopped and hugged Joyce as soon as Joyce was near. "Oh, I'm having so much fun."

They visited the many formations and arches in the park until the sun began to set. They sat down in the mouth of an arch to watch the many gradations of color as the sun disappeared.

"Absolutely beautiful," Violet said, breaking the silence as they watched in awe. "Okay, hotel and food are in order. Thanks on coming this way, Arthur. You're a great tour guide."

"What a vista," Violet said as they stared out from the Canyonlands National Park Grand View Point Overlook, gazing down at the confluence of the Green and Colorado Rivers and the many canyons and myriad colors. She grabbed Joyce around the waist.

"This view is sublime." She punched Arthur gently. "Doc, what say you?"

"Yes, Violet, the view is unworldly," Arthur responded. "How about a stroll along the trail. Work off some of that breakfast."

"I was thinking the same thing," Joyce said.

They walked along the rim of the plateau for a time before returning to the car and driving to many other points of interests and short walks. Then thy drove out of the park the way they came in.

They caught interstate 70 and headed west. "It's about 125 miles to Salina," Arthur said. "We should probably stop in Green River for lunch." Arthur turned to look at Violet. "Hopefully we can find a restaurant with something we can eat."

In Green River they pulled into a Taco restaurant. They were able to get bean and vegetable tacos and were soon back on the road.

"Are we going to Salt Lake?" Violet asked.

"We could or we could cut over to Nevada, pass by Grand Basin on US 50 toward Reno. The road to the summit will be closed, but we'll be able to see it from a distance. There will be a lot less traffic. I think we've given the authorities the slip, or otherwise they would have tried to nab us in Moab. It's probably wiser to stay off the interstates as much as possible. We'll still be able to go to Lake Tahoe, which is beautiful. Have you seen Lake Tahoe, Violet?"

"Yes, I have. It's beautiful as you say and so big."

"As an alternative we could cut down on US 6 toward Yosemite. The Tioga pass road will be closed so we can't visit Yosemite, but there is Mono Lake, which is fascinating."

"It's April 9th," Joyce said. "Shouldn't we be back in Berkeley by the 11th?"

"Yes or the 12th," Arthur answered. "The only thing we need to do in Berkeley is pick up our capsules from storage and go to the laboratory around 11:00 PM. If we go toward Yosemite, we can spend tonight in Ely. Then drive to Lee Vining, spend the night there, visit Mono Lake in the morning, and then drive up to cross over the Sierra Mountains on 50, and then on to Berkeley, which would put us there on the 5th. The road across Nevada will be sparsely travelled."

"Good idea Doc," Violet said. "I think taking as many back roads as possible is advisable. They may have figured out we rented other cars."

"Let's hope not," Joyce said and leaned forward and put her arms on Violet's shoulders.

27- APRIL 10, 2025

Violet laid back fully in the sand and let out a prolonged breath in the cool morning air. "Well, Doc, we made it across the US so far without being caught. The car changes have seemed to work." She pushed herself up on her elbow. "What do you think of the Mono Lake, Joyce? Aren't these tufa limestone formations something else?"

"Spectacular," Joyce said. "Unusual that the lake is fed from underground springs with no inlet. It's saltier than the Salt Lake. I love that we came here after Lee Vining. We drove right by last night." She grabbed her knees and looked over at Arthur. "You think the authorities could be waiting for us in Berkeley?"

"Perhaps... I did use my real name at the Berkeley hotel. We didn't visit any scientists in the Bay Area though. Our first visit was to Ramada in San Diego. Still we need to be on the lookout for any suspicious people or cars. We've got about 300 miles to go. We'll need to use a different hotel in Berkeley. Violet can book the hotel with her Bridget Larson identity."

"I've got a feeling we've made it," Violet announced. "I couldn't believe how unpopulated the stretch from Ely to here was. I think we only saw four vehicles on the road the whole way. The landscape was beautiful especially the multiple mountain ranges. Who would have thought?"

"Yeah it was a lovely drive," Joyce added. "What the hell do you think the people in Tonopah do? It's in the middle of nowhere."

"Commerce center I suppose," Arthur said

"I'm feeling so good," Violet said as she rose up, stretching. "Let's boogie. Breakfast in Lee Vining was quite delicious. I'm fueled up and ready. We should arrive in Berkeley late afternoon." She extended her arm to Joyce and pulled her up. "We'll have a day to relax in Berkeley, and then Arthur and I will be off back to 2060. I can't wait."

"So, Arthur, you expect to send Violet back in two weeks, April 24th at 11:00 PM. Is there anything I need to do other than wait in the hotel for her?"

"Not really. The trip back to the future is much more arduous than the trip out. It takes an extreme toll on the body. I ended up in the hospital in a coma for three days after my return from 1990 to 2050. I don't know if the number of years transversed has an effect. We'll be coming through 35 years. Whereas last time, I came through 60 years. I'm thinking that the amount of years has an effect, but we don't know. Perhaps repeated travel affects the body as well. The soonest I think Violet would be ready to travel again is two weeks. It might be as much as three weeks or more. She's a fit lass, and I expect once out of the return coma, she'll bounce back quickly, but there are no guarantees. You sure you want to hang around Berkeley until she returns?"

"Yes, I want to be there when she returns," Joyce said. "I have friends in the area I can visit if she needs more time before travelling again. I'll be at the hotel on the return dates. I still can hardly believe you both came from the future. How in the world did you ever discover your Einstein-Rosen Bridge?"

"I've been working on trying to establish such a Bridge for many years. I never imagined that I could send anything back to the past, nor bring it back. I didn't think a life form would be able to withstand the enormous forces of the Bridge. Without the advent of the fusion power station in Oakland, it would not have been possible. The amount of electrical energy required in stupendous. Plus, what Violet added was essential for the Project. Her ability to write the code for the software to control the Bridge was brilliant. I could not have done this without her."

"Thanks, Doc." Violet laughed. "I just followed the Meister's lead and direction. The Doc is one unbelievable genius."

"Violet exaggerates as I'm sure you've noticed."

"In this case, I suspect she's not exaggerating," Joyce said, patting Arthur on the back. "I think you are a genius too. I salute you for caring about life on this planet, and I assure you Violet and I will do everything within our power to get societies to wake up and stop polluting our planet. We will continue to disseminate the new technologies you have brought me, and we will organize demonstrations to publicize the need for change and get other scientists to join us. With Violet at my side, I believe we can accomplish much." She leaned over and gave Violet a kiss. "It's getting late. Shall we head off?"

Violet bounded toward the car. "And away we go."

Arthur gave Joyce a hug at the Berkeley hotel. "It's been a pleasure and honor knowing you, Joyce. Take care of Violet when she returns. She will need a few days to recover."

"Yes, I will, Arthur. Thanks so much for including me and agreeing to send Violet back to me. I will miss you, Doc."

"And I you. Okay, you ready, Violet?"

"Ready and willing, Doc." Violet grabbed Joyce. "I'll be back. Don't worry. See you in two weeks." She hugged Joyce tightly and then spun around, hooking her arm in Arthur's. "Mr. Wizard, away we go." They left the room, Violet glancing back at the sober Joyce with a wink and blown kiss.

They went to the storage locker and retrieved their equipment and walked to the Physics Building. After descending to the basement, they stopped outside the door to the laboratory. The light inside the lab was on. "Doc, there's somebody inside. What the hell are we going to do now?"

"Damn... here take the capsules and go hide in the bathroom down the hall. I'll go see what going on in the lab. We've got an hour. Let's not panic."

Arthur entered the laboratory and saw a lone person sitting at a desk.

"Hello," the man called. "Can I help you?"

"Hi, I was just looking around. I'm hoping to join the faculty here. I saw the light and thought I'd have a look."

"Normally this laboratory would be closed up at this hour. Isn't this a strange hour to be looking around?"

"I'm a night owl and don't go to bed until the wee hours. I enjoy strolling around late at night."

"You'll have to leave. I'm just finishing up myself. I'm Doctor Frasier, Physics Department Head. Who are you?"

"My name is Doctor Franklin. I've been at the Swedish Technological Institute for many years. Well, thanks for letting me see the laboratory. I'll be off. Good night." Arthur left the laboratory, hurried down the hall, and entered the bathroom.

"What are we going to do?" Violet said as soon as Arthur entered. "Should we bail and come back next week?"

"Shh," Arthur whispered. "The man said he was just finishing up." Arthur grabbed Violet's arm. "We'll wait awhile and see if he leaves."

After thirty-five minutes Violet whispered, "This is cutting it close, Doc. Should I go check if he's gone?"

"Let's wait another five minutes." He reached out after the interval and patted Violet's shoulder. "Okay go check."

Violet quietly left the bathroom and crept down the hall. The laboratory was dark and the door was locked. She rushed back to Arthur. "All clear. Let's boogie, Doc."

They took their capsules to the laboratory door. Arthur jimmied the door, and they entered the dark laboratory, shinning their flashlights. They went to the small crosses still on the floor. "I was worried after all this time that the marks might have been erased," Arthur said. "Not that we really need them, but it's good to be in the exact spot of arrival for retrieval, I think. Okay let's don our suits and get into the capsules. You still have oxygen?"

"Yep, Doc, I'm good to go."

They pulled on their helmets after they had their suits on, turned on the oxygen, and slipped into the capsules.

"Hope we have a good journey back," Violet said. "See you in 2060."

Simon, Rose, Diane, Billy and Harold were present in the laboratory to witness the retrieval. Rose was so anxious that she had trouble breathing.

"Relax, Rose," Diane said. "You look like you're ready to pass out."

"We've done this before, Rose, as you've seen," Simon said. "Everything should go as planned if they have made it back to the rendezvous point."

"What if they didn't make it back?"

"Then we won't retrieve them tonight. We have two other set dates they can make." He approached Rose and rubbed her back. "We'll bring them back."

"What if you don't?"

"Don't even think about that. They're enterprising people. They'll make one of the rendezvous times."

Rose touched Simon's shoulder and let out a quick breath. "Okay Simon, I believe you." She wished that she had his confidence. Her whole life was on the line. If they didn't retrieve Arthur and Violet, her life would be essentially over. She would carry on for her children, but she would be hollowed out. She told herself to be more positive like Simon. Yes, Arthur and Violet would appear. They will appear. They had to appear.

Simon told Billy and Harold to take their positions. He started the sequence as soon as the helium was circulating. As the noise of the surging helium filled the room, Simon began typing on his terminal. He wished Violet was here, but reasoned he had done this several times before and knew what he was doing.

"Okay power ramping up." He turned and looked back at Diane and Rose. "Everything is looking good."

Simon announced the stages in turn and felt all was going well. The sweat was dripping from his brow. "Stage four stabilizing," he announced. "Bridge formation beginning." He concentrated on the parameters. "Bridge confirmed. Retrieval in progress." He suddenly stood and shouted, "They're here. Thank god." He slumped back in his seat, exhaling loudly. He was greatly relieved that he had successfully controlled the Bridge. He turned to Rose, smiling and nodding. "They're here. They've made it back." He turned back to his terminal. "Shutting down." After twenty minutes, he said, "Down to 40°. Billy, open the hatch."

"They're inside," Billy shouted as he entered the enclosure. Simon rushed to the enclosure as well as Harold and Rose. They carried the capsules to the break room and opened the hatches.

Rose felt for a pulse on Arthur while Simon felt for a pulse on Violet. "Arthur's alive."

"So's Violet," Simon said. "Gently remove their helmets and let's extract them carefully from the capsule. Have you got the adrenalin syringe, Rose?"

"Yes, I'm ready." As soon as they were out of the capsules, Rose announced, "I'm cutting the suit. I've found a vein. Injecting now." She stared down at Arthur momentarily, before kissing him. She put a finger to his neck. "Pulse is rising."

"Same here. Let's carry them out to Diane's car," Simon said.

Rose was sitting in her bedroom holding Arthur's hand. They had set up two hospital beds in the bedroom. Both Arthur and Violet were connected to drip lines of saline and glucose.

Diane was sitting next to Violet's bed. "It's been two days and no movement. You think they're okay."

"Arthur was in a coma three days last time," Rose said, her face flush. "I hope they'll come out of the coma soon, but who can say. Traveling twice might be more detrimental. All we can do is wait and hope." Rose squeezed Arthur's hand and brought it to her lips.

Violet did not know where she was and whether what she was seeing and experiencing was real or not. Maybe she was dead and witnessing the horrors of the Bardo. The monsters and the crushing pain were horrendous. Sure feels real, she thought. She had brought this on herself. She would never see Joyce again. Then she saw a faint light in the distance. She instinctively knew she needed to go toward it, but she could not move. The crushing pain was too great... unbearable.

Suddenly, Violet opened her eyes and screamed as her body jerked into a rigid plank.

"Jesus!" Diane shouted. "What should we do, Rose."

Rose hurried to Violet's bedside and tried to hold Violet as Violet started shaking violently.

"It's okay, Violet. You're back. You made it. Relax... relax. Violet, it's Rose. Violet...."

Diane had taken hold of Violet as well and tried to keep hold of her to ease the violent shaking.

"No... no," Violet shouted. "Please make it stop."

"Violet, I am here. Violet, it's Rose. You're okay."

Slowly Violet stopped shaking and tried to focus on the beautiful face before her. She knew that face and voice. It's Rose. Did Rose die? She looked to her left. There was the dark, smiling face of Diane, her curly hair like an entity unto itself. She took a deep breath and felt the memory of intense pain dissipate. She was back. She had made it. She was alive... alive.

"Rose... oh Rose, I'm so happy to see you. My god, I've never felt so much pain and misery in my life." She inhaled deeply several times and began to relax. "What a journey... Rose... Rose, what about Arthur?"

"He's still in a coma," Rose said. "He's breathing a lot shallower than last time. I'm very worried."

"Where is he?"

"He's to your left, about six feet away. We are in my bedroom. Arthur felt that he could not go into the hospital again. He believed it was important to not have another hospital stay on his record. We brought you both here to recover.”

“How long have I been out, or in a coma, or whatever?”

“Two days.”

“Jesus, I thought for sure I was dead and wandering in the Bardo. The visions and the pain.... I can’t begin to tell you. Oh thank you, Rose. I feel so exhausted. I need to sleep. Thank you... thank you....” Violet closed her eyes and slowly drifted to sleep as her breathing slowed.

“My god, that nearly scared me to death,” Diane said. “Is that what Arthur did when he woke up last time?”

“Pretty much. After witnessing his awakening last time, I was very surprised that he would allow himself to go through the harrowing experience again.”

“Man, you couldn’t get me to time travel,” Diane announced as she followed Rose back to Arthur’s bed. “He’s much paler than Violet was. You think we should take him to the hospital?”

“I don’t know. He made me promise that no matter what I wouldn’t take to the hospital. Please call Simon and ask him to leave work early. I need his opinion.”

As soon as Simon entered the bedroom, Diane rushed to him and hugged him tightly. “Violet came out of the coma and is sleeping. Arthur is still in a coma and his breathing is very shallow. Have a look."

Simon walked to Arthur's bed and checked his pulse. He frowned and looked at Rose.

Rose came over to stand next to Simon. "What do you think?"

"His pulse is weak, but steady. His color is not too bad. No fever." He exhaled sharply. "Eeah, I'd say he's … how should I put this… he's still acceptable for a person in a coma. I know he'd be irate if we took him to the hospital. Plus, Muncher has been giving me the third degree ever since Arthur's and Violet's absence. He keeps saying he can't believe Arthur let both of them take vacation at the same time. I caught him the other day in early trying to access my computer terminal. I sure felt like killing the asshole, and I'm a pacifist."

"I can't let Arthur die, Simon. I need him. How would I live without him?"

Simon hugged Rose. "I know, Rose. He's not dying yet. Last time he was in was in a coma for three days."

"Violet came out of her coma."

"I know… I know. Arthur's older and this is his second trip. Who knows what the additional trauma of a second trip is."

"Thanks for coming, Simon." She hugged him. "I feel better now." Rose pulled him to Violet's bed. "Look at her. Sleeping like a baby. She looks so calm. She's so beautiful, isn't she?"

"No doubt there," Simon replied.

"Watch it, Mister," Diane said and laughed.

Violet at Diane's raucous laughter opened her eyes. "Simon, you're here. It's so good to see your face." Her eyes flutter, and she was asleep again.

"That was weird," Diane said.

"I always said, your laughter could wake the dead." Simon looked at Diane with a devious smile.

"Now, now children," Rose said. "Let's play nice."

Diane frowned. "Yeah, Satchmo, take it easy on me."

Simon rushed to Diane and swept her up in his arms. "You know I'm only joshin', Honey. I love your laugh." He kissed her. "I love everything about you."

"Well, thank you."

Violet was sitting up in bed with a vacant look as she watched Rose carry in a tray of food. "Oh, Rose, I don't think I can eat anything yet."

"You need to build up your strength."

"Yeah, I know. Set it down, maybe later," Violet looked over at Arthur. "No movement yet?"

"No, but he's breathing a little deeper."

"I tell you, Rose, coming back in is 100 times worse than going. The excruciating pain is unbelievable. I'm glad I'll only be going one way next time."

"One way?" Rose stared at Violet. She suspected Violet was still a little disoriented. "Just rest, Violet. Eat something later." Rose patted Violets arm and went to Arthur to caress his face with a warm wash cloth.

Come on Arthur, come back...come back. It's been four days. From what she could tell their trip had resulted in maybe a ten year reduction in greenhouse gases. A significant help but still not enough to stop the catastrophe ahead. The additional weeks and additional contacts hadn't helped that much. Violet was gaining strength with each hour. Why was Arthur lagging? Oh Arthur, you can do this. I love you... I love you so much. She bent and kissed him. As she straightened, she saw his eye lids flutter.

Suddenly, Arthur stiffened and expelled a prolonged moan. His eyes opened wide, and he yelled as he body went into a spasm. Rose struggled to hold him. "I'm here, Arthur. It's Rose. You're home... your home."

Arthur stopped struggling after a few minutes and went limp, staring at Rose, blinking, and wetting his lips. "Water please." Rose held his head and gave him a drink of water. "What day is it? Where am I?"

"Thursday, April 16th. You're home in our bedroom"

He seemed to relax a little. "How's Violet?"

"I'm good, Doc," Violet said. "Welcome back."

Arthur turned with a grimace and looked at Violet. He sighed and turned back to gaze at Rose. "Oh, Rose, you look so wonderful. I can't tell how much your smiling face means to me." He expelled a long breath. "Oh, my body aches so. I'm so glad we both made it back." He closed his eyes and soon drifted to sleep.

Rose went to Violet's bed, the tears sliding down her face. "I'm so happy, Violet."

Violet watched Arthur eating. "Doc, doesn't food taste different."

"Yeah, I noticed that after my last trip. It's a rather strange phenomena, don't you think."

"For sure, Doc." Rose entered the room. "Ah, Rose, I think I'm ready to get out of bed. I thought I'd wait for you as not to freak you out if I was walking around your house half naked."

"Great, Violet, let me help."

Violet, slid down from the bed and stood still holding onto the bed and Rose. "This feels weird." She took a few steps. "Yeah, I remember how to do this." She laughed. "I'm good, Rose. You can let go. This is much better than lying in bed. I want to get dressed and go outside."

"Your clothes are in the spare bedroom." All of a sudden Rose started turning pale. "Excuse me, Violet. Morning sickness." She hurried from the room.

"Is John home?" Violet asked as she followed Rose toward the bathroom.

After throwing up and wiping her mouth, Rose replied, "John's at school."

"Oh yeah. I should have known." Violet went into the spare room, pulled on her jeans, and slipped on her shirt." She went out into the back yard and stood, allowing the warm sun to flood her face. "Ah, nice." She was almost feeling normal. Man, what a trip. She wondered how things were going at the laboratory. She imagined Muncher was probably very suspect at Arthur's absence. She would be glad to travel back and never have to see Muncher again. Although there'd be plenty of Muncher types back in 2025. Next week April 24th, she'd be back in Joyce's arms if Arthur agreed that she was ready. She thought she would be.

28- APRIL 24, 2060

Muncher acts like he knows something's up," Violet said as she and Arthur were in the breakroom.

"He's acting funny all right, but he's not going to be a problem," Arthur said. He knew Violet's excitement had aroused Muncher's suspicions. She could hardly contain herself. He was both sad and glad that Violet was returning to 2025. A lot more reduction in greenhouse gases was needed. Their last trip had increased the switchover to clean energy, he had surmised from what he vaguely remembered from before their travel, but there was still too much CO2 and methane in the atmosphere. The amount of CO2 being produced had been substantially reduced, but the poles were still melting and sea rise was continuing to increase a few inches a year. The amount of money spent in sea retaining walls and flood surge paths could have been much better spent on eliminating fossil fuels completely.

"I hope you're right," Violet said pursing her lips.

Arthur put his hand on Violet's shoulder. "Why don't you leave for the day and go relax. I'll stay and make sure Muncher doesn't cause any problems tonight. I'll send Simon off early too. He's about ready to strangle Muncher."

"I wish he would. While you were still recovering when I came back to work, that son of a bitch touched me up. I would have torn his nuts off except I thought it might cause a problem and possibly delay my return."

"Shh, here he comes."

"Arthur, I was thinking that we could try moving the electrical inputs to the structure closer to the electromagnets," Muncher said. "That might concentrate the power more and give a boost to forming the Bridge. I think you made the structure too large, but we can't do much about that. Maybe trying to reduce the size of a Bridge might help. I mentioned it to Billy, but he said I should talk to you." He looked repulsively at Violet.

Violet returned his stare, her face contorted in a snarl. "I'll take off, Arthur," she announced. "I've got an appointment at the eye doctor." She smiled at Arthur and ignored Muncher as she spun around, raised her hand, and sauntered away. "See you all tomorrow."

"Okay, Violet, see you tomorrow," Arthur called.

As soon as Violet was out of ear shoot, Muncher moved closer to Arthur. "She's been acting funny lately and especially today. I doubt she really has an appointment."

"Why be so critical of Violet?"

"She's so stuck up."

"Stuck up? How absurd. You need to be more appreciative of your coworkers."

"She wouldn't even tell me where she went on vacation when I asked her. Do you know where she went?"

"I believe she went to Alaska."

"I know you trust her, but I'm not sure she has the best interest of the Project in mind."

"Violet is an effervescent creature and essential to the Project. She most certainly has the best intentions toward the Project. You need to concentrate on your own work."

"Where'd you go on vacation?"

"I went to Vancouver. Rose and I went hiking in the mountains there. Beautiful."

"So what do you think about moving the electrical inputs?"

"It's an interesting idea. I'll do some calculations and see what I come up with." He patted Muncher on the back. "Hey, would you like to go for a drink and discuss your ideas further. There's not much more we can do today. We'll let Simon close up shop."

Muncher smiled. "Yes, I would like that."

"Okay, let's go." Arthur walked out into the lab. He placed a hand on Simon's shoulder. "Randolph and I are going to the pub. Please finish up and lock up. We'll start fresh tomorrow."

"Will do, Arthur," Simon replied. "See you both tomorrow."

They gathered at 10:00PM in the laboratory: Arthur, Rose, Violet, Simon, Diane, Billy and Harold. Violet was excited as she prepared herself for her return voyage.

"I think we should post Harold outside to make sure Muncher doesn't show." Simon grit his teeth. "That asshole has been running password deductive software on my terminal and Violet's. He must have been coming here at night. If we hadn't gone to twenty character passwords, he might have cracked the passwords and accessed the hidden system."

"That won't be necessary," Arthur said. "I slipped a laxative in his whiskey sour. He'll be home the rest of the night."

"You sly dog, Doc," Violet said and laughed. "I can picture him now, grunting his guts out."

Simon and Diane doubled over in laughter. Rose looked at Arthur askance. "Was that necessary? He's going to suspect you."

"Let him. After tonight, he can do anything he wants. The software will be destroyed and the structure will be rendered useless." He stepped closer to Violet. "Go ahead get your suit on. We're putting humanity in your capable hands, Violet. I have every confidence in you and Joyce. Change the world and save us all. Give my love to Joyce. I'm glad you found someone to share your life with." He hugged Violet and stepped back to wipe his tears. "We'll all miss you tremendously. You will always be close to my heart. I have been blessed to know you, my dear fellow traveler." He turned away and sucked in his breath. "Okay, everybody to their stations," he said, his voice cracking. "Let's get this show on the road."

"You all right in there, Violet?" Arthur asked as Simon brought up the power to maximum.

"I'm cool calm and collected. Ready to blast off."

"Bridge beginning to form," Simon said. "Bon voyage, Violet." Simon turned back to look at Arthur. "Bridge is stable. Violet's away."

Arthur started crying profusely. Rose hugged him to her. "She knows how much you love and respect her." She started crying as well. "All our hearts are with her."

Diane came up and hugged the two, crying as well. "She is so brave."

"Shutting down," Simon said, wiping away his tears.

Arthur gently extricated himself from Rose's arms. "Okay let's start dismantling the Project. Billy, reconfigure the power panel rendering the power boost inoperable. Simon, please start deleting the software for the Bridge."

"You sure you want to do that. We could download it onto hard drives like before and hide it away?"

"No, I will be terminated from the Project after tonight, I imagine. We can't risk Muncher or someone else much more capable finding the disks. Even if they don't terminate me, I will be resigning."

"Shit," Simon said. "What about me?"

"It's your choice, Simon. It has been an honor working with you. You can stay on if you like or resign."

"I'm not going to stay and work for Muncher," Simon said with disgust.

"I'll take early retirement," Billy said. "It's been the biggest honor of my life to work here with you, Arthur."

"Thank you, Billy. The feeling is mutual."

"Shouldn't take me more than an hour to reconfigure the power panel. I doubt that Muncher will even notice it was changed."

"Why don't you and Diane go on home," Arthur suggested, placing his hand on Rose's shoulder. "Simon and I will be along shortly."

Diane and Rose went up the steps, stopping to gaze back at the immense structure. "I don't know what Arthur is going to do now," Rose said. "He's spent so many years working on this Project. Its dismantling will leave a big hole in his life."

"Simon as well," Diane said. "He was the happiest he's ever been working here with Arthur. We'll have to support our men more than usual to help them transition." Diane slipped her arm around Rose, and they left the lab.

"All right here we go," Simon said as he brought up the Bridge Program. He typed in some lines of code, then turned back to Arthur. "If I hit enter it will all be erased. Would you like the honor, Arthur?"

"Why not." Arthur walked to the terminal and hit enter. He looked up at the screen as the code started to disappear. He stepped back and wiped away his tears. "Violet... our hopes are in your hands."

29- APRIL 24, 2025

Violet slowly surfaced and took a quick breath. She tried to move her legs, but they didn't seem to be responding, nor were her arms. She could hear her heart beating. She had to be alive. Had she travelled too soon? Should she have waited longer for her body to fully recover? In a few minutes, she was finally able to shift her hips. Her eyes felt like they were bulging out of her head from the effect of the adrenalin. She concentrated on her arms. She was able to move them slightly. A good sign. Gradually she was able to lift her arm to look at her watch. It was nearly midnight. She had been out longer this time. She told herself to take it easy, don't go overboard. She wiggled her legs and felt her heart beating faster. She opened the capsule and tried to pull herself up. She slumped back. Then with a surge of energy she pulled herself halfway out of the capsule and rolled onto the floor. She turned off her oxygen and removed her helmet.

She lay there for a time on the concrete floor before she was able to sit up. The adrenalin headache was excruciating, but she got to her knees and stood shakily up. She stripped off her flight suit, depositing it in the capsule. After she retrieved her backpack, she turned on her flashlight, and went to the laboratory door. She opened the door and looked both ways down the hall. Nobody about. She went back for the capsule and left the laboratory, climbing the stairs with rising vigor. Outside, she took several deep breaths. Joyce would be waiting. Off she walked as fast as she could manage.

Violet knocked softly on Joyce's hotel room door, waiting— one hand against the wall steading herself as she held the capsule in the other. No response. Where could Joyce be? Had something happened? Had the FBI caught up with Joyce? Now what should she do? She knocked again harder. Still no response.

Suddenly, the door swung open, and there stood a sleepy-eyed Joyce. "Violet, oh thank god. I thought you weren't coming. I must have fallen asleep." She pulled Violet into the room.

Violet dropped the capsule and hugged and kissed Joyce. "My love I'm back for good. It is so wonderful to hold you again." She stood back. "My head is killing me. I need to lie down."

"Of course." Joyce led her to the bed and joined her, holding her in her arms. "Go to sleep. You can tell me all about it in the morning."

Violet awoke with a shudder. Her dreams of being caught in an alien space filled with mist and shrieking screams was fresh in her mind. She saw Joyce smiling at her and her apprehension disappeared.

"Good morning, Violet. My prayers have been fulfilled. I was so worried last night that you wouldn't be coming. You don't know how wonderful I feel seeing your beautiful face again."

"I imagine it's similar to the feeling I get seeing you."

"I'm afraid we have to leave. Last week I was picked up by the FBI. They threatened to charge me with auto theft. They grilled me for hours. They wanted to know where you and Arthur had gone. They said that a woman named Bridget Larson had abandoned a rental car several blocks from this hotel. They had camera surveillance of me with Bridget Larson, alias Violet Remy, alias Violet Drummer and Samuel Johnson, alias Arthur Simpson, alias Arthur Brown. I told them that you had left, and I didn't know where you went. I said that I heard you discussing going to Canada."

"The cash deposit I left more than paid for the rental retrieval. They couldn't charge you with auto theft."

"I knew they couldn't charge me with anything. They asked me endless questions— why I was with you and Arthur. The same thing over and over. Eventually, they let me go. Afterwards I checked out of the hotel and went and stayed with a friend in Marin until yesterday when I came back to this hotel and rented the same room to await your return."

"Damn, I'm sorry, Joyce."

"Don't worry. I imagine they may have followed me, but in Marin I didn't see any people or cars watching my friend's house. I went to see an attorney in Marin, who my friend recommended. He's ready to help if the FBI come after us again. Still, I think I should leave separately and check out. I've rented a car. It's near that coffee shop right off campus. The one we went to. I'll walk there and wait for you."

"I'll have to go to the storage locker and hide the capsule."

"You won't need it anymore. Can't you just chuck it in a garbage skip?"

"No it would be found fairly quickly. The capsule could raise many questions. The storage locker was rented for a year. It will be safer there. I can always extend the rental by sending them more money."

"Okay, I'll check out then. If I notice anyone following me, I'll skip the coffee shop and wait outside the University Library. When I see you, I'll go inside and wait in the first floor woman's toilet."

"Turn the rental car in here first. They undoubtedly are tracing you with it."

"Oh...yes, I forgot they could do that. I'm not thinking clearly because I'm so happy you are back."

"Hey, not to worry. It's all good." Violet got up, dressed quickly, and put on a blond wig. She sat down and exhaled. "I still have a splitting headache and feel a little dizzy."

"We can stay a few more hours."

"No, they're probably out front waiting for you to leave. I'll go out the back with the capsule. I'll see you in a couple of hours."

"All right. Give me a kiss before you go."

Joyce and Violet left the University Library hand in hand. Before they had walked a short distance, they were stopped by men in suits, who identified themselves as FBI. They were escorted to a parking lot and driven to the FBI office where they were kept alone in separate rooms.

"Violet Drummer," the Agent said as he entered the room, "you are a hard person to find. We've been looking for you for weeks." He sat down opposite Violet. "My name is Agent Donelson. It seems you, Arthur Brown, and Joyce Salmon have been stirring up a number of scientists about supposed global warming and providing questionable information on new technologies."

Violet stared back at the Agent, but remained silent.

"What have you to say for yourself?"

"What would you like me to say?" Violet leaned back and smiled raising her brow.

"I'd like an explanation why you are visiting these scientists and providing them with these questionable technologies."

"What's a questionable technology?"

"Technologies that no other country has developed or even heard of."

"Could these technologies be considered innovative, ground-breaking technologies? And, if so, why would that be worrisome? I would think they would be considered valuable and worthwhile."

"Who developed these technologies?"

"Arthur Brown and his associates."

"Where were they developed?"

"At Arthur Brown's Swedish Institute."

"We can find no record of this Swedish Institute."

"Maybe that's because Arthur Brown likes to keep his Institute secret."

"What was the purpose of visiting climate scientists, stirring them up to be more proactive, and disseminating the technologies?"

"The purpose? I would think that is self-evident. If the governments of the planet do not eliminate fossil fuels, the world will experience increased deadly heat waves, destructive loss of habitats, enumerable species extinctions, extreme sea rise, all resulting in millions of climate refugees and eventually the death of most of the life on this planet."

"Don't you think that is terribly alarmist and unrealistic?"

"Alarmist, yes, but truth. Are you charging me with a crime?"

"You need to answer my questions."

"I'm trying to. If you are not charging me with a crime, then I should be free to go."

"We want to know how the new technologies were developed."

"The same way all new technologies are developed— through research and experimentation."

"Where is Doctor Brown?"

"I don't know."

"Why have you and Doctor Brown used various aliases?"

"We like to."

"Using an alias to defraud someone is against the law."

"I haven't defrauded anyone."

"You abandoned a car that you rented with false identification."

"The cash deposit more than paid for the car retrieval by the rental agency after I informed the agency of the car's whereabouts. I don't believe that is a crime. I ask again, may I go. If you will not let me leave, I need to call my lawyer."

"You are causing yourself problems with your false identities. You need to stop stirring up trouble."

"As John Lewis said: 'never, ever be afraid to make some noise and get in good trouble, necessary trouble, trouble stirring up good trouble is always beneficial'." Violet leaned forward and stared at the agent with a squint and pursed lips. "Do you remember John Lewis, the civil rights icon?"

Another man entered the room and whispered to Agent Donelson. Donelson looked up with a frown, then nodded. "Ms Drummer, you are free to go. We will be watching you."

"Thank you, Agent Donelson. Have a nice day." Violet got up and left the room to join Joyce sitting on a bench in the lobby.

"Oh, Violet I'm so glad they let you go. I called my friend's lawyer. He told me you would be released soon. He made some calls. I'm sorry that they caught us. I didn't think anyone was following me."

"It's okay. We've got that over with and won't need to be worrying about being caught again. Let them follow us. I don't have to travel back in order to not upset the web of time. They can arrest me, put me in jail for a time for all I care. I will not be deterred. It's all good, now. We're free as birds. Let's take the train to LA and stir up some good trouble."

They got a hotel room after their arrival in LA. As soon as Violet entered the room, she started disrobing. "Let's get naked and celebrate our reunion. I've been dreaming of this moment for weeks. Let's see that buxom body of yours. I can't wait to have it in my arms again."

Joyce quickly disrobed and joined the naked Violet on the bed. She kissed and rubbed Violet's naked body all over as Violet lay back and sighed with pleasure. As she kissed her way toward Violet's red triangle, Violet arched her back and pushed Joyce's head to her labia, squealing in delight. Their love making lifted Violet to new heights of ecstasy.

When Violet recovered her breath, she reciprocated, tonguing Joyce to a shuddering climax. Both spent, they lay in each other's arms for several hours.

Joyce extricated herself from Violet's arms and sat up. "Whew, you are something else, Violet. I never experienced such soul lifting love making. I'm so thankful you came back to me." She ran her fingers through Violet's sumptuous red hair. "I enjoyed the train ride down here. Good idea. Too bad it wasn't a high speed train. China has sure covered the market for high speed trains."

"The US will get there, I'm sure."

"I hope so. I didn't see anyone following us."

"There was a man on the train," Violet said, "in jeans and a sweatshirt. I bet he was following us, but it doesn't matter in the least."

"You know I know almost nothing about your life," Joyce said. "Where were you born? Who were your parents? I want to know everything about you. Tell me your life."

"I was born in Eugene, Oregon. I was an only child. My parents were quite conservative, and we didn't see eye to eye on many things. I kept my sexual orientation from them and pretty much from myself until I finally realized I was born this way. I did well in school and was accepted to Berkeley. On my second summer return home from college, I told my parents I was a lesbian. My mother cried and my Dad told me to leave and never come back. I haven't seen them since."

"Oh darling, I'm so sad for you. That must have been very hurtful for you."

"Yes... I should have gone back and tried to reconcile with my parents. Now it's impossible. Maybe that's for the best. I'm reborn, and I have a wonderful woman to share my life with."

"Yes, you do." Joyce pulled Violet to her and hugged her tightly.

"Tell me about your life?"

"My parents are deceased. They never knew about my sexual orientation. I was in denial in college although I had a few lesbian encounters. During my graduate years while I was working on my thesis, I met a graduate student, who seemed very nice. We started dating, and he asked me to marry him. I thought I could be heterosexual and knew it would be better for my career, so I accepted. We were married for about two years. I found sex with him unsatisfying, but acceded to his demands for sex at first, but as time wore on, I kept making excuses why we couldn't have sex. Eventually he became physically abusive and forced sex on, raping me often. It was horrible. I filed for a divorce."

Joyce hung her head and wiped her tears before gathering her strength and continuing. "The divorce was a nightmare. He and his lawyer were very aggressive. I gave up my equity in the house we had purchased together even though I paid the down payment and almost all the mortgage payments in order not to get saddled with alimony payments. He wanted alimony payments because my salary as a full professor was considerably higher than his salary as a research technician for a drug company. He never completed his graduate work. After I married him, he turned into a complete asshole. Soon after we were divorced, he was fired from the drug company. He had a never ending succession of jobs and was often out of work when he repeatedly asked me for money, which I usually agreed to, just to get rid of him. I was so relieved when he moved to California and married another unsuspecting woman."

"Do you still have any contact with him?"

"We exchange Christmas cards."

"Is he still married?"

"I believe he's now in his fourth marriage. He's a predator."

"Have you had any other affairs since your divorce?"

"Not really. I've mostly thrown myself into my work. I have been asked out occasionally by men, but I usually have declined. Sometimes I have gone out with men just to have some company. I've never had sex with any of them. I also thought it might stifle any rumors about me. I didn't want the Institute to know my sexual orientation." She reached out for Violet. "When you and Arthur visited me, I was struck dumb by your beauty and scintillating personality. The barriers I had erected around me slipped away so easily. I was astounded. It's as if I was waiting for you. When I learned you had come from the future and would be leaving, I felt my heart would break."

"Not to worry. It's all good now." Violet sprang into a sitting position and gave Joyce a quick kiss. "Enough lollygagging, I'm recovered pretty much and feel energized enough to go visiting scientists. Any ideas on who we should visit first?"

"I've made a list. I think we should see Simon Reeves here at UCLA first. He's a Professor of Integrative Biology, a well-known climate scientist, and we can see Professor Grossman as well."

"All right then, give them a call and set up the meetings. I'm raring to go." Violet rolled out of bed. "But first we need to take a shower. You and I smell like funky spice pots."

"Nicely put." Joyce laughed and gave Violet a shove. "I brought a luffa to scrub your svelte back and bottom."

"Sounds wonderful."

After a relaxing and sensuous shower, Joyce toweled Violet dry, and Violet reciprocated. "Feel like eating?" Joyce asked. "Shall I call room service?"

"Yes, let's get plenty of dishes. I need to build up my strength."

"After Reeves and Grossman, we can visit Professor Simpson at Cal Tech then we can go up to

Portland and visit Jason Bachman. Should we fly or rent a car."

"Let's rent an electric car. I'm glad you put your time waiting for me to good use, researching who we should see to rev up the push to eliminate fossil fuels. Come on, get that buxom body moving. We're burning daylight."

"Violet you are such a breath of fresh air." She slapped Violet's bottom gently. "I'm so lucky."

"Exactamundo, Babe, get that sumptuous round butt moving. We've got places to go and people to see." Violet laughed and pulled Joyce to her, kissing her deeply. "Can you believe I'm really here for good?"

"I can now," Joyce replied. "What fun we are going to have. A tale for the ages."

"Yes indeed. We are going to make history and work wonders. I can feel it in my bones."

"Yes, my love, we are going to work wonders."

30- APRIL 29, 2025

Violet hooked her arm in Joyce's as they left Jason Bachman's office at Reed College in Portland. "This was a productive week. The scientists we've met with have all been supportive and seem to be willing to increase their activities, but going around the country visiting climate scientists to get them more involved is not going to cut it. What we need is a big public event, a rally, before we leave the west coast to publicize the need to eliminate fossil fuels." She stopped walking and turned to Joyce. "I've read that Mercer with 350.org was in Los Angles. Let's contact him."

Violet started walking again, then slowed her pace. "Maybe we can plan a free concert and rally in Golden Gate Park or some other place. Like the free concerts I read about in 1968 and 1969 to publicize the need to end the Vietnam War— the summers of love. Or something like the largest peaceful grouping of young people at Woodstock. We've got to rev up the young people in this country to demand and force change. Get them off their cellphones and get them wound up." She stopped again and grabbed Joyce's hand. "Yeah, a free gathering with music and speeches would definitely provide a lot of publicity and engage young people. The incremental changes to reduce fossil fuel use that happened over the years from now to 2060 weren't nearly enough. When I left in 2060, we were nearly at 2.5° C and on were on our way to an extremely dangerous 3° despite Arthur's activities in 1990 and 2025. We've got to make a big splash, get young people to be more demanding that real action be taken to end fossil fuel use."

"That's going to take a lot of planning and expertise we don't have," Joyce said.

"Yes indeed and money. We need to hire people with the expertise. I've got a sack full of gold coins. There's people and organizations with experience in staging and promoting concerts and rallies. I imagine there are many bands, who would be interested in helping to mitigate climate warming. We could get Politians like AOC and the California Governor to give speeches. We need to engender a hell of a lot more publicity on what the fossil fuel companies and their supporters are doing to the environment."

"I like it."

"We can use the rallies to drum up support for State Attorney Generals to file law suits against the likes of Exon, Chevron, BP, and Shell. Fossil fuel companies need to pay for what they are doing and have done to the planet like the tobacco companies eventually paid. The money will be miniscule compared to the harm they have done, but the publicity will be invaluable. Banks and hedge funds need to stop funding fossil fuels. Fossil fuel companies without access to capital and the diminishing demand caused by a progressive carbon tax would end up dead in the water. The only way to accomplish what is needed is to stir up the populace to force politicians to act and pass the necessary legislation."

"I like what you're advocating, but wonder if we can pull it off."

"We can do it. We need to get as many advocates to help us as we can. There's plenty of advocates and environmental organizations out there. We just need to bring them together. California is a progressive State, and its economy is larger than many countries. It's the place to start."

"You actually think we can organize such a rally and concert."

"Yes, with help I do. We have to get a significant carbon tax passed in the US Legislature. The Government needs to spend the money necessary to launch a Green New Deal. A Green New Deal would provide enumerable new jobs. The government along with private companies would be the employers for these jobs, and government could guarantee livable wages. That would get people behind a Green New Deal. We need to reallocate the majority of defense spending to the Green New Deal. Most of the so called defense expenditures are basically being flushed down the toilet on weapons that if life on the planet is to survive will never be used. We need to shrink defense spending and use the money for the Green New Deal and tax the wealthy and corporations. An upper income bracket tax of at least 70% is needed like it was before President Reagan got the legislature to cut it to 50% in 1981. In 1945 the top bracket paid 90%

in income tax. Today the top income bracket tax is 37% and there are so many loop holes that very few of the extreme wealthy even pay that percentage. We need to get rid of all the loop holes that allow tax avoidance. The time is ripe. Harris, the new President, would be fully behind a Green New Deal if it's popular. She's not going to risk trying to get something unpopular passed. She wants to get re-elected."

"How do we counteract the money behind fossil fuels? It seems the FBI are in league with the fossil fuel companies. They're already following us. If we start organizing such a rally, we could be arrested on some trumped up charge."

"Yes, we could. That's why we need to go big while we can. Harris would be an ally if we get the people riled up. Even though the forces of white supremacy are gearing up against her, she has a slim majority in both the House and Senate. It was fortunate that enough centrist Republicans finally realized that Trump was a toxic wanna be dictator, con man, and he lost big in even greater numbers than last time. I hope they convict him and his family of tax fraud and send them to prison. We need to go all out and get the people off their staid asses to support the necessary steps to save life on this planet. Revving up the young, who have the most to lose with climate warming, is the way we can do it. I've lived in the future, and it is not pretty. We have to do our utmost."

"Okay, Violet. You've convinced me. I'm with you one hundred percent. I know Mercer quite well. Let's give him a call."

"Wow, did you see the crowd out there," Joyce said grabbing Violet around the waist. "My god, there's thousands and thousands of people of all ages. The bands were fantastic. The city was great providing the buses to get the people here from the many parking venues. What a great idea." Joyce lifted Violet off the ground and spun her around before setting her down and hugging her tightly. "Mercer got them attuned to what was needed to mitigate climate warming. The California Governor was eloquent, Greta was great, and AOC got them on their feet. The crowd was full of enthusiasm. You did it, you amazing woman."

"We did it, Joyce. Without your contacts and reputation and the other climate scientists and organizations you got on board, we couldn't have pulled it off. This is just the beginning. We're on a roll, Babe. Next on to LA, Chicago, Saint Louis, and then New York."

"Yes indeed. Oh, I'm so happy you came back."

"After we've covered the US, then we should go to Europe, Russia, India, China, Australia, Africa, South America, and anywhere else they'll have us. If we get the populace of the world behind ending climate warming, the governments of the world will have no choice but to spend the money necessary to transition to clean energy and save the planet."

31- JUNE 10, 2030

"Look at that crowd," Joyce said as they were standing back stage at the Sydney concert and rally. "I can't believe how successful we have been. It's been a long and arduous five years, but what we've accomplished is beyond my wildest dreams. Greenhouse gas emissions have been cut drastically since 2025."

"For sure, but we're not done. Until every damn carbon emitter is gone, we will continue. The young of the world have responded wonderfully and have kept up the pressure on the politicians with their ubiquitous demonstrations, forcing politicians to abandon the fossil fuel money and begin passing legislation for the people rather than the wealthy and corporations. Europe and the US have led the way. The overturning of the Citizens' United ruling by the Supreme Court once Harris increased the appointees helped immensely. Campaign finance laws have prevailed. Money is no longer free speech and corporations can no longer have such a big impact on legislators. The people have taken back their democracy. Reinstituting the Fairness Doctrine on the public airwaves also helped to mitigate the influence of far right media like Fox News that had programed so many gullible fools with their lies. The US and the world have reduced defense spending and used the money to foster the clean energy transition. It is amazing what the world youth have accomplished."

"I like this rally," Joyce said. "It's quite fun, but the rally in China was unbelievable. They have stopped building coal plants and plan to replace the existing plants temporarily with gas fired plants until they have enough solar and wind generation to replace them. They are making great progress. I was amazed that we were able to stage a concert in Beijing."

"The momentum we caused with our rally concerts in the US, Europe, and Russia was the catalyst," Violet added. "Of course Harris backing our endeavors and helping with and agreeing to come with us sealed the deal for the Beijing concert." Violet looked out at the concert crowd, thinking how much they had accomplished thanks to Arthur before turning back to Joyce. What would her life had been without Joyce? She took a deep breath and thanked Arthur in her mind for changing her life. "If Harris hadn't gotten Congress to pass a major progressive carbon tax and make a settlement with fossil fuel companies to write off their reserves as well as getting money out of politics, the China Premier would not have agreed to the Beijing Concert Rally. What an incredible coup the rally was."

"Yes, Harris has been a fabulous second term president."

"I like to think our rallies and the pressure of the young demonstrators induced her to promote the changes she instituted," Violet said. "I quite enjoyed the Beijing concert. Opening with the traditional music and dances followed by the Chinese rock bands was apt. When I think of all the rallies and concerts we've done, I think the Beijing one was the most monumental to me."

"It certainly was the largest. The Chinese press said there were close to one million people in attendance."

"Yeah, when I looked out at the crowd, I couldn't see the end of it. The immense video screen behind the stage was the largest I've ever seen. The cheers of the crowd were deafening. Oh, Joyce, I am so thankful I came back to you. My life with you has been so fulfilling."

Joyce hugged Violet to her. "You have made my life an adventure that I could never have imagined. I'm so happy. We've worked wonders as you said we would. You are such an amazing person."

"Easy, Joyce, don't go overboard. Without you this never would have been possible. But we are not done."

"The Australian Prime Minister said tonight that the last coal plants here would be eliminated in the next five to ten years and all new electrical generation would be solar and wind."

"Talk's cheap. We need to make sure he keeps his promises. They're still mining massive amounts of coal."

"If the trends continue, the world could be carbon neutral in less than fifteen years."

"I certainly hope so. We have engaged the young in the countries we have held rallies in, and they have forced governments to make many necessary lifesaving changes, but we are still dealing with the detrimental effects of climate warming like this damn smoke from the brush fires west of here that's causing my eyes to water. How far away are the fires?"

"The man I talked to said the wind should be shifting, and we won't get so much smoke tomorrow, but it will be a while before they can contain the fire."

"So we're going to be smoke free just when we're leaving. That should make flying out easier, not to mention easier breathing. Too bad we weren't able to fly back to the US on Airforce One with Harris. I certainly enjoyed flying to China on it. I tried to get her to come to Australia with us. Of course she's got many other things that need her attention. I'm not looking forward to a commercial flight for twenty some hours, but it will be nice to relax a few months in Cambridge before we go to DC and stir up more good trouble."

"Indeed. You are very good at stirring up good trouble."

32- APRIL 30, 2060

Rose greeted Arthur with a kiss as soon as he entered their house. She had been waiting anxiously for his return. "Have you seen the news?"

"Yes, we are down to almost zero carbon emissions," Arthur said, pulling Rose to him and kissing her strongly before holding her at a close distance. "Carbon in the atmosphere is now at 430 parts per million. The frozen tundra has stabilized. There's only a few gas power plants still operating in Russia and they are to be retired."

"Violet and Joyce did it." Rose placed her hand on Arthur's chest and studied his face. "They really did it. They changed the world thanks to you. They got the world's youth behind them clamoring for change with their concert rallies around the world." She grabbed him tight and kissed him, thanking providence for her swing through the Physics building and their meeting. Would Arthur have been able to establish time travel without her? Who could say what factors united to make things possible? Thankfully her children and the majority of children on the planet would inhabit a livable future world. "They did what we climate scientist couldn't."

"Starting in 2025 gave them a decided advantage. Things came together for them in astonishing continuity. The reversal of the Citizen's United

Supreme Court ruling was a monumental help. The fossil fuel industry couldn't buy politicians like they had in the past. It is totally amazing what they were able to accomplish. The world owes so much to those two phenomenal ladies."

"That's for sure. Not to be mawkish, but next week is your last week at the University. How do you feel about leaving your Project?"

"I feel good. Simon has his old job back at the Computer Science Department. Billy retires in two weeks. Harold is staying on. There's a new Project head coming next week. I met him today. Nice guy. He's already figured out that Muncher is an idiot. I doubt they will ever be able to produce an Einstein-Rosen Bridge again."

"Let's hope you're right."

"I'd put money on it. We were only able to do it with the collaboration of the team."

"I think you are being too modest, my genius husband."

Arthur laughed. "You almost sound like Violet." He shook his head and looked away for a few seconds as he remembered sending the cat to the past— the first time he realized what they had accomplished and what it could mean. "I will enjoy my free time with you and John immensely. I will be able to travel with you as you crisscross the globe now that we have nearly stopped the absurd use of fossil fuels. I look forward to flying on the hydrogen hybrid jets."

"I'll relish you being by my side. Just imagine if you hadn't been successful, and Violet hadn't decided to stay in 2025. You as well as Violet and Joyce changed the world. You are so amazing."

"Thank you, but the bulk of accomplishments rests with Violet and Joyce. The synchronicity of the two was amazing."

"I know I wasn't always as supportive of your work as I should have been."

"Oh, Rose, I couldn't have done what we did without you. Your support and love was so important. I'll miss the team, but most of all I'll miss Violet. I'm glad I'm leaving the Lab. It is not the same without the vivacious Violet. She and you were the catalyst that spurred me on."

"Violet's still alive. We could visit her in Cambridge."

"I've thought about that. I don't know how that would affect the time continuum. I expect though that the continuum was firmly established and seeing Violet wouldn't cause problems. It would be a shock to see Violet and Joyce as older women."

"Yes, but I'm sure it will be so rewarding for you and Violet. You know I was a little jealous of her. I knew there was a friendship and bond that rivaled the love you held for me."

"It was a different kind of love and friendship."

"Yes, I know, my Darling" She gave him a strong hug. "We've been invited to Simon and Diane's tonight for dinner. Simon is barbequing plant based burgers and hot dogs. Diane has made her spicy potato salad."

"Great."

"John's already over there with Josh. We have time for a shower together."

"Ahh, sounds wonderful." Arthur folded Rose in his arms. "How's our little girl in there." He rubbed Rose's belly.

"She's doing just fine. I've got some pictures from the ultra sound for you."

"Great, break them out. You know we should drive our new electric van to visit Violet and Joyce and see the sights along the way. You have vacation time coming don't you? We can take John with us. He'll love it."

"You mean take him out of school?"

"Sure, he's nearly finished for the year."

Arthur pulled the car up in front of Joyce and Violet's house. Their road trip across the country had been fun. John was amazed by all the wonderful sights they had seen. Arthur turned off the car and sat looking at the house a few minutes.

"What are you waiting for?" Rose asked.

"Yeah, Dad, let's go and see your friends."

Arthur wondered how Violet and Joyce would look. He recalled their beautiful faces and their flight from the authorities across the country not that long ago.

"Dad, what's wrong?"

"Nothing, John, I was just collecting my thoughts." He opened his car door and, after opening the back door, helped John from the back seat. He looked apprehensively at Rose as she joined him, grabbing his arm. "Here goes." He inhaled deeply and grasped John's hand. "Let's go knock on the door."

When the door opened, there stood Violet, a youthful looking seventy year old woman with long gray hair, an enticing smile, and those scintillating blue eyes Arthur remembered so well.

"Doc, what took you so long? We've been on pins and needles awaiting your arrival." Violet laughed and flew into his arms. "Oh Doc, I missed you so much over the years." She dragged him inside and pushed him toward Joyce, who stood holding out her arms.

"Arthur, so glad to see you again," Joyce said as she hugged Arthur tightly.

Violet hugged Rose. "Oh Rose, you are as beautiful as ever. So good to see you again." She grabbed John. "Well look at this little tyke. What a handsome young man. You look just like your mom. I bet you drive the girls wild."

"I do no such thing," John responded.

"Oh, I see. Well, you'll change your tune soon, I bet."

"You know Dad worked with a woman named Violet," John said looking up at Violet. "She kind of looked a little like you, but was much younger. She was very beautiful."

"You don't say. You don't think I'm beautiful?"

"Well, perhaps for an older woman."

"Oh really. Well, thank you." She grabbed John's hand. "Let's go out back to the garden. Joyce has turned it into a wild flower delight since she stopped working."

Rose stopped in front of all the awards on the hallway wall. "Look, Arthur. Here's a picture of Violet and Joyce receiving the Presidential Medal of Freedom. Oh, and look, here they are with Harris and the China Premier." She grabbed Arthur by the arm and pulled him to the pictures.

"Wow, great pictures," Arthur said. "How does it feel to be famous, Violet?"

"Fame is overrated, Doc."

"Violet used that ceremony to berate the President for not doing more to get China to eliminate fossil fuels," Joyce said. "The President didn't know what to say." She laughed and pushed Violet before scurrying to Rose and enveloping her into her arms. "I've heard so much about you, Rose. It's an honor to meet you finally.

"It is my honor," Rose replied. "You are an amazing woman and renowned climate scientist. I've followed your career closely. I am so thankful for what you and Violet have done. You have saved us all."

"We couldn't have done it without Arthur. He's the real unsung hero."

Rose grabbed Arthur from behind and kissed his cheek. "That... he most certainly is." They went into the garden. "How beautiful, Joyce."

"Thank you." Joyce pulled the Champaign from the ice bucket and poured each a glass. "Here's to a long awaited reunion. Long life and happiness."

"Long life and happiness."

ABOUT THE AUTHOR

Donald Houser is a writer of four previous self-published novels, *Love And Mayhem On The Silk Road* (2021), *Cloud Of Death* (2020), *Death In The Peru Rainforest* (2019) and *Escape From The Presidio* (2015). He is a retired engineer, who is interested in the peoples of the world. He enjoys reading informative and captivating books, traveling and learning about other cultures, and hiking in the wonders of nature. He is a long time resident of Santa Fe, New Mexico.